Sidekicks

Ashley Skolrud

Finch Benson Publishing

To Jess.

You've been making memes about *Sidekicks* since before you even knew what the book was about. As the Official President of the "Toby is my Book Boyfriend Club," it's only right this book is for you.

CONTENTS

TRIGGER WARNINGS

*S*IDEKICKS CONTAINS TOPICS COMMON in superhero stories such as death, murder, violence, terminal illness, cult behavior, stalking, drug use and overdose, animal cruelty, child abandonment, and child endangerment.

In addition, some backstories will include discussions about the following topics without them being on the page: reproductive coercion (without sexual assault), physical child abuse, and suicide.

Readers who may be sensitive to these elements, please put yourself first when it comes to reading this story. No book is worth you sacrificing your mental health.

PROLOGUE

A GUNSHOT.

An explosion.

A fire.

I was sitting in the back of the ambulance, unable to hear what the paramedics were saying, but probably something about how if my hearing didn't come back in the next few days, I should go get it checked out.

Every single person on the scene knew who I was, and yet not one knew my name. Not really. Chronos was recounting every single detail of the mission to our handler, Jacqueline. Twinge was trying to keep Tribulation from continually punching a brick wall and breaking his hands. Again. NanoByte was pacing—a sure sign she was having a panic attack. And Ghost was gone. Smart.

I closed my eyes, only to be greeted with the last thing I saw before the world exploded: an aura—black, shaking, terrified. My eyes flew open as I gasped, and knew, no matter what, I needed to get away from here.

1

A warm shower, a mug of cocoa, and a hug.

I wasn't important enough for anyone to notice I was leaving, slipping away once the paramedics were wrapping Tribulation's bloody hands. I went to my stashed motorcycle and started making my way home. The rushing air gave me relief from the burnt plastic smell of my wig, and I hoped this was enough of a reason to ditch it. A fire hazard, the medics had explained. I was lucky it didn't melt into my head. The Eagle should have known better to get such a cheap wig.

Dad should have known a lot of things. And my wig was the least of them.

I was in less of a daze when I got home, parking my cycle in the garage before walking into the house, only to see my father walking out the front door. We stared at each other, each still covered in the grime from the explosion. He looked haunted in a way I hadn't seen since my mother died.

"I'm sorry," I saw his lips say, though I could barely hear his voice. "Nicole, I'm so, so sorry."

He turned and left. Never to check in on the kids he left behind. Never to face the consequences of his actions.

Never to know he had killed the wrong man.

Never to be seen again.

Chapter One

T HERE WAS A PURPLE haze over the audience, pops of gold, burgundy, and gray peaking through the general aura of the crowd.

Purple was happiness, gold was excitement, burgundy was stress, and gray was boredom. Exactly what I had expected. I blinked a few times and let my power fade away, and once again, it was a room full of people.

People who were specifically here for me.

I was sure if I could look at my aura it would be a goldish-green—excitement and anxiety all rolled into one. But I didn't need my powers to know how I felt, even if I wouldn't let them peek through my perfectly practiced calm exterior.

I was a Caldwell, after all, and it had been drilled into me from birth that we would never allow people to know how we were truly feeling. Especially at the event that would remind everyone here that the Caldwells were the philanthropic center of Calder Bay.

Especially at the first family event in five years.

However, the real question was whose shadow was I actually going to be in this evening? I had been to plenty of my father's parties growing up, the events he was expected to plan for the rest of the one percent of the city. However, it was my mother's parties that had been legendary. To this day, people would ask me about them, even though I had been too young to have ever attended. They were the parties everyone begged to go to, and the lack of an invite could destroy your social reputation for years.

If it was anyone's shadow I had to be in tonight, I preferred it to be Katya Caldwell's. I had been living in her husband's enough for the past five years. The woman who had been full of life, warm and open, and forgiving to a fault. Until my father sucked the life out of her to the point she felt she could no longer go on.

I could relate. It was the same thing he had done to me the moment he left us to clean up his mess. He left, Nate left, and Zain disappeared. I'm still not sure he left of his own volition. I was the only Caldwell left to pick up the pieces of a business empire I didn't know how to run, to keep our reputation spotless so nobody would think to look closer than they had to and preserve his image, which I wanted nothing more than to set on fire.

If anyone asked where he was, he was sick. It was the same excuse I had used for five years, which I am sure plenty of people interpreted as him having cancer or something similar. That worked for me. Nobody actually cared about him enough to check-in. Sebastian Caldwell was the person you went to when you wanted a good time, not someone you were close to.

4

I hated how easily it let me make excuses for him. Even if someone getting suspicious would make my life harder. I had every single day scheduled down to the minute, the exact kind of foundation I never had growing up. I had a house of my own, I had a career of my own, and I had a life of my own. Nobody else was in it—there wasn't room. And that was exactly how I liked it.

I felt my phone buzz, and I rolled my eyes at the name of the person who, for the last month, had been determined to try and shatter everything I had built. I never would have accused Brittney Merrick of being smart, however, I had always thought it was obvious we were in the "after" of her association with my family.

I declined the call and immediately noticed the flashes of a photographer catching me and stuffed my phone back into the pocket I had made for it in my skirt. Those were pictures I was going to have to buy off of him for more than they were worth. The only trick I had learned from my mother about making sure any pictures we didn't want would never see the light of day.

"Oh. My. Gods. Nikki Caldwell!" a voice interrupted my thoughts. I wished I was surprised that Jeannie Michaels was here, especially as I had intentionally left her off the invite list. But she was better known as Miss Lumeriana, the first superhero social media influencer, and she had turned what originally was a cash grab into a multimillion-dollar brand. If I was still in the business, she would have been my archenemy—even if we were technically on the same side.

"Jeannie, it's so surprising to see you," I said, plastering my fakest smile on my face. "I thought you were busy tonight."

"And miss a Caldwell party? Sweetheart, I've given your cause a million new views just by being here," Jeannie said, as if she was doing me a favor. "What is it tonight? Orphans? I mean...your father does love his orphans."

"An abused woman's shelter, actually," I stated, falling back into the script I had rehearsed thousands of times in my office. "All the funds from the auction tonight will go toward renovating the building, in addition to fully furnishing it, and should everyone be so generous, give them enough funds to help it run for at least a year."

"Well, whatever it is, we all know it's just a chance for you to show off," Jeannie quietly hissed in my ear. "You'd think you would be more willing to share the spotlight now that your Daddy's not here, Nicole."

"Oh no," I said, feigning shock. "That new supersuit you've been begging me to design for you has accidentally been deleted from the waitlist. Looks like you'll have to keep your outdated designer, but that's fine. I'm sure you can keep this look a few more years while everyone else gets a stylish refresh."

I innocently smiled at her, knowing I was calling her bluff. Everyone was here to see the launch of my fashion line, but most people here didn't know I had been designing super-suits for their favorite heroes for the past year and a half. That was the majority of the business I was building, where the money was coming from so I could dress celebrities on the red carpet and put on shows like this one.

"You know there's plenty of designers who..." she started before my phone started to buzz again. And in the mental calculation of continuing to talk to Jeannie or having to talk to the person who I had declined the last fifty times she had called in the past month, I was going to choose Brittney every single time.

"Excuse me, I have to take this," I said, walking away from her as I answered the phone. "Brittney, what could you possibly...?"

"Ms. Caldwell," an unfamiliar voice on the other end of the line said, "My name is Officer Lewis. We have been trying to get a hold of you through your assistant, but she had said the only way to contact you tonight is through your phone. We need you to come to the station. Unfortunately, we need you to identify a body."

And with that, the anger from being forced to talk to Jeannie and the annoyance of Brittney's endless calling instantly disappeared and was replaced with the ice of terror running through my veins.

Chapter Two

ONE OF THE VERY first things I could remember Sebastian Caldwell teaching me was the police were worthless. Too many of them were corrupt—whether they were paid off, racist, or just living misogynistic power fantasies—and there was too much red tape for the few good ones to be effective.

It was part of the reason he had first created the Eagle. At the time, the Department of Superhero Affairs was looking for credibility, and while he had no powers, he had money. Now the Department was thriving, and the Head was an official position within the President's Cabinet—and the police were now worthless because they were irrelevant.

It was so different from how he had started, back when he was determined to turn our family's reputation into something new in a single generation. Taking the blood money of his family, and turning it into something he could take pride in. And he had grown up around the mobs, could think like them, act like them, and disband them. It was what made him such a good hero. For what he lacked in superpowers, he more than made up for in the way he could think like those he took down. And while, to my knowledge, my father didn't kill anyone until Nightshade, he definitely found ways to make them wish they were dead.

Sometimes the worst punishment was letting them live—it seemed to be a motto Dad had lived by.

I looked at the photographs of Brittney's pale body, plastered on their wall as a victim, and had to question if Dad's motto was as sound as we had been led to believe. I knew of some heroes who had killed the worst of the worst, and while there was always an investigation because of a lost life, it always seemed to be decided they had acted for the good of the people. Dad hated it and was certain it was going to be a slippery slope to make heroes nothing more than vigilante murder machines.

No wonder murdering who he thought was Nightshade broke him. It was so against who he was as a person, so out of character, he must have thought it was the only way. But Nightshade still was a mystery, both to the police and to everyone on our team. With our seemingly infinite money and resources, we were never able to learn his real name or any details about his identity. He wasn't affiliated with any of the mobs, and the few contacts in the underworld my father had were terrified of him. And he always targeted women, typically ones who went outside his idea of typical gender roles—and never killed the same way twice. If anything, he kept trying to make it as dramatic as villainously possible, always having to outdo himself.

The one thing I knew about him for certain was he enjoyed it. Every time I read his aura, it was full of his sick pleasure. This was a game, and I hated him all the more for it. And there was a part of me, deep down, who truly wished my Dad had killed the right man, just so the monster wouldn't have decided to pop back up again.

"Ms. Caldwell," I heard a voice say beside me, and I jumped in surprise. While I had been lost in thought, it was clear they didn't realize I had been analyzing the crime scene pictures they had on the board. How everything fit what we knew Nightshade would do. She seemed to have been pecked to death by birds, her skin ripped right off her bones. The only thing he left untouched was her face, with his signature Nightshade plant painted on Brittney's right cheek.

The pictures took me back a decade—back when Ariadne Carlson was murdered for the oh-so-scandalous reason of being a plumber. It was our last case before everything was derailed. She had been beaten to death with her equipment and then run over with her van, just because I think he liked the tire tracks formed from her blood. But it was the blood memory that brought me back to the present: with a message that had been written in Brittney's on the wall: *Birds of a feather don't fly together.*

Even though I was the only one whose codename followed in the footsteps of my father's and took their name from a bird, the media loved to call all of his sidekicks the Eagle's birds. None of us really liked that, though there was nothing we could do about how reporters saw us, but it was clear he was taking a page from that now. It was a threat. To all of us who had ever worked with The Eagle. One that made me wonder if we were next.

"Are you alright Ms. Caldwell?" the officer said again, and I realized I had forgotten to answer him the first time.

"Yes. Sorry, it's so much to take in," I said, taking the glass of water he handed me and using the time it took to take a sip to ground me. I wasn't sure if he was expecting me to cry, or throw up, or faint at the sight of the pictures—especially as I apparently had already been calmer at the morgue when I had identified the body. "Isn't this like what Nightshade used to do? I remember my father following those stories pretty closely in the newspapers."

"Wouldn't have thought a pretty young thing like you would even know what a newspaper is," the officer said, and I couldn't help but glare at how insulting that was.

"My father's a big supporter of local journalism," I deadpanned, thinking back to the multiple times he had insisted newspapers were the most honest form of journalism. To this day, I'm not sure I believed him, but it was nice to have the routine of waking up and seeing him have his paper and coffee every morning.

"Well, I can assure you Ms. Caldwell, Nightshade's body was found five years ago. I'm sure your father read all about how the Eagle took him down," the officer sounded entirely too sure of himself, like he was the one of the two of us who had been there, and I resisted the incredibly strong urge to roll my eyes.

"So you think it's a copycat?" I asked, feigning ignorance, "And what's with the bird thing he was writing about?" It was easy enough to play dumb and ask questions—one of the best tools I had in my arsenal. It was only a matter of time before the

12

Department took over this investigation, and I wanted to get as much information as I could out of him before that happened.

"Doesn't really matter. Nightshade was known for leaving nonsense on the walls." Technically true, though we figured out a pattern where he was always hinting at the profession of his next victim. "I'd bet good money this means nothing," the officer continued, and I did everything in my power not to roll my eyes. "The copycat was probably just following a trend."

Maybe it was because I was so trained in his patterns—it had been my father's obsession for so long, and it was so obvious what the clues meant. He already knew who we were, and I would bet good money he knew people referred to us as the Eagle's Little Birds and how our hideout was literally called The Nest. The officer's bad hypothesis told me I had all the information the police did, and staying here wasn't going to be worth the time.

"But don't let that worry you," he said, quickly backtracking. "I know it hurts to see your friend like this..."

"Brittney wasn't my friend," I immediately corrected, with much more ice than I had intended. Clearly, my constant annoyance at her calls had not yet fully dissipated with her death, and the cop was now looking at me in a new light.

"Really?" he asked, getting entirely too interested in me. I hadn't meant to make myself seem like a suspect, though at least I had the alibi of being around hundreds of people when this murder happened. One of the few perks of being at nonstop engagements. "It seemed like you both were close."

"My father has been running a charity for underprivileged youth for almost as long as I've been alive," I stated, brushing off his questions with fake naivety. "When I was younger, he mentored a lot of the teens who came through the center. Brittney and her twin brother were two he worked with. And as we're in the same business, sometimes she'll call me in a professional capacity. It was my first fashion show tonight, you know," I said beaming at him.

"Was she supposed to model?" the cop asked, jotting down a few notes.

"Why is that relevant?" I asked, the ice returning to my voice—it was a tone Dad had practiced with me multiple times growing up: the tone stating I was ready to call my lawyer. "I came to identify a body, and unless you're vaguely accusing me of..."

"What part of I am from the Department of Hero Affairs do you not understand?" a loud voice interrupted me, and I whipped my head toward it. I had heard through the grapevine Toby had gotten a job at the Department, but I had not expected the first place I would run into my teenage almost-boyfriend was in the middle of a police precinct. And even just his voice was enough for all of the emotions I had shoving into the back of my mind since I was sixteen to create a tsunami inside me.

Butterflies tinged in guilt.

The reminder of my very first kiss. And days later when I decided to ghost him.

And as he rounded the corner, my jaw dropped at the sight of Toby. The suit was expected, but he was a few inches taller, had

14

ditched his glasses, and had muscles I never would have expected from his formerly lanky frame. Or what he had preferred to be his frame back when he was a teenager. Considering he was a shapeshifter, Toby could look like anything he wanted—and apparently, he was now in his buff era. It was jarring, but it made me wonder exactly how much he had changed in the five years since I had last seen him.

But where I was shocked at what he looked like, the officers were scrambling, and it was clear the precinct didn't have a lot of experience with The Department. Which explained so much about the questions I had gotten from the officer.

"Is there a reason you're questioning Nicole Caldwell? Is she a suspect?" Toby asked the moment he saw me, and while I caught the confusion in his voice, his better-than-you tone made the officer who had been talking to me almost faint. Toby was in his element more than he ever would have been if he had gone into hero work.

Even if he clearly now had hero-level abs.

"Um, no... sir," the man said, vigorously shaking his head. "She was here to identify the body of the victim."

"I see," Toby nodded, motioning to the team with him to start packing up the limited evidence and pictures the police had out. "Is there any reason you stalled in contacting us? I'm sure you're aware any cases regarding Nightshade, whether it be him or a copycat, as you seem to believe, fall under the Department's jurisdiction, correct?"

"There was a note in the file," Office Lewis stammered, and I had to admit, I was enjoying watching the man squirm, "but it was from five years ago, so I wasn't sure if it…"

"I'm going to stop you right there," Toby interrupted, sounding both bureaucratic and annoyed. "Clearly you have not been trained properly, so I will be recommending the entire precinct goes through proper Department Protocols training starting tomorrow. What you should know is, per the law, all Department notes are active for twenty years unless explicitly stated otherwise. As there was no early expiration of said note, it should have been reported immediately. You were lucky your receptionist realized what was going on and reported it. Should I be concerned about your lack of following protocol, or was this, in fact, a lack of training?"

I knew if Toby had been wearing his glasses, he would have pushed them up to look more intimidating. But this version of him, the tall, buff mirror-world version of him, managed to be both terrifying and incredibly attractive. Which was the absolute last thing I needed to be thinking about right next to the evidence of an open murder investigation.

"It was… I mean… I thought…" Officer Lewis stammered, and Toby waved his hand away.

"Thank you for your evidence, and I trust any and all of your files pertaining to this case will be turned over before we leave," Toby said, singlehandedly ending the conversation. "Now, if you'll excuse me, I'll be escorting Ms. Caldwell out of the building before anyone else starts getting ideas about interrogating her over something she quite literally could not have done."

I watched as he gave a few short-handed instructions to his team, and then hooked his arm in mine and started pulling me out of the building.

It wasn't until we were almost out of the building when I realized Toby had shrunk three inches, the suit was now baggy, and he had pulled his glasses out of a pocket and put them back on. And as much of a hot fever dream he had presented to the police officers, I had to admit, I liked him better this way—it suited him so much more.

"Talking to cops, Nikki? Really?" he hissed in my ear as we walked out the front door, "I know you've been out of it for a while, but I am confident your dad taught you better."

"Oh, do you think he'll actually show up to tell me how disappointed in me he is?" I sarcastically gasped. Toby was one of the few people who knew my Dad had disappeared, and as a result, had also been given the unofficial assignment to cover it up. "It looks like you figured out my master plan on luring my Dad here so I can chew him out." Toby gave me a look, one I easily knew meant to cut the sarcasm. "I forgot every conversation is an interrogation until it was too late," I sighed. "I had meant to try and identify the body and leave."

"But you stayed," Toby asked, before giving me a knowing grin. "Trying to get information?"

"Someone had to," I pointed out, "especially since you and your team were taking your sweet time getting here. It took me a good

17

five seconds of looking at the evidence to realize Nightshade is finally back."

"How is that even poss..." Toby said, before looking at me suspiciously. "What do you mean "finally?""

I hadn't meant for it to slip out, the one secret I had carried closer than my own skin over the years. The truth about what had happened that night.

"The man my Dad killed? It wasn't Nightshade," I quietly told him, looking around to make sure nobody was listening. "I read his aura when it was happening, and the colors were wrong. I had never seen Nightshade's aura those colors before. The colors of fear and panic and helplessness. With everything that was going on, it should have been pride. Happiness he finally broke his enemy."

"Why is there no notes about this in the files?" Toby asked, a blue tinge of his true skin color starting to creep onto his skin as he lost the concentration needed to keep it a human color. "Nikki, why didn't you tell someone?"

"Who would have listened?" I asked. "I was the only one who knew, my Dad left, and it was clear the Department wanted the case wrapped up in a pretty bow."

Toby closed his eyes and let a sharp breath out through his nose as his skin once again turned a golden tan. "And that's why he knew to target Brittney. He knew all of your identities. If I had to guess, I would say he's trying to wrap up loose ends," he sighed again before shaking his head. "I'll bring all of this information to headquarters, and I'm sure they're going to want to question you about the auras. And then we'll figure out who to assign this to."

"What do you mean? Obviously, I'm taking this case." The words leapt out of me faster than I knew what to do with. Without even thinking. There was just something, the smallest embers of something, starting to wake up from seeing Brittney's body. A feeling I couldn't even place after years of numbness. Something in me wanted this, needed this. So fast my brain didn't give me a chance to talk myself out of it.

"Nickel..." Toby quietly said, his voice filled with worry. "I'm not sure that..."

"My license hasn't expired yet," I pointed out, a fact I knew from the multiple times the Department had tried to get ahold of me when it came to renewing it. "And, per the law," I said throwing his words back at him, "as I had worked on the case before, I get the option to pick it back up before it's reassigned. I. Want. It."

"Nikki, your license expires in three weeks," Toby countered. "The chances of you being able to capture him in time..."

"Fine, give me three weeks," I said, an idea popping into my head as I started typing on my phone. I knew he was going to mention not having backup, and if there was ever a time to finally get back in touch with my brother, it was now. "And if he hasn't been found in time, I'll hand everything over and it can be reassigned to anyone whose name isn't Miss Lumeriana, because if you even think about giving this to her, I will end you."

19

"You know she's our best..." he paused, clearly thinking through everything. "Fine. Deal. But you can't do this alone, Nikki. That one I won't budge on."

My phone beeped, just like I had expected, though the timing couldn't have been more perfect.

"I won't be alone," I smiled, showing him the text from an unlisted number. "I'll have Zain."

Chapter Three

I F ANYONE HAD TOLD me I would one day be standing in the middle of the Annelton airport, I would have thought they were lying to me. But that was after I had them explain where the country Annelton was. I hadn't heard of it before, and I was surprised it was big enough to even have an airport, though I was confident that was the only thing going for this town masquerading as a city. There were more people here than I had expected, considering there was enough to constitute there being an airport in the first place, but it felt so wrong to be standing in a sea of flannel in my designer clothes.

And to make it worse, it was the middle of sweater season—with a cool chill in the air to show winter was coming, without any of the coldness. Annelton hadn't gotten the message though, as they were expecting a large amount of snow to fall, to go with the already too much snow on the ground. I hadn't prepared for this kind of temperature, and I wanted to bundle myself in at least five blankets and pretend I had never arrived in this fashion disaster of frozen wasteland. Whatever Zain was doing here, I was not sure it was worth him making me come pick him up.

After finding a taxi, when it was clear none of the rideshare apps even had drivers in the area, I gave them the address Zain had texted me. Or at least, I assumed it was Zain. It hit me about halfway through my flight this easily could be a trap set up by his mother or some other person who worked with her and was planning on luring me to my death. Which was the last thing I wanted to think about. I had to be optimistic considering how terrible my week already had been.

We passed houses that I think had once been a variety of colors but now were all the exact same shade of dull, with roofs covered in snow that somehow hadn't made the houses cave in on themselves. The town was quiet, and while I normally thought quiet was bad, here it just felt old. Like the town itself was wishing it would be forgotten, and its residents were slowly dying away. I didn't see anyone around my age here, and it didn't seem like the town had been well taken care of.

By the time I arrived at the martial arts studio Zain had directed me to and paid the taxi driver what felt like entirely too little money, I got the suspicion I was going to have to break in. Which was a very Zain thing to do, but the last time I had picked a lock was years ago, and I did not have those supplies with me. The sign said it wasn't going to be open until the afternoon, which made sense as I was certain everyone had to thaw out after freezing in their sleep. I was about to turn and see if the taxi was still there when the door opened, and I found myself staring into my brother's supernaturally green eyes.

There was no questioning this was my brother, even though, for the first time in my life, I had to look up at him instead of down. The growth spurt he had wished for had finally happened, and while he had always been obnoxiously short as a child, he was now a good half a foot taller than I was. Which honestly, was a bit rude of him. His skin was a deep bronze, which surprised me, considering I wasn't sure Annelton even knew what the sun was. But despite the changes and the hard reality he had grown up so much, he still had the same mischievous smile I remembered.

That was until he opened his mouth.

"Glad the snow didn't stop you from coming in," he said, his voice now a deep tenor—though entirely too professional for what I thought was reuniting with my brother, "It's been a while since I've had a private lesson, and I wasn't sure if you were going to make me actually take you up on the no-show fee."

"Private...?" I started to ask before he casually flicked his head at one of the neighboring rooftops. I saw the glint of something shining back, and the way he was speaking became clear. Zain was being watched, and if we were lucky, the people who were spying on him had no idea who I was. And the "Toby is right" part of me immediately pointed to this as yet another reason as to why I should have passed on the assignment to someone else. It took me much longer than it should have to realize Zain was being watched.

I nodded at him and followed him into the studio, only for all of my senses to be assaulted with the world's loudest death metal playlist.

"Okay, that should cover the bugs," Zain yelled, though I could barely hear him above the music. I know it was the point, but I still gave him a very nasty glare over the fact I was being forced to listen to this. "You will have to fight me though, they're watching through the windows." He said this as nonchalantly as he could yell it, as if he was saying the sky was blue or that water was wet.

I didn't need to ask who was watching him. The Circle of Shadows was the only answer. His mother's ancient murder cult, which Dad had forbidden us from learning about. Even knowing the name the Circle of Shadows made him upset, because if it was up to him, he would have preferred Zain to appear out of thin air instead of us acknowledging the fact he had cheated on Mom.

Another pang of anger shot through me as I remembered the first thing I hated my father for, and I distracted myself by taking off my shoes and wondering if fighting Zain was going to ruin my jeans. They weren't flexible enough for me to do anything, and I wished he had given me a dress code with his clandestine instructions on how to find him.

"Wait, that's really what you're wearing?" he asked as he took in my outfit, and I could hear the cackle of teasing in his voice.

"You want to spar, you give me advanced notice," I shot back, and for a moment it was just like the five years had never passed, and we were teasing each other from across the Nest.

"Martial Arts School, Nikki," Zain said, motioning around him. "I thought it was self-explanatory. I mean, did we ever have a morning where we didn't start the day...?" Zain paused for a moment, cocking his head as he analyzed me. I had seen him do this plenty of times as a kid, he was looking at my muscles, the way I moved, figuring out my weak spots. "You're out of practice," he concluded, looking up at me in surprise. "I expected better from you."

"It wasn't like I was going to use any of Dad's lessons in the real world, " I self-consciously muttered, but Zain didn't reply as he went to a cabinet and pulled out a t-shirt and sweats I'm guessing he assumed would fit me, as he motioned to one of the changing rooms.

"Dad's world *is* the real world, you idiot," he quietly said into my ears. "Pretending otherwise is going to get you killed." I hated how correct he was, and Zain didn't even know the reason I was here yet. I wasn't fully out of shape. I took kickboxing classes a few times a week to relieve stress. I just had wrongly assumed my days of punching people in the face were over. Not to mention, I had a security team, two bodyguards, and plenty of others who were likely to jump in front of a gun to keep me from getting hurt.

Okay, maybe not plenty. But enough.

It felt wrong being here without my security team, something I knew for sure Zain was going to make fun of when he found out. But they didn't know about my past, and I told them I was spending the next three weeks on a private island where nobody would find me, so they got a three-week paid vacation. Seemed like a fair trade-off.

As I changed into the clothes, I retched at the intense smell of body odor that screamed they hadn't been washed in a few uses and had been marinated in sweat. This had to be a tactic Zain was using to get the upper hand, even though he had never needed it before.

"Better," Zain said as I walked out, motioning me to the mat. The music was still blaring, but I was at least able to start to tune it out and focus on Zain.

"So, is it worth it to ask any questions, or are you planning on avoiding them all?" I asked, hoping he would go easy on me.

That hope was immediately dashed as he had me pinned to the ground before I even got into a fighting stance, and I hit so hard that I was convinced my entire body was going to be bruised within the next few minutes.

"Probably avoid them," he answered with his signature mischievous smirk. "Plus I'm much more curious as to why you were trying to find me."

"Considering you're standing right in front of me, I would say I *did* find you," I said, getting up and getting into position. Zain dodged at me, and I was able to block it before I found my arm twisted behind me. He was faster, moving as fluidly as I would expect a ghost would. And while I knew his powers only included talking to the dead, I was almost certain he was as much a specter as those he could speak to. I tried breaking out of his hold, but I was once again on the floor.

Another easy loss. I could feel Zain's disappointment without having to look at him.

"Not to mention," I continued, pushing myself back up off the floor, "I knew searching your name would be enough to get your attention, considering you're the one who taught me how to set up internet alerts in the first place. Especially when you're keeping such a low profile." Being slammed into the floor twice in a row made me feel like I needed to rest for a minute. And that was not a good sign. Not. At. All.

"Unfortunately for you, as my mother has been trying to ignore my existence by sticking me in this frozen wasteland, I am not allowed to use the internet," Zain chuckled. "Fortunately for you, I have my sources anyway." A surprise attack came my way, and I was able to dodge it. The instincts were slowly waking up, though it wasn't great. Zain smiled, and it scared me—he was definitely about to go a lot harder. "She thinks I had too much publicity with Dad, so she dumped me here so I could train and only train. I think she was hoping my brain would rot into something she could control from the boredom."

"Oh," I said, a little surprised. Yasmine Hadi had always been a bit of a secret. I knew she was the head of the Circle of Shadows, and the organization had tried to recruit Dad. I knew she was dangerous, and somewhere in the recruitment process, she convinced Dad to cheat on my Mom, and as a result, we got Zain.

But the number one thing I knew about Yasmine Hadi was we had been under explicit orders to run away if she decided to show up.

"No, don't give me the 'you forgot my mom is a murderer' face," Zain said, practically reading my mind. "Just like you shouldn't forget *your* mom was the world's most wanted jewelry thief." Zain calmly shrugged, before coming at me with such an intensity it didn't match the nonchalant tone of his voice. "Dad always wanted to believe people could be redeemed. I think it's why he was attracted to our mothers: he always saw them as projects. People he could fix. And he did a good job with Katya." I was on the floor again, hitting harder this time from the distraction of talking about my mom. "Not so great a job with my mother. Or me." It wasn't the first time I had heard Zain talk about himself or our mothers as objects. It was something that came from his background: it was easier not to get attached if a person was an idea instead of a life. Once, I would have thought he had moved out of thinking of himself as an object, but it seemed like I was wrong.

I attempted to get up, only to find myself on the floor again. Zain looked at me with complete disbelief, twinged in disappointment. I realized the hard truth I had been hoping to avoid: he had been going easy on me. Once upon a time, I would have been able to counter this. But that ability had been buried the day I watched my Dad leave and never come back.

"So," I said, rolling out my muscles as I got up, "the Circle of Shadows really has a stronghold in Annelton?" Honestly, the question itself felt like a sick joke, as it didn't make sense an ancient shadow organization would choose somewhere in the middle of nowhere as a base of operations. From what I had come to understand, they worked underground in cities, places with power, places that were important.

"Yes," Zain bluntly answered, "and you just walked right into it." The way he phrased everything, the way he had been talking about himself, it wasn't the first time I feared this was a trap. That my brother was once again an enemy instead of an ally. But Zain's eyes darted to the window, to the speakers, just enough for me to know he was testing how much he could say. How much he could get away with. That he was expecting someone to burst in and kill me for getting these answers at any second. "So, why are you here, Nik?"

"Nightshade's back," I answered, as I hit Zain and knocked him to the floor for the first time. I had wondered if Zain had known, if the ghost of the victim had spoken to him. If I hadn't actually been carrying this secret alone. "And his latest victim was Brittney."

"Any clues?" Zain asked, coming at me again, but I dodged, wrapping his arm behind his back in the same hold he had me in earlier.

"He wrote ''Birds of a feather don't fly together,' on her wall in her blood," I answered, "so, if his past clues are to be believed, he's after us. My guess is he thinks we're unfinished business."

"He could be after Dad..." Zain muttered, his brows scrunching together as he started to think through the situation. "Trying to lure him out of hiding? Same idea of the night when he captured us, getting Dad too emotional to think straight. Only this time, he's raising the stakes."

It was a much better hypothesis than the police had come up with, and it fit Nightshade's patterns so much more than anything else had.

"The joke's on him, though. Dad made it clear he doesn't actually care about us with how quickly he bolted," Zain continued, and a flash of intense anger passed over his face in a millisecond. "He'd probably thank Nightshade for taking care of his loose ends. If I ever met either of them again, I'd just put a bullet between their eyes and solve the problem of dealing with either of them ever again."

"Not funny," I snapped at him, though I wasn't sure he was joking. From the moment Zain arrived in our lives, his instinct was always to jump straight to murder. It was uncanny to hear it from a child, but now that he was an adult? It was much more chilling.

"Come on, Nik, you know I've killed people before," Zain scoffed, punctuating it with a very teenage eye roll. Just like I did. Just like Nate would have. The one mannerism we all managed to inherit from Dad was the way we rolled our eyes. "I had before I ever showed up on Dad's doorstep, and I have since I left. Sometimes, it's the easier option." I bristled at the darkness Zain was forced to live with. It had been something I had always wanted to ignore about my baby brother: the fact he had been forced to live in such darkness. He was forced back into it after he disappeared from his bedroom days after dad left. "Plus, the official reason my mom has me training so much is she wants me to be ready to kill *her*."

I blinked, barely dodging a hit to the face I knew Zain had planned on landing while I was distracted by his admission. It was just like him to play dirty—or as he called it: an advantage.

"Don't talk like that. You're more than just a weapon," I said.

"How do you know, Nik? You haven't seen me in five years, and even back then, you only saw what you wanted to see." Something changed in Zain, the darkness growing behind his eyes, making them almost seem to glow green. I wasn't sure if he thought he was being listened to, or if it was something he truly believed. But even if he did, I couldn't. He was the biggest constant in my life before it all exploded. He was always there to spar, train, and sass me; but he was also my biggest source of comfort, to remind me of my worth when Dad had once again forgotten about me, to show I was just as important as Nate was.

"I know because I'm standing here," I countered, "You've beaten me to a pulp, but if you were only a weapon, you would have stabbed me before I walked through the door. You care, Zain, even if you don't want to admit it, and you always have."

"And it made me soft," he spat out the last word, lunging at me, and I let go, letting my instincts take over, and while I wasn't sure how I did it, I managed to pin Zain to the floor.

"Then why am I still alive, Zain?" I asked in his ear, unable to tell if he could even hear me over the music. I wanted to hear him tell me it was because he cared, I wanted him to say he missed me, and I wanted to have my brother back. Because in opening the box of what I had left behind, the biggest thing I needed was my brother.

"Yes, Zain, that is an excellent question," a new voice said, turning off the music. My ears rang from the sudden silence, as I looked at the sultry voice which sounded like it belonged singing jazz music in a nightclub. "I believe you were told to end the Caldwell line, should they come looking for you. Why is this one still breathing?" She was tall, taller even than Zain, and her eyes were a pale blue that looked like the icicles hanging from the rafters outside.

I could tell she wasn't Zain's mother. Her coloring was too pale, and she couldn't have been much older than I was, even if she clearly was planning on treating me like I was five years old.

"So, little girl," she said, proving my point. "Are you here to steal our Prince of Shadows?" The woman pounced, and a knife I hadn't seen was now pressed against my throat. She was so casual in how she held it against me, hard enough for me to feel it, but soft enough I wasn't bleeding. Yet. I could tell she was going to break my skin cell-by-cell and relish watching me squirm.

"She's here because she's my sister, and we haven't seen each other in five years," Zain droned, his voice sounding so stereotypically bored and annoyed that I remembered he was only eighteen—this is what he would have been like if he had been allowed to act his age. " You know, regular family things."

I was hoping Zain had a plan that didn't involve me bleeding to death, considering I didn't escape one murderer at home just to get my throat slit here.

"My Prince," the woman said, her voice gleefully taunting him, "When have you ever had the luxury of a normal family?" I knew this was a challenge, daring him to attack so she'd have the perfect excuse to slit my throat. "Tell me her reason, and I'll kill her quickly. Painlessly even, out of respect for your bond. Or you can watch your sister die a horrible and painful death as you watch. The choice is yours. How would you like to take care of your weakness?"

Well, I truly did not like being labeled as a "weakness," even if I had just had my butt handed to me on the mat.

"I truly was just here to see Zain," I said, trying to distract her so Zain could get me out of this. "I didn't even know the Circle was here, and I really want nothing to do with you." I could see Zain look at me, silently pleading for me to keep my mouth shut. A valid ask, considering I felt the slightest trickle of blood starting to run down my neck.

"To turn down the Circle means your family will be hunted across generations until all of your names are extinguished," the woman laughed in my ear. "Your father sealed your fate long before this moment, little girl."

I had not thought I could hate Dad more. I thought there was nothing else he could have done to make me hate him more. And yet, somehow, five years later, there was yet another thing to add to the list. Because I would have loved some warning that an ancient murder cult had marked me down for murder when I was a child—and it made me wonder if that was the reason Zain had been dropped with us: to kill us all when we didn't expect it.

But the real question was why hadn't they gone after me before? Now wasn't the time to ask, because all I could think of was how to get out of this.

"Nicole is harmless," Zain said, rolling his eyes yet again. I was starting to think his eyes were defaulted that way when talking to members of his cult. "However, the Circle is matriarchal. Lines are determined through the mothers, and as Nicole and Nathan do not share mine, it was determined they weren't worth killing. If my mother didn't think it was worth it, then I believe you shouldn't either." He was so casual as he walked toward a counter, sitting on it like he was talking about the classes he was supposed to teach during the day instead of whether or not my life was forfeit. "But... you have always been a bit of an extremist, Lilith..." He didn't finish his thought as two throwing stars seemed to shoot out of his hands—landing in the woman's eye and temple. She fell to the ground, dead on impact, and I screamed. I hadn't meant to, but I could still feel the way the blood was trickling down my neck.

And Zain was smiling. The expression was so out of place with the fact he had so blatantly murdered her, that I finally saw exactly what my father was scared of. Why he had never let us speak about the Circle past the basics to explain Zain's presence.

I saw his son, who loved killing and was in his element.

"Alright, that's taken care of, and before you say anything, Dad's killing rules don't apply here," Zain insisted before going over to the cabinet he had pulled my clothes out of and started pulling out an arsenal of weapons. "We're also going to need to steal a car."

"Zain, you just killed someone!" I exclaimed, "What are you talking about?"

"Obviously, I'm helping out with Nightshade, I just had to lure Lilith out and get her out of the way. Thanks for being such a great distraction, I really appreciate it, sis," Zain said, giving me finger guns as he clicked his tongue. Which felt wildly out of place considering there was a dead body on the floor in a giant pool of blood.

Zain used my attempt to wrap my head around what was going on to push me out the door, a wall of cold snapping me back to reality. He was already looking at different cars as I rubbed my exposed arms, hoping I wasn't going to get frostbite. The door to the ugliest SUV I had seen in my life opened at Zain's touch, and he motioned for me to get in.

"Come on, we have about three minutes before she was supposed to confirm your death," he said, thinking out loud as I got into the passenger seat. He had already exposed the wires and was fiddling with them, causing the car to roar to life. I buckled my seat belt, figuring there needed to be at least one thing in my report for Toby that wouldn't give him a migraine. But as Zain floored the gas pedal, I realized keeping track of a list of things Toby was going to hate was pointless. He was going to hate all of it.

Chapter Four

"So, why Brittney?" Zain asked, his eyes darting between the road and the rearview mirror. It took me a second to realize he had bounced back to talking about the case. "Nightshade should have gone after you first. You're the easier target."

"I've got a security team. I'm hard to get to," I deadpanned, insulted that my very murdery brother thought I was easy to kill. "Brittney didn't have money, and her apartment wasn't the safest. Pretty easy to break in, and I doubt anyone was going to complain about the weird noises."

"Was Jacob moved to a safe location?" he asked, "or did he just cuss Nightshade out so creatively that he was too offended to make him a target?" For the first time since the nightmare had started, I thought about Brittney's twin. The police hadn't said anything about him, and from the pictures of the crime scene, it was obvious Brittney had been living alone.

"Nobody's mentioned him," I finally said, feeling a little guilty I was included in the statement. "I think something might have happened that made the twins stop talking."

"Think he snapped and is a copycat Nightshade?" Zain asked, a teasing smile on his face was met with a glare as he realized it wasn't fun. "Right. Sorry. I forgot, Nate was the one who also saw that probability. Not you."

"He was rough around the edges, but that doesn't mean he's going to become a supervillain, no matter what you and Nate say," I scoffed. I thought about continuing when the unmistakable sound of two motorcycles behind us cut me off before I could continue my pseudo-lecture.

"Better crouch, they've got guns," Zain said, flooring the gas pedal, which knocked me back into the seat and locked my seatbelt.

"How am I supposed to crouch, I'm buckled into...?" I was interrupted by a round of gunshots as the back window of the SUV shattered all over the back seat.

"You have got to be kidding me," Zain muttered, before pressing my seatbelt button and pushing me forward. "And before you start looking for people to help us, it's the middle of hunting season, and they probably are going to think the gunshots mean a deer wandered into town."

Hunting season. Of course. Another reason never to come back to Annelton.

"There's a pass through the mountains, hard to do a chase through," Zain said, swerving the car onto a new street. "Should be able to get us to relative safety in Wallabrook."

"That can't be a real name," I muttered. I didn't know where Wallabrook was, but it somehow sounded worse than Annelton. "Why don't you head toward the airport?"

"Because your pilot's probably in an unmarked grave by now," Zain shrugged. "Plane probably was stolen, too. Hope you weren't too attached." Never in my life had I ever heard of a plane being stolen. It sounded entirely too ridiculous to be true. "This area? Perfect for the Circle. Nobody's going to think to look here, easy to go off the grid if you need to. Don't recommend it. Had to do it for a year when I was fifteen. Mom's orders."

If we weren't currently being chased by gunmen, I would have thought Zain was describing the plot of a bad horror movie. The breaks squealed as Zain turned onto a new street and watched as the motorcycles drove past the intersection.

I crouched down further, figuring if I was going to have people firing guns at me more in the future, I was going to need to really start paying attention to Zain now. And then it hit me: the future. I was thinking about doing this in the future. Whatever it was that was woken up last night talking to Toby didn't just want this case, it wanted *this*.

And that was not a realization I could focus on right now, considering there was a good chance I was about to die.

Again, we swerved, and I heard more motorcycles, their engine roars coming from different directions. Zain sped up, adjusting the gears as he ran a red light, and I heard the tell-tale sounds of a crash behind us.

"Wait, they didn't see the red light?" I asked, trying my best to see from my hiding spot.

"Are you kidding? That was on purpose," Zain scoffed, his eyes never leaving the road. "Giant bonfire let everyone know where we're at, and sacrificing yourself for a terrible death is Circle training 101." So, clearly, they weren't just a shadow organization, they were also a cult. Great. Creating human bonfires was a whole new level of indoctrination I wasn't prepared to face when I woke up this morning.

We turned again, and I slammed into the passenger door, adding to the collection of bruises I was gaining today. But I saw a smirk and a light behind his eyes. He had some sort of plan.

Thank. Goodness.

"I need you to drive, switch places with me," Zain insisted, pulling one of his feet underneath him.

"That is a terrible idea unless your plan is for us to die," I grimaced and I heard him audibly groan in annoyance.

"Why? Can't you drive stick?" he frustratingly yelled at me.

"Actually... I can't drive a car. Never learned," I admitted. "Dad was supposed to teach me, but back home, it's more responsible not to own a car. So, I never learned."

"Oh, my god, Nik, it's like you've designed your life to be a walking death trap. You are so lucky to have me with you to save you from your idiotic life choices," Zain grumbled. He slammed on the brakes, and seconds later, I heard the sound of another crash—this time against a building. "Here," he said, handing me a gun, before accelerating at top speed again. "And you better know how to aim, or we're as dead as we'd be with you driving. So, climb in the back, shoot out their tires, and before you say anything about not wanting them dead, trust me—the world's better off without them. You can be all high and mighty about it after we survive this."

Even with Zain's apparent encouragement, I was still glad shooting out their tires did leave a small opportunity for survival. While his very lax attitude on killing people was disturbing, there was no way I could handle actively killing someone on my conscience. This, though? It was one of Dad's favorite tricks: injure, but don't kill. And if this town was a Circle stronghold, there was definitely someone here who could patch them up.

I attempted to gracefully climb to the back of the car, only for Zain to swerve and launch me into the back seat. It took a few seconds to reorient myself, and as I finally looked out what used to be the back window, I realized nobody was behind us.

"Give it a second," he said, his eyes looking at me through the mirror, and I saw a car turn onto the street—and accelerate so we were bumper-to-bumper. Apparently, they had speed on their side.

First shot: I hit nothing, which was expected considering I had my eyes closed.

Second shot: I hit the top of the car, which only seemed to aggravate the driver. Guess he thought I was shooting at him and not his tires.

Third shot: surprisingly hit the tire underneath the driver's seat. The car spiraled out of control, flipped, and then burst into flames.

Oops.

"Hey, better than I thought you'd do!" Zain exclaimed from the front, as if all I needed to be okay with this was some positive reinforcement. I kept watching, checking for anyone who might be following us, but as he ran a red light, we finally made it onto the highway.

I took a few shaky breaths as I climbed back into the front seat and put my seatbelt back on for a sense of normalcy. I saw Zain roll his eyes at me, but I didn't care. At this point, I was expecting a helicopter to start firing missiles at us.

"First rest stop I find, we're switching cars," Zain said once I got my breathing under control. "Then we need to get to Wallabrook, change clothes, and change cars again. From there, they're going to expect us to hit up an airport, so we're going to road trip down to drive to Lumeria City."

"Oh, you have an entire plan, and I'm just along for the ride?" I asked, realizing how tired I was now that the adrenaline was wearing off.

"I mean, I was going to have you drive for part of it," Zain deadpanned, "though maybe I can teach you to drive. It's going to be a long trip."

"So what's in Lumeria City?" I asked, settling into the car.

"Nate," Zain answered, "and he is going to be so pissed to see us."

Chapter Five

I WAS WEARING A plaid flannel. And second-hand jeans. And a beanie. Not to mention a pair of sunglasses with the lenses popped out to give the illusion I was wearing glasses. I had never liked the hipster aesthetic, though it seemed in the mountain regions of Lumeria, this was just what everyone wanted to wear.

It was wild to think I had just been at a fashion show, and now I looked like a fashion disaster.

Zain and I had driven in silence after getting out of Wallabrook, which somehow was a bigger city, despite the name sounding like it was another backwoods town in the middle of nowhere. I had dozed off after two hours of landscape, only to be woken up by my phone ringing.

"Hello?" I sleepily asked into the phone, before realizing it was a video call I had put up to my ear. Which meant Toby could now see me in all my lumberjack glory.

"Nickel, what are you wearing?" Toby asked, though I could tell he was holding in laughter.

"Don't say anything else," I groaned. "I know I look like I belong in some artisan coffee shop working on my next indie novel."

"You know, I don't think I want to know," Toby wisely admitted, shaking his head. "I was calling for a status update. Have you found Zain yet?"

"Hey, Space-Guy!" Zain called from the driver's seat, and I tilted my phone so Toby could see him, too.

"Question answered," Toby said, "or at least *that* question answered. Is there a reason you hadn't told me about the plane heist? Or the murdered pilot?"

"I was napping," I lamely said. "We had a hot exit getting out of Annelton. Circle of Shadows."

"Nikki, are you kidding me?" Toby asked as he processed it, "You're only approved for the Nightshade case and..."

"Dude," Zain cut in, "she didn't know. We made it out. There's like a fifty percent chance they won't be a problem anymore. It's fine."

"Those statistics and your definition of fine both worry me," Toby muttered, and I could feel his stress through the phone. "Listen, Nickel, please be careful. What's the next move?"

"Lumeria City," I answered. "Nate's there, so I'm hoping we can convince him to join us. I think it'll be better for us all to be in one group than in a position for Nightshade to pick us off one by one."

"Good call, and if he doesn't want to come, we have plenty of safe houses in the area we can move him and his family into," Toby said, clearly writing something down on a notepad. "Gray's back in Calder Bay, so you should be able to get back to her quickly. It's only a four-hour drive between the Bay and Lumeria City, right?"

"On a good day with no traffic," I scoffed. "It's more like a six-hour drive."

"Alright, any idea where Jacob is?" Toby asked, and I grimaced as I was hoping he would have the answer to that question.

"You don't know?" I asked, glancing over at Zain, who shrugged.

"We lost track of him about a year and a half ago," Toby sighed. "I can see if we can find anything while you're talking to Nate and Gray. But with the training you got, if he doesn't want to be found…"

"I know," I nodded. Considering nobody's figured out where my Dad had gone in five years, I was certain Jacob was using every single trick we had learned to do the same.

"I'll get to work on that. Talk to you later, Nickel." The screen went dark, and I could see Zain smirking at me in the reflection.

"So… you and Toby are still together?"

"No," I snapped, "it never happened." A ripple of sadness and regret tinged through me, and part of me wondered what would have happened if I hadn't shut him out all those years ago.

I was sure he would have left me. Just like everyone else in my life did.

"Really?" Zain said, looking more confused as he took his eyes off the road to really look at me. "He turned you down when you've gotten hotter with age?"

"First of all, ew," I said, wincing at the compliment. "Second of all, I turned him down. Dad left. Nate left. You disappeared. I was stuck with all the business responsibilities and making sure our world didn't fall apart. Toby was just a distraction I couldn't afford."

"Then why are you so embarrassed for him to see you in flannel chic?" Zain asked, and I smacked him on the arm as he laughed. "Admit it Nik, you've still got it bad."

"You know what?" I said, adjusting myself in my seat. "I'm going to go back to my nap." Apparently, I needed the sleep, because one moment I drifted off, and the next, Zain was shaking me awake in a driveway.

I was positive he was trolling me when it came to our location. I had never seen something so stereotypical in my life. The two-story house, the white picket fence, the children's playset, and even the minivan that was parked right next to us. This was the exact level of "normal" I thought only happened in movies, the kind where living in a house like this meant you were hiding a deep dark secret.

Or in Nate's case, hiding from all of us.

I could tell someone was home. The lights were on inside, and I could smell something cooking through the open window. I wasn't entirely sure who would have been the one cooking, because between them, Nate couldn't cook, and Kitty would always choose take-out over a home-cooked meal.

"You think it's Kitty in there cooking?" Zain asked, clearly having the same thoughts I had.

"You're the one who knew Nate was here, and I asked no questions about how," I reminded him, "but the van is modified to be wheelchair accessible, so I think it's a safe bet to say, it's Kitty in there cooking."

"Didn't think they'd both get boring," Zain grimaced as he got out of the car. "Weird."

I felt like an intruder as Zain and I walked toward the front door, which swung open before I rang the doorbell. Two pairs of my brother's bright blue eyes stared up at me. Identical twins. I figured there was one kid with the playset, but two? I didn't see that coming at all.

"Mooooooooooooooooooooooooom! There's strangers at the door!" one of the boys called out.

"And one of them is the computer lady!" the other called out.

"Sawyer. Milo. If I have told you two once, I have told you a thousand times not to answer the door..." Kitty was beginning to lecture before she caught sight of the two of us.

"Nikki?" she quietly asked, a giant smile forming across her face. "Oh my stars, Zain? I think you're taller than Nate is now! Why didn't you tell us you were coming?"

"Long story," I said, motioning my head at the two small children who had almost immediately decided Zain was their new jungle gym. Looking at the boys I started to do some math, just by how old they seemed—and it quickly became obvious Kitty was probably in her first trimester when Nate disappeared. Which gave some answers, but also more questions. "Something's happened. So, we figured it best to tell you and Nate in person."

Kitty immediately understood, and I couldn't help but smile. She was still just as bright as I remembered, and even though she hadn't been one of Dad's birds, she had figured out he was the Eagle within five minutes of Nate introducing her to the family.

"Well, Nate's coaching cross country, so he won't be here for another half an hour or so, but you're free to stay for dinner. In fact, I'm going to insist on it." She led us through the house, which was just as stereotypical as the outside. It felt like I was walking through a sitcom, and I did not mean it as a compliment. "However," she continued from the kitchen, "you both volunteered yourselves for cooking duty for showing up without warning, so I hope you're ready for pasta night!"

"This is weird, right?" I whispered to Zain.

"Yeah, I think the door was a portal," he whispered back. "Mirror universe? Or are we on one of those prank TV shows?"

"Nikki, you're going to be on noodles. I remember your cooking—it's terrible," Kitty instructed. "Zain, you're on vegetable cutting duty. You should be able to find everything easily, I got a little crazy with the label maker Nate got me for my birthday, so everything's labeled."

"Definitely a prank show," I whispered to Zain before getting to work. This was just a weird, upper-middle-class world where the chances of serial killers coming after you were nonexistent, and the heroes were just stories you watched on the evening news.

"So, how have you both been?" Kitty asked, once she was sure the twins were distracted. "Having incredible sibling adventures together?"

"No," I awkwardly answered. "I hadn't seen Zain until... Was it today or yesterday? I lost track of time."

"Yesterday," he nodded. "My mom came calling. None of you would want to meet her."

Kitty winced, and I had a feeling she at least had the context of who Zain's mother was, even if she had never been included in those conversations.

"I've just been working a lot," I said as I filled up a pot with water. But as I glanced over at Kitty, I could see she was waiting for me to say more, only to realize I was done. I knew what her face looked like when she was pitying me—and I knew I sounded both sad and lonely. It was hard to explain I didn't need anyone else, that if I let too many people in, it was just going to hurt more when they all inevitably left me again.

"Well, I saw the pictures from the show," Kitty smiled, trying to be encouraging, "and I swear, your design work looks like it came from the heavens. And what about you, Zain? What kind of adventures have you been on?"

"Just finished high school, did dual enrollment so I got my first two years of college out of the way, work part time at a martial arts studio," he answered, attacking the vegetables with his knife like they were the Circle members who had chased us out of Annelton.

"Oh, that's amazing! Any idea what you're going to major in once you're in university?" Kitty asked, almost immediately. It felt like she had been saving them up, creating a mental list for when she saw us again. That she cared enough to see us again, unlike my brother, who I was starting to think hadn't missed us at all.

"Biochemistry," Zain answered. "Figured it would be a good way to help with creating more potent poisons. Adjusting them to do the most damage."

Despite it being one of the most Zain answers in existence, it was clear Kitty had not expected it. She looked around, clearly checking that her sons hadn't heard the admission. And I wondered if she had expected all of us to retire, just like she and Nate had, in a world where we didn't have to worry about these things.

"That's... interesting," she finally settled on saying after she processed it. "Nate's a history teacher and became department chair this year. And he also coaches track and cross country at the school. Then I work for the Department, which unfortunately, I don't think either of you has the clearance to hear more since you haven't renewed your licenses yet."

"You're a hacker, and Nate's still bossy, got it," Zain nodded, reading between the lines of Kitty's words immediately. He looked around the kitchen before opening a cupboard called "bowls and other storage containers" and got out two: one for him and one for me to put the noodles in once they were done. Which was proving to be a problem, because even though they had one of those stoves that boiled water quickly, I had forgotten to set a timer for the noodles, so I had no idea how to tell if they were done.

"That's one way of putting it," Kitty laughed. "Though Nate has mellowed out..."

The front door opened, interrupting her thought.

"Hey, babe!" Nate's voice said, sounding almost the exact same as it had the last time I saw him. "And hi..." He paused, and I could tell he was using his powers to tell who it was visiting, trying to play off that he knew there were guests. I guess it was one of the few perks of being able to see five seconds into the future, there weren't any surprises. "No..." he muttered, before storming into the kitchen. "Absolutely not. You two, get out of my house. Now."

"That is no way to talk to your siblings," Kitty snapped, wheeling in front of him with a hard glare. "And before you even think about having them arrested for trespassing, I happily invited them in so nobody would do anything."

"She might be my sibling," Nate snapped, and it was clear we were watching a fight play out that had been happening for years, "but *he* isn't." Zain decided the insult was a sign he should twirl the kitchen knife, because of course he took pleasure in pressing all of Nate's buttons. Some things never changed.

"Last I checked, he was," Kitty nonchalantly said, before going over to a different cupboard, opening it up, and handing Nate a stack of plates. "Now, if you would please set the table, we do have guests, and I would appreciate you trying to make them feel welcome."

"No," Nate said, though he did start setting the table despite the fight. "We moved here to get away from them. We changed our last name to get away from them. The last thing we need is for them to suck us back into that life."

"Ironic, when your wife works for the department," I deadpanned, dumping the pasta in the strainer and hoping it was done. And if it wasn't, at least Nate would be forced to eat crunchy noodles for how terrible he was acting. "She's more in it than I am."

Zain snorted, and I could tell he disagreed. Which was a fight we could have when we didn't have our older brother practically frothing at the mouth at the sight of us.

"Okay, I don't care. Whatever this is," Nate said, waving his hand at both of us, "go do it somewhere else. I have a life, I have kids, and whatever reason you showed up on our doorsteps, I'm not interested. Now leave. Please." It was clear the "please" was an attempt to placate Kitty—and from the glare she was giving him, it wasn't about to happen.

"Told you he'd get gray hairs," Zain muttered so I could hear, before looking at our older brother, "but fine. Be that way. Enjoy getting murdered."

"That's enough. All of you," Kitty snapped, and it had been so long since anyone had talked to me in a "mom voice" I couldn't help but listen, "When Toby told me you'd be coming today, I had been optimistic enough time had passed where you could at least be civil. However, as the three of you cannot seem to behave like adults, I will. Nate, they are staying. I'm excited for the boys to get to know their aunt and uncle. And then once they're in bed, we are going to talk. The three of you can't avoid each other forever."

"Yes, we can," all three of us muttered in unison.

"Not on my watch," she said in a sing-song voice as she went back into the kitchen. "So, Nate, finish setting the table or you'll have to do the dishes too. Nikki and Zain both helped with dinner, so you need to contribute."

Chapter Six

O NCE UPON A TIME, family dinners were a Caldwell family constant. Mom had insisted on it—it didn't matter what schedules were like, how busy anyone was. We would eat dinner together as a family. It didn't matter if Dad was black and blue from whatever villain he was punching the night before. It didn't matter if Nate and I had a million extracurriculars. When Zain arrived, she immediately involved him in the family traditions, even though, looking back, I was sure she struggled with his entire existence.

After her death, it was a habit. But as time went on, we all just grew quieter and quieter, and Dad started training and recruiting us to his mission. Dinner together became a luxury—training and patrol schedules didn't allow for it to happen regularly.

And by the time Dad abandoned us, family dinner was a long-forgotten idea.

Part of me wished it stayed that way, because it was awkward sitting at a table with my nephews, who I hadn't known existed until an hour ago, rambling about preschool. All while their mother tried to include us in the conversation, and their father was glaring at us for daring to be at his dinner table. The war of our being there was far from over between Nate and Kitty—though it was clear she would win. But everything was as stereotypical and normal as the house. It felt like another world, a world where Zain and I were outsiders. I had always known this sort of life wasn't for me. It wasn't for a Caldwell—Dad had always said we couldn't be like regular people because we were role models. The kind of people that others should strive to be. We needed a spotless public image so nobody would want to look into what we did with our private time.

But there was a monotony to this, a set routine that didn't change day after day. And I hated it. It felt like I was trapped in a life I couldn't get out of, and I realized my life was a routine. Not the domestic kind, but a routine that was set around making sure I was so busy, I never had time to think about how boring it had become.

That was not the kind of realization I wanted to have over undercooked noodles and jarred pasta sauce.

Glancing at Zain, I could see the same emotions mirrored on his face—the need for adventure, the hatred of a life of routine. Nate had always been the one who longed for adventure when he was younger, or maybe he was only pretending since he was Dad's favorite. But as I looked around, I wondered if that longing had something to do with Dad's DNA—if the nature vs. nurture experiment that came from Dad adopting him showed nature won out in the end.

Maybe this sort of life was one Nate's biological father had wanted, which was something our Mom never would have settled for. Or if, in all of Nate's stubbornness, he just threw himself into having the exact opposite life of what Dad would have wanted. And if that was the case? That was all our Mom.

I watched as the after-dinner chores and bedtime routines took over the house. I watched as Nate would glare at us every time he passed us. We were intruders in his life, but it was like he had forgotten we had plenty of reasons to be angry at him, too.

"Why are you two still here?" Nate growled as he came back into the living room, followed by Kitty, who was giving him a very intense eye roll, clearly over her husband's attitude.

"Because we need to talk," I dryly stated, tired of the insinuation we were here just to disrupt his stupid, perfect life. "Brittney's dead."

"Oh. Wow," Nate said, and I wondered if I had been slightly too blunt. But since it got him to listen to me, I decided I didn't care. "It's terrible, but what does that have to do with me?"

I glanced down the hallway, just to make sure there weren't any prying toddler eyes spying on us, before pulling out the file of pictures from my bag. I could tell he was wary, with how official it all looked, until he saw a picture of the crime scene. Nate's face immediately paled as he took in the details, and his eyes flashed gold for a moment. I hated it when he used his powers in a conversation. It always meant he wanted to know the answer before he ever asked the question. Then he'd choose to ask a different question, instead.

Perks of being able to see slightly into the future, you could choose a different path. I'm sure Nate thought he was saving time, but it was always annoying.

"How is he not dead, Nikki?" Nate asked, pleading with me to tell him he was wrong.

"I know this is going to sound terrible, but I need you to process faster. Britt's dead, Nightshade's made his grand reappearance, and the Circle of Shadows is kind of after us. Or at least me and Zain—not entirely sure if they're mad at anyone other than us."

"What did you do to piss off your mother?" Nate snapped at Zain, extremely accusatory. And maybe with the car chase, it was slightly deserved, but I hated how Nate felt he had to be on the defensive.

"Existed," Zain deadpanned, refusing to elaborate more.

Nate let out a deep sigh as he leaned back in his recliner—because he was, in fact, basic enough to have an old worn-down recliner. But I had seen this sort of face on him before: he was strategizing. One of his strengths was that he was always good in a crisis. However, it always came with a helping of "I know more than you" and a side of "I told you so."

"What are you planning on doing about all of this?" Nate asked.

I was shocked he didn't immediately take the lead, but instead wanted to hear us out. Or he wanted to hear our plan so he could tell me all the things wrong with it. It was hard to tell with him sometimes.

"At the moment, the plan is to get everyone back together. Or at least warn them, and get everyone who isn't interested in helping to a safe house," I explained. "Zain was first on my list, and he knew where you were, so..."

"Why didn't you just ask Toby for my address instead?" Nate interrupted, and honestly, I felt a little stupid. Of course, with Kitty and Toby still working for the same place, they would still be in touch. And Nate had such an insane obsession with rules, he probably had filled out every piece of transfer paperwork the Department asked for, even if he didn't plan on putting on his suit ever again.

"I didn't think about it. I haven't worked with the Department in years, and he didn't offer up the information," I snapped at him. "And I forgot we could ask them to do that kind of legwork for us. Or maybe he just assumed I knew where you lived."

"Okay, you really haven't been as involved as I thought you were," Nate muttered, and I could catch the condescension in his voice that had been a hallmark of my teenage years.

"Anyway," I muttered, "we were coming to get you, then we're going back to the Bay to pick up Gray. She's finishing up her PhD at the college, so she's easy to find. It's just Jacob who is a bit of a mystery."

"Yeah, I haven't talked to him, but you can ask Britt..." He paused as both Zain and I glared at him. It was an autopilot question, but the wrong one. "Right. Not an option. But you could ask Toby. As I'm assuming he's your handler."

"Yeah, and I bet he still wants to handle her, too," Zain muttered loud enough for me to hear, and I immediately threw one of the decorative pillows at him.

"We. Are. Not. Together," I stated, smacking him with another pillow to get the point across.

"By the comet, you two are such children," Nate groaned. "How are my students more behaved than you?"

"Because you bore them to sleep?" Zain guessed, and Nate's face tensed as if he was ready to throw us out again.

"Okay. Children. Back to the mission," he said, pulling out what I assumed was his teacher voice, "Did you at least check through her apartment to see if there were any signs of Jacob when you took the pictures?"

"Fun story, these aren't my pictures. They're the cops'." Nate was clearly resisting the urge to facepalm. "But Toby is having a team look through the scene for anything, and I figured the cops' pictures were fine."

"Forgive her, she's gone too soft and forgotten how terrible the police are with crime scenes," Zain interjected, acting as if I had committed one of the most serious sins. "Luckily, she had Toby getting actual experts in for information, so we can look over that once we get to Calder Bay."

"Once *you* get back to Calder Bay," Nate corrected, though it wasn't quite as forceful as he had been earlier. "Hopefully, Toby's team finds something, but then, you should have gone in yourself. It's always better to see the site before there are hundreds of hands on it. Is there anything else you could think of that could help?"

I started to shake my head no, considering the cops had been no help with their "it was my fault, as Brittney had called me last" theory, only for me to realize she had left me a voicemail. One I hadn't listened to yet. I hated that Zain's "gone soft" theory was right, but I pulled out my phone and let it play on the speaker.

"Nikki!" the clearly terrified voice of Brittney screamed out of my phone's speaker, *"He's here. He's been following me for weeks, and I know you've been ignoring me. I need help. I don't know who he is, or why he's after me, but I've seen him everywhere. For weeks. Please pick up the phone."*

In the background, there was a loud crack of a door being forced open, and another scream. A struggle, the telltale thump of the phone dropping to the floor. And then a new voice.

"Well, aren't you a naughty little bird," Nightshade's voice crooned, *"and you're calling for help."* His terrifying giggle sent a chill down my spine. *"Well, well, isn't it Nightingale. I can't wait to see you."* And then it ended.

I had known I was a target; the writing on the wall had made it perfectly clear. But now I wondered if it meant he had planned on me next. If my decision to fly out of the city had saved my life.

"I had hoped it was a copycat," Nate muttered, his eyes clearly in shock.

"Yeah, we'd all know that voice anywhere," Zain agreed. For the first time since we had stepped into the house, there was an understanding between the three of us, there was no denying it was the exact same voice that had echoed through the warehouse before Dad had shot his decoy.

"He's going to come after you, Nate," I quietly said. "Maybe Kitty too. She knew all our secrets, and we have no idea how Nightshade figured us out. Let alone if he knows who we worked with."

"You're the next target, and my guess would be Gray after. You're all in Calder Bay," Nate agreed, "but there is safety in numbers. You were right about that, Nikki, and it's five against one. If we can get to Gray before Nightshade, she probably will have some gadgets that will help us out, and keep the two of you from going off the rails."

"We?" I asked, giving him a smirk.

"I think he senses all the laws we bent yesterday," Zain chuckled. "He's not going to let it happen again."

"I'm sorry, bending laws?" Nate asked, and his *"I'm going to give a lecture face"* clearly hadn't changed in the past five years.

"Everything was covered under the Hero Code," I insisted.

"I mean, Nikki did kind of lie to the police," Zain decided to list anyway. "I'm traveling with a fake ID, we stole like five cars, and I killed at least three people. Probably more."

"You're killing people again, Zain? We've talked about this. Multiple times," Nate snapped, "We. Don't. Kill. People."

"You don't. I do." Zain shot back, and I felt my phone buzz in my pocket—and was thrilled to get away from the fight that was most certainly coming. I walked out of the room and saw two sets of eyes looking at me from down the hallway, so I walked outside, instead.

"Go to bed," I hissed at the twins, watching them both shoo as I answered the phone. "Tobias. Why did you not tell me you had Nate's address?"

"Wow, hello to you, too, Nicole," Toby said, clearly startled by the greeting he got.

"Sorry, Nate's being impossible. He and Zain are in the middle of a fight. You're just getting... residual fighting?" I wasn't even sure if that was a thing, but it certainly felt like a thing.

"Well, to answer your question, I had reached out to Kitty about moving her, Nate, and the boys to a safe house, and she turned it down," Toby explained.

"Okay, that explains a lot about how Kitty has been acting," I sighed, "but you do realize that didn't answer the question right?"

"Kitty said you already had their address, and she'd see you when you showed up," Toby explained, and I realized exactly how much of this Kitty had planned. Nate was not going to like that at all.

"Well, I didn't, but Zain did," I sighed.

"So, you found him, and that's a win!" Toby exclaimed, and I could tell he was trying to make me feel like I wasn't a complete failure at all of this. It was sweet, and I appreciated it—and I hated that Toby could still read me that well.

"Yeah, it is," I said. "Gray's next, which you knew. But are there any updates as to where Jacob is?"

"I wish," Toby sighed. "All of his numbers were disconnected, and it's clear that Brittney hadn't heard from him. And after looking at her apartment, it's clear she hasn't talked to him in over a year."

"Do you know why he and Brittney lost contact? They always seemed like they were inseparable," I asked, realizing if he had talked to her about renewing her license, he might have the information.

"He's using again. Got hooked on Silence," Toby sighed. "She wanted him to get help, he didn't get help. She kicked him out, thinking it would be a wake-up call, and nobody's heard from him since."

"Stars, of course, he wasn't going to make this easy," I groaned, knowing it only made it that much harder. But the only good news was that if the Department and all their resources were having trouble finding him, I was willing to bet the same could be said about Nightshade.

"Listen, focus on Gray, I'll see if we can find anything, and just keep going one step at a time," Toby advised, and I could tell how good he was at his job just to keep people from being overwhelmed. "How are you holding up, Nickel?"

"I don't know," I answered, completely honest. "I've been running on adrenaline for two days, and I don't think I've processed anything. Everyone hates each other. And I keep forgetting even the simplest of protocols, so I doubt I'm doing a good job."

"Says the girl who traveled across the country and then road tripped back, got your brother out of a magical murder cult,

64

and found your other brother. I'd say you're doing fine," Toby insisted, and a small smile started to grow on my face.

"Yeah, but the people Zain killed aren't," I sighed.

"You mean the magical murder cultists he killed in self-defense? I think the world can do without those specific people," Toby pointed out. "And it *was* self-defense. You're safe, and if anyone even thought about attacking the house, I think Kitty would beat them to death with her cast-iron skillet."

"That sounds very on brand for Kitty," I chuckled.

"Yeah, she really loves her kids. I'm glad you finally got to meet them," Toby admitted, and it was clear he had met them already.

"Right. I forgot I was mad at you about that, too," I sarcastically said. "Why didn't you tell me I had nephews?"

"Again, I was under the impression you already knew about them," Toby pointed out. "I truly did not think that when you said Nate cut you off, you meant there hadn't been any communication between you two in years. Kitty made it seem..."

"Kitty is a meddler," I said, and if on cue, the front door opened, and Kitty smiled in a way that let me know she had been listening.

"I need you to please control your brothers," Kitty said, not caring that I was on the phone.

"You also have two spies who probably learned some fun new adult words from Uncle Zain," I said, rolling my eyes. "Okay, Toby, I have to go. I'll call you after we see Gray tomorrow."

"So, Toby...?" Kitty asked, a mischievous smile on her face.

"Nope, you've meddled enough for one day. You don't get to do that," I said, walking past her and into the living room.

"Okay, that's enough, both of you!" I yelled, immediately getting both Nate and Zain's attention. They clearly had been at it the entire time I had been on the phone, and I was sure I probably had each of their points burned into my subconscious. "You two have had enough of an ethics debate for one night, and the handler sides with Zain. So, Nate, shut up." That was enough to silence his next argument, which I was sure completely disproved his next point if he hadn't gotten to it yet. While it was true the Hero Code didn't allow for murder, it was a bit hand-wavy when it came to death by self-defense. "Now, we have a six-hour drive back to Calder Bay, so Nate, you need to pack. Zain, you need a nap because you've been driving nonstop, and we will be ready to go in two hours."

"Listen, I haven't said I'm even going…" Nate started to protest before Kitty entered the room.

"Oh yes, you are," she snapped at him. "Between how many times I've caught you listening to a police scanner and the fact you've been trying to get classified information out of me for the past two years, you need this. I agreed you needed the break when we left, but this whole thing is a part of you, Nate. And this case? It's haunted you, and you need the closure, Babe. Please stop acting like you don't."

"Kitty…" Nate groaned, and Zain and I gave each other a look. It was awkward watching your older brother and his wife argue like an old married couple. It was even more awkward knowing that they technically *were* an old married couple.

"And," Kitty continued, "if you're gone, you'll lure all these people away from me and the twins. I know Nightshade knows everything about you, but there's a good chance he doesn't know anything about me. You have plenty of vacation time, I can do most of my work from home, and I have an inside line into the Nest's computer systems, so I can help with the tech aspects. It'll be just like old times. One last mission." Kitty's eyes were entirely too excited by this suggestion, so I was sure there was no "one last mission" actually happening for her. And that was exactly why she didn't tell Nate anything about her job.

"And this is why Kitty works for the Department," I muttered to Zain, who stifled a laugh.

"As if you ever doubted why," Kitty turned to me with a wink. "And most importantly, it'll give you three time to remember that you're a family and need each other."

"That we don't," Nate snapped, and I couldn't help but give him a look—one I had seen on Mom's face any time we tried to get out of any of her family activities. He and Mom had always been the two to work to keep us all together, so it just made him seem like a liar the more he insisted he didn't need us. If he had been lying back then, just because he thought everything was what he was supposed to be doing.

"Stop being a complete hypocrite, and go with your siblings," Kitty instructed, and it was clear there was no room for argument. "I'll talk to the school tomorrow, give them some sort of excuse.

Maybe fake some paperwork from a doctor who's forcing you to have some time off."

"No forgery. There's already been enough crimes committed, and we," he said, motioning to him and his wife, "are not about to be included in that."

"Says the man about to go on a mission after relinquishing his hero's license. Good luck with that one. Maybe Toby will just sweep it under the rug for you," Kitty smirked, and I could see Nate's skin pale. "But we'll just have a major family emergency. I think being hunted by a serial killer counts."

"Fine. Family emergency," Nate relented, though it was clearly against his will.

"So just to be clear: are we a family or not? You're giving so many mixed signals, bro," Zain deadpanned with a smirk, and I let out a groan. The ability to chill with pushing Nate's buttons had not dulled with age at all.

"Shut up," Nate snapped. "I need to pack. You need to nap, because, Zain, I decided you're driving first."

Chapter Seven

According to Nate, the nice thing about having three drivers was that it would have made the six-hour drive to the Calder Bay Technological Institute a very easy drive. And the fact that I could not drive was deserving of a lecture when he traded off driving with Zain.

I hadn't missed Nate's lectures, though this one was clearly designed to keep me awake so he wouldn't be driving alone. I wouldn't have been able to doze off, anyway. Between falling asleep in the cars Zain had stolen, and now being crammed in this tiny rental car, I wasn't sure if I would be able to sleep again if it wasn't in a bed. I missed home, even some of the meetings I had thought I'd be glad to avoid.

"Where exactly do you think we'll find Gray?" Nate asked as we walked onto the campus. The sun was rising, and I couldn't help but wish I had stolen something out of Kitty's closet to get out of this flannel. Somehow, it had just started smelling like cow. Or maybe *I* smelled like cow, because I hadn't showered since before I left to pick up Zain. That was going to need to change in the next day or so.

"The labs," Zain shrugged as if it were the most obvious answer in the world, though I had to agree with him. "You know, the special ones that need a keycard to get into."

"And how are we...?" Nate started asking, just as Zain held up what looked like a master keycard, and I hadn't even realized we had passed somewhere he had gotten one from. "Never mind," our older brother grumbled, and I could tell he was as unsurprised as I was.

Gray had always been a morning person, which had been a running joke back when we were a team. She'd be out on a patrol and still managed to be awake and coherent at 6:30 in the morning, without any coffee and ready for class. There were a lot of times we wondered if she ever slept, or if she was just an android who was running on batteries.

It was trial and error to find her lab. We were attempting to look like we belonged and knew exactly where we were going. But instead, we ended up on the wrong side of campus, were chased out of a lab I was sure was going to result in a monster invasion, and finally entered a hallway and ran into a grad student. Literally.

Though that grad student wasn't upset, because a smile lit up every inch of Gray's face, even though she had dropped the mug she had been holding and her tea had shattered on the ground.

"I knew it!" she excitedly exclaimed as she forced all of us into a group hug. I wasn't entirely sure how, considering she was practically a foot shorter than Zain and Nate, but I wasn't going to question her infectious energy. "I knew one day you three were going to show up. Wasn't expecting today, not going to lie, but don't worry, I'm ready, and I've been waiting. And I have so many things to show everyone. Still in the prototype phases, obviously, but you're going to love them. They're going to make our lives so much easier now that the team's getting back together."

I had prepared myself for Gray to be a morning person, but I had forgotten she talked a mile a minute. Her curly hair was pulled into a ponytail on the top of her head, and her deep brown skin looked completely refreshed, even though from the looks of it, Gray had been here for hours. But I hadn't had anywhere near enough coffee to handle this kind of energy first thing in the morning.

Though I was much more concerned that Gray was acting like nothing had changed between any of us. Like we had just taken a monthlong vacation, and not that we hadn't spoken to each other in five years. To be honest, I wasn't sure Nate had even fully processed his being back yet, considering Kitty had practically thrown him out of the house.

"I knew it!" Zain happily exclaimed. "Dude, I told them you'd have been working on something, and they both told me to shut up. I've been stuck in the middle of nowhere for five years, so please show me something cool." And just like that, Zain and Gray were best friends once again. Their friendship had always been easy, always revolving around innovation: Zain with the ideas and the testing, Gray with the building and implementation. And while Dad had never actually allowed any of Gray's inventions to come out with us, there was always the intention that eventually she would be our gadget girl.

I just wasn't sure what to think of the fact that Gray had been living the past five years waiting for us all to come back. Like what happened was inevitable, and she'd been in preparations for years. There was no way Gray knew about Nightshade, she was entirely too cheerful to see us. And I hated that we were going to burst her bubble.

"You okay, Nik?" Nate quietly asked me, and I detected a bit of concern in his voice. When I was younger, I would have been comforted by it, but now? It just felt like a slap in the face. Yesterday, he would have done anything to keep us out of his life forever. Today, he didn't get to act like he cared.

"Considering you made it perfectly clear you don't want me in your life, don't act like you want to be a part of mine and expect an answer," I quietly hissed, the ice that had been building in my soul over the past years filling my words.

"Okay, I deserve that," he admitted with a wince, looking like he wanted to say something else and deciding against it. Zain and Gray had already continued down the hallway, and I quickly worked to catch up with them. I was a little jealous watching the way they could act like no time had passed. Even Zain and I hadn't been like that. And I was certain that once this mission was over, Nate would go back to pretending I didn't exist.

My inner mantra that I was better off alone started to play in the back of my mind, but for once, it was hard to believe I had thought Brittney was better off alone, and she ended up dead. Every single plan I thought of to deal with Nightshade ended up calling for safety in numbers.

"Alright, so here's my lab," Gray said, dramatically flinging open the door, "so I know things may have changed a bit, but I've been thinking of everyone's biggest strengths and weaknesses, and figuring out how to improve everyone's experiences. And just to check, are we going to pick up Britt and Jake, too? I want to be prepared for everyone, and I couldn't leave them out."

The awkward silence that followed the question was deafening, and I sighed as I realized between Nate not wanting to be here and Zain's habit of being entirely too morbid, I was becoming the new team leader by default. And honestly, I was starting to understand Nate's teenage years in a way I never had when I was younger.

"Brittney's dead," I quietly said, trying not to be as blunt as I had been with Nate. "And we have no idea how to find Jacob, but we need to. Something's come up."

"Wait... dead? What do you mean by dead?" Gray asked, attempting to sit in her chair, only for it to roll out of the way and her to land on the floor. "She posted on Flickify this morning."

"It had to have been scheduled," I sighed.

"Nightshade's back," Zain explained, the same tone Dad had used back when we had mission briefs. "He got Brittney first." It was clear by looking at Gray, she was thinking through every possible scenario. Her eyes were darting back and forth as if she were seeing something that wasn't there, and electricity seemed to fly out of her fingertips. Pieces of metal, machinery, and computer parts all gravitated to the currents coming from her fingers and started to transform. Together they created a face, the one of the man my father had killed. A tear fell down Gray's face as she let her power go, and the little robot she created shattered into a million different parts.

One thing became perfectly clear: while the rest of us had tried to move on from what happened, Gray never had.

"Well," she said, wiping away her tears. "I guess we'll be field testing the prototypes. What sort of evidence do we have?"

"Crime scene pictures, a voicemail. I don't think there were any witnesses..."

"You mean you didn't examine the crime scene? Like at all?" Gray asked, looking at me in pure confusion, "Why not? I know your license is still good, and Department protocol states you get assigned the case if it's been reopened."

"Correct, and Toby's the new handler," I added. "But up until this happened, I wasn't planning to get back into the whole hero thing. I don't think any of us were."

"Oh," Gray said quietly, her entire essence deflating in a way that reminded us how tiny she was. Gray's personality and energy always made up for what she lacked in height, but seeing her without it made her just seem so small. Like I had just kicked the human equivalent of a puppy.

"If it makes you feel better, I wasn't ever out. I was just... forced into working on the other side for a bit," Zain offered, which seemed to cheer Gray up a little.

"Okay," she sniffled, before sighing and picking herself up off the floor. "I remembered you had a thing for throwing stars, so

I found a way that would harness electricity to short-circuit a target's nervous system. So as long as it's embedded somewhere near a nerve, it'll paralyze the target. Perfect in a fight, and they're solar-powered. So, have them lie in the sun for an hour, and they'll stay charged for two weeks... or first use. I'm still working on getting them to hold multiple charges, but I have an issue where they keep catching on fire. So, at the moment, one use only."

I was impressed as Gray showed off the throwing stars. The woman was brilliant, and it was the perfect tool for Zain. The attention to detail she had given was incredible, and I was glad to see how in her element she was.

"Are you sure you don't want to see what I made for you?" Gray asked, in a small voice that immediately put me through all stages of a guilt trip.

"Gray, I never said I didn't," I assured her, "and if it'll help us against Nightshade, go for it."

"And also the Circle of Shadows, who Nik conveniently left out, are after her and Zain," Nate spoke up, only for Zain to flip him off.

"Oh great. *Greatgreatgreatgreat*, everything is great," Gray started muttering, and I could tell she was processing the new information at a rapid pace. "Since multiple people are after you, and by association, us, I would have loved more of a heads up. But you know, we'll get over that, and we're going to need everything I've made. Good news, I'm going to get so much field test data," the anxiety in Gray's voice was contagious, and I truly hoped Nate hadn't just sent her into a giant spiral. "I updated the comms so it's on a locked frequency. Nobody else will be able to access it, but I added some fun modifications." She opened up a box that was full of earpieces and glasses lenses. "The lenses go in your mask and record, see other people's viewpoints, and you can pull up a map to see where everyone else is on a map. It gives accountability, which is big in the Department right now, and also makes it easier to find each other if we're in trouble."

Gray quickly closed the case, Nate's fingers almost getting caught in the box. "I also thought Nate would love these, because you're a huge micromanager and love to make sure everyone's doing what they're supposed to instead of trusting us." Gray gave him a knowing look as Nate's jaw dropped in offense at the remark. But Zain and I both burst out laughing, which gave Gray more of the momentum she had previously lost.

"However, I did also make you something," Gray smiled at him. It was a little drone that looked just like the logo Dad had designed for his codename of Chronos. And before anyone could ask what it did, it started flying around, scanning everything in the room, before eventually resting in the holder Gray had set out for it. "Alright, give me a moment," she muttered, pressing a few buttons on the stand, before a 3D image of the room was projected out of the room. "So, what I love about this is it'll scan everything for you, but then you can manipulate the 3D imaging so you can make it bigger, smaller, take away things that aren't necessary. It would help scout a location or for crime scene analysis. It's a shame I couldn't have helped out with Britt's apartment, but..." She shook her head, trying not to think about it. "There's also heat mapping, so you'll be able to see the hot and cold spots of a room and any person who happens to be there."

Nate's eyes lit up at the implications, though he was trying to hide how excited his data-driven mind was loving everything this drone was capable of.

"Then, Nikki, I've got two things for you. Well... one is for everyone, but mostly you, and the other is specifically for you. But you're the one who will understand how amazing the first one is," Gray said, dragging a giant box off a shelf and opening it to reveal multiple bolts of fabric. And I had to admit, she did know me, if she could see me so well.

"You invented fabric?" I asked, running my hands against the material. It was cool to the touch, like I had always imagined that wearable metal would feel. "Is this why you're still a PhD candidate and haven't graduated yet? You've been working on all of this instead of your dissertation?"

"I've been working on my dissertation... sometimes," Gray insisted, "or at least enough where my advisor thinks I'm making good progress. Plus, I'm specifically looking into tech innovation as a way to help with hero work, so the field tests will help with my research, and technically, this entire thing sounds like it's me working on my dissertation. Powers and technology always make for a smart combination," she giggled, with sparks of electricity dancing on the tips of her fingers.

"Hey, as long as none of this is sold to Miss Lumeriana, I'm all for it. But she'll ruin it and immediately try and get like a million of her viewers to buy it if she thought it'd make her more famous,"

Zain scoffed, starting to slide the unsupervised throwing stars in his pocket.

"Why would I give it to her? I want to help people, not make a billion dollars," Gray said with a grimace, and I was relieved she wasn't interested in the super-influencer trend that Jeannie had inspired. Too many inventors had already been tempted by the dollar signs, and I was glad Gray still had a soul.

"Anyway," Gray smiled, as she started bouncing on her toes, "I want you to try and take a picture of the fabric." My eyes narrowed as I pulled out my phone, opened the camera, and pointed it at the fabric.

Only for it not to appear.

I could see my feet, the floor, even the table, but the fabric itself was nowhere to be seen.

"So the fabric makes you invisible to any type of camera. It's a chameleon technology that lets you hide by mirroring what you would see on the other side of you to create the illusion you're not there. Hypothetically, I should be able to tweak the technology to eventually make you invisible to the naked eye as well, but I haven't even begun working on that. I was kind of hoping you had designed new suits for us so we could test them out..."

"I will buy this from you right now. How much do you have?" I asked, much to Gray's surprise. "It's not public knowledge, but I've been doing supersuit redesigns on the side, so I could easily find someone to test it out for us. Or I could design you a suit, if you wanted one.

"Wait, really?" Gray asked, almost buzzing with excitement. "Because you did promise you'd make us all new suits." That had been one of my biggest goals when I had been younger, to make stylish and effective suits that made heroes look like they belonged in the present, instead of using the same designs that had been passed down since the Celestia Meteor had granted us superpowers over a century ago. I guess in some way, I had done it—just not for us.

Maybe it was time to think about us again. At the very least, to test out the fancy fabric.

"You know, I thought Dreamscape and Quiver's newest suits looked somewhat familiar," I heard Nate mutter to nobody in particular.

"Listen, I'm not going to say no to a new supersuit. As much as I love Seb, fashion was not one of his strengths," Gray smiled, and I could already tell she was my next project. Designs started swirling in my head, and I needed to get to my sketchpad before I lost them all.

"Alright, I'll start sketching once I have a moment, but what else did you want to show me?" I asked, trying not to get too distracted.

"First, I need you to promise you won't get mad," Gray said, crossing her arms and looking at me.

"What did you do?" I asked, afraid she was going to pull out one of the diarrhea colored wigs my Dad always forced me to wear.

"Since you're not the fastest runner," Gray said, and now I understood why she needed the promise—because despite the

79

fact I was a faster runner than the average person, I had been the slowest one on the team, "I made you a glider so you won't fall behind!" As she explained it, she pulled out what I could only describe as a metal backpack and pressed a button. It unfolded until it was about the size of a snowboard, but with the distinct shape of my old Nightingale emblem. "You can strap your feet in, and not only will you be able to go faster than all of us, but it'll also get you up to a hundrend feet in the air if we need to get to a roof quickly."

I pressed the button to compress it back into a backpack and went to pick it up. Or at least, attempted to pick it up, as it felt like it weighed at least a hundred pounds. And while I could barely lift it, in sliding it off the table, I almost dropped it on the floor.

"You couldn't have made it lightweight?" I grimaced, setting it down. As helpful as it might be, it wasn't going to help much in the field because having to stash it sounded like it would be time-consuming and life-threatening.

"Do you know how hard it is to find metal that doesn't weigh a ton but has the structural integrity to handle flight and the weight of a human?" Gray said, her hands flying as she seemed like it would be helpful to explain. "I'm still working out the logistics, and I didn't have enough research grant money to get that kind of material."

"Okay, you keep that, and I will gift you the money because I am not going to carry it," I said. "I think Toby would have a panic attack if he learned I was trying to carry that around while doing hero work."

"That sounds like Toby," Gray chuckled. "Why did you two break up? The last time I talked to him, literally all he could talk about was how amazingly talented you are, and he couldn't even concentrate on the fact that I was trying to get my hero license renewed because he kept asking if I had heard from you recently. And you were so cute together!"

"Um... we never were actually together," I awkwardly said, though I had to admit I was shocked Toby was talking about me like that. Or he had followed my career enough to gush about it. "Anyway, I do want to test this thing out. Are we allowed to do that here, or will I get shot out of the sky?"

"Nobody's installed any anti-aircraft guns on the roofs of the buildings... that I know of," Gray quickly added, before mentally calculating whether or not it was a good idea. "But considering we're still trying to keep our identities a secret, we probably shouldn't. Seems like it's a great way to go viral on Cinegram."

"Right. Secret identities," I nodded, knowing it was yet another thing that had completely slipped my mind, and Gray just looked at me in exasperated disbelief.

"Did you two," she said, motioning at me and Nate, "just both wake up one morning and decide, 'I'm going to get out of shape and pretend to be a completely different person?' Because honestly, this is getting ridiculous."

"Why does everyone keep insisting I'm out of shape?" I snapped, "I do yoga, I run, I do kickboxing. I am active. And just because I'm a slower runner than all of you doesn't make me a bad runner!"

"And I'm on my feet all day teaching, spend at least an hour at the gym every morning, and coach multiple sports. I can assure you, I'm still in shape too," Nate added on, and I was glad it wasn't just me getting commented on. Even though Gray rolled her eyes and lifted the folded-up glider with one hand.

Show off.

"But to answer your question, I did make that conscious effort," Nate continued, "the day I left. I was twenty years old and supposed to take care of all of you, keep the Bay crime-free, and somehow run all of Sebastian's businesses? I couldn't handle that. None of us should have had to."

"Really?" I asked, and an angry laugh bubbled up in my throat, "None of us should have to handle that, so you dropped it all on me? Because guess what, you running from your problems made them all my problems. You left me with no warning and no guide, and I had to give up so much just to make sure the world didn't completely fall apart. I had to get emancipated because I had no legal guardian. I had to drop out of high school because I couldn't balance having to track down replacements for all of Dad's business and charity work. And I had to work with the Department to figure out who would patrol the city since we weren't there anymore. So, because you got to run away and have your stupid white picket fence life, I didn't get to have a life of my own."

"Oh, stop with the victim complex, Nicole," Nate immediately shot back. "You've launched a fashion line. You've managed to become incredibly famous without a social media following.

You've even managed to string Toby around for six years, and I have no idea how he hasn't seen through everything to see how much of a shallow fame-obsessed mean girl you've become."

Even though Nate hadn't physically hit me, his words felt like a slap to the face. My eyes burned as I felt tears start to fall down my face. I didn't want Nate to win, I didn't want him to see me cry. I didn't want to have to explain that the girl in the media wasn't even me; it was the mask to protect me from people like him.

"I have been living on my own since I was sixteen years old because everyone decided their lives were better without me," I choked out, the tears falling faster the more I fought to get them out of control. I could feel a sob coming up, and I took a deep breath to try and get it under control. To try and fight the way my brother had completely demolished me again. "So, yes, I have a meticulously crafted public image, so people don't want to talk to me. Because it's just me and Dad's shadow looming everywhere. Because that's who they care about. Him. How is he? When is he coming back? What is he up to? And I don't even know if he's alive anymore because we all just decided to cover for him, and I am now stuck in a lie. Everything I am is just a lie." I felt myself hyperventilating, and I knew I had to get out of the room. I shoved Nate out of the way to get to the hallway.

"Have they not talked in a while?" I heard Gray ask Zain as I ran down the hallway. I didn't hear the answer, but I was sure he was filling her in on what our last few days had been like. I rested my head against the wall, letting out a frustrated grunt as I realized I had been followed.

"You do not get to blame me for your life, Nicole," Nate snapped, clearly not getting the hint that I didn't want anything to do with him. "Nobody told you to do all that."

"Dad did," I snapped back. "In all of his instructions, it was if Nate's not available, ask Nikki. Have it be Nikki. All those companies and charity projects still had to be run. People had to be hired since I don't know anything about how to run anything. Because you were taught, I just had it all dumped on me. And if you thought about someone other than yourself for more than five seconds, you'd be able to think about how much you destroyed me before you try and do it again." I turned and walked down the hallway before yelling, "Do not follow me," at him, just so I could be alone.

There was a safety in being alone that I had wrapped myself in over the years. A blanket that made it so others couldn't hurt me. The sobs I had been holding back broke out, and I slid down one of the walls and curled myself into a ball. In the past three days, I have done more than I wanted to with my past. The stupid part of me that wanted this, the part I shouldn't have listened to, got me sucked into a murder investigation, wanted by the Circle of Shadows, and was expected to act like nothing had changed.

But it had. I had been ignoring so many calls from people wanting decisions made, wanting me to get back, ready for me to balance all the plates I had barely been keeping spinning for the past five years.

But the old me, she still went rogue, and despite me being in my relative safety by myself, she still went and did the one thing I wished she wouldn't: she called Toby.

"Nickel..." his sleepy voice asked into the phone, before he heard me sob. "What's wrong?"

"Nate's terrible, and I don't want to be here anymore," I cried. "And Gray is just so... I'm just so tired of everyone forcing me to be the new Dad and not caring how I feel about it. And I want to go home." Another sob broke out, and the little part of me that was holding me together just broke. The sobs were pouring out, and it wasn't just this, it was years of emotional buildup that finally was forcing its way out.

"Just a moment," I heard him grumble on the phone, and then there was an intense alien sound, and Toby was right in front of me. I knew as a fact that teleportation was not one of his powers, but I wasn't going to question it as I buried my face into his shoulder when he hugged me.

"Nikki, I..." I heard Nate had followed me again, and he was clearly surprised Toby was there. Or that I was still crying. Or his being horrible had consequences.

"I do not want to talk to him," I choked out, and Toby nodded. The alien noise sounded again, a flash of red light, and the next thing I realized, I was in Toby's apartment.

Chapter Eight

I wasn't sure how long I sobbed, but it felt wrong that nobody told me to stop. Toby instead held me, encouraged me to get it out, and the years of repressed emotions all wanted to come out at once.

"I'm sorry," I sniffled after completely covering his shirt's shoulder with tears and snot. "I know you have work. But Gray's so... and Zain's so... and Nate just..." I wasn't as done as I had thought I was, as a fresh sob broke free, and I wasn't even able to complete a coherent thought.

"You've been carrying a lot," Toby whispered in my ear, "and if they can't realize it, that's on them."

I didn't answer, instead, I just let myself rest in his embrace. He was warm, safe, and comforting.

He was home. And I hadn't had that feeling in a long time.

And he was blue. It was so rare for anyone to see what Toby actually looked like. Yes, he was still tall and scrawny, but his skin was a beautiful teal, his hair was a wavy navy blue, and his eyes glowed gold like the sun. He was a smaller version of the entire tribe of the Asl'Hagt. One who looked as alien as the rest of them, without looking like the warriors they were known for. I couldn't blame him for using his powers to look more normal; anyone who saw him like this would either think he was a superhero or an invader. And Toby wasn't either, he was just kind, normal, Toby.

"You look like you," I sniffed, a ghost of a smile almost forming on the sides of my mouth. It wasn't often Toby let people see him like this, and it always felt special when I got to see what he looked like behind the mask.

"I always look like me at my apartment," Toby shrugged, before telekinetically hovering a mug of tea where we were sitting. "Here, it might help."

I wasn't surprised he had been using his powers to get a mug ready for me while I cried, but it was incredible how such a simple gesture felt like so much more.

"Thank you," I whispered, taking a sip and relishing in the comfort of the peppermint. "I'm sorry for being this embarrassing. You have better things to do than to deal with me."

"It's not embarrassing to show emotion, Nickel," Toby soothed, "it's human."

"It's weakness," I whispered. "Do you know the last time I cried? My mom's funeral when I was twelve. Dad pulled me aside and told me that Caldwells showed strength in times of struggle, and crying made us look weak."

"Full offense to your father, but I don't think his parenting was that great," Toby grimaced, and I dryly chuckled in agreement. "Some of his ideas put my father's to shame. Which is pretty impressive considering my father is once again trying to figure out how to conquer his planet."

"I guess we're both disappointments, then," I said, snuggling more into Toby. His cheek rested against the top of my head, and I finally let myself relax. A deep breath, and then a spike of panic. I shouldn't be doing this to Toby, I shouldn't be letting him in only for him to be disappointed by me again. I immediately jumped up, doing my best to untangle myself from his embrace.

"Do you want to talk about what happened?" Toby asked, and even though I knew I should probably talk about it, he was the first person to ask me that question where I knew the answer could be no. He would drop it if I wanted him to. It's what Dad would have done.

But doing things Dad's way was exhausting, and I just didn't have the energy to hold anything in anymore.

"Nate said I have a victim complex because I don't think it's fair he disappeared and left me with all his responsibilities," I quietly explained, letting myself open up for the tiniest bit for the first time in years. "And insisted I had a choice in walking away if I didn't want them."

"Yeah, he's made his opinions perfectly clear about that over the years," Toby scoffed, "because with the little I knew about what you were going through..." He paused, and I realized he probably had known bits and pieces of what was going on, just from the role of his job. Despite not wanting to do things for the Department, I had never fully shut them off. And he had been there getting crumbs along the way. "Once, I had asked him who he thought would be the public face of the institution that came with your family if you hadn't taken it up, and he told me it didn't matter since you decided to be in a public-facing job."

"That's so stupid," I grumbled. "So much has been in freefall that I am still dealing with the aftermath. I couldn't access anything until I was eighteen, and the only reason I had money was because I knew Nate's bank password. But I was still expected to make decisions in his place, and on my birthday? I celebrated by doing the paperwork they had been putting off. And then there was the interim CEO debacle, the embezzlement scheme in the charity we had to fix, and if Nate had done the bare minimum for two years, things never would have gotten that bad."

"You know you didn't have to do it alone, Nikki," Toby whispered, and it was just quiet enough that I wasn't sure if I was supposed to have heard him or not.

"And how was I supposed to know you were going to stay?" I whispered back. "Nobody else cared enough to."

"Because..." he trailed off, but I felt him shift to look at me. Really look at me. His golden sunburst eyes were full of feelings I had convinced myself he didn't actually have. Feelings of mine that I hadn't gotten rid of. And for a moment, I was certain he was going to kiss me—and I wanted him to.

But he didn't.

The wait was too long, the moment was long over, and the silence that had been safe and familiar turned into something incredibly awkward. Fast.

"Just. Because," he said, moving away from me on the couch, and I sighed—clearly misinterpreting everything that had just happened. Toby was always sweet, always helpful, and after five years of repressed emotions, he was the first person to see all of me and not make me feel ashamed about it.

I was a mess, and the two of us were long over. And it wasn't fair to him to put those expectations or feelings on him. And it wasn't fair to myself to try to read into things I was clearly imagining.

"I've missed you," I quietly admitted, before realizing that was the exact wrong thing to say. "I mean, I know I was the one who ghosted you. But you were my best friend, and I missed that."

"I've missed you, too." Toby smiled at me. "Maybe we can try to start over? I mean not fully from the beginning, but as... friends?"

"Yeah, of course," I nodded, but there was a part of me that didn't believe him. I was entirely too damaged, and eventually, it would be too much for him. He would leave. There was something he wasn't saying, and whatever it was, it made me doubt him.

After all, Nate still hated me. Gray only saw me as a way to do hero work. Zain could be kidnapped by the Circle of Shadows at any minute. I wanted to trust him, I wanted to believe he would stay. But all the people in my life had shown again and again that it wasn't worth it to be attached.

Even now, when we were forced to be together again, forced was the key word.

I sniffled again, and it was clear my body wanted to cry more, but there were no more tears to fall. I was exhausted. Mentally, physically, and emotionally.

"Do you mind if I take a nap?" I asked, figuring it was better than trying to talk through the awkwardness that had built up across our conversation. "I haven't slept well."

"Go for it," Toby nodded. "Bedroom's right through there." Normally, I would have insisted I sleep on the couch, but after two days of not sleeping in a bed, I wasn't in the mood to argue. I just wrapped myself in a blanket and quickly fell into a dead sleep.

Chapter Nine

"**A**s her handler, I do not have to tell you where she is!" Toby was yelling, which woke me up from the nap. I was completely disoriented, trying to figure out where I was.

"Tobias, I am certain nowhere in the Handler description does 'teleporting your girlfriend away from her mission' exist as a guideline. And the fact you did seems like a serious conflict of interest!" Nate yelled back, and I groaned as I tried to bury my head in the pillow. I didn't want to get up, and I still didn't want to deal with my brother. Honestly, dropping him in the ocean and hoping a mermaid would drown him seemed like the better option.

"Two things," Toby countered, and I could imagine him using his powers to make himself taller than Nate. I hoped he was—it was hard to argue with someone who could just keep getting bigger than you with every point. "The first is that looking after the mental health of the people I am a handler for is in my job description, and if you didn't notice, you were..."

"Don't you..." Nate attempted to interrupt.

"No, I'm talking now, so you can shut up and listen for once, Nathan!" Toby shouted, with an ice I had only heard in Toby's father's voice before. The kind that made everyone not only stop, but be afraid of what was coming next. "You were the cause of Nikki's emotional distress, and for the sake of her and the mission, I extracted her before any additional damage could be done. Maybe you should think about the consequences of your actions for a few seconds before deciding you're blameless. It doesn't give someone a 'victim complex' to point out that your choices can negatively impact someone else."

It was strange to hear someone defend me like this. I'm not sure anyone ever had before. Especially if they thought I wouldn't be around to hear it, and I was confident Toby still thought I was asleep.

"Now, second," Toby continued, "I'm not dating Nikki. We've never been in a relationship, and honestly, I don't think either of us is in a place to be in one right now." Part of me wondered if this meant he had been thinking about kissing me after all, but I wasn't going to let myself think about that. I just slowly moved off the bed, so I could listen better through the door.

"Fine. You're not dating Nikki, but you wish you were," Nate amended, and I rolled my eyes at his version of reality. "You know, you can admit she's been stringing you along for…"

"She's actually done the exact opposite by shutting me out, Nate," Toby interrupted again. "The fact she opened up enough to call me is a huge deal. Because I don't think she's done that at all in five years. Five. Years. And that's something you wouldn't understand, because you just turned everything off, created a narrative where you were the hero, and then let it feed your bitterness. And because of that, she's turned into your father—so wrapped up in the armor she was forced to build for herself that trusting anyone with her secrets and emotions feels like a personal betrayal."

Well, now it was obvious he thought I was asleep, because Toby would never have said that if he thought I was awake. He knew something like that would hurt me. Even though he was right.

I hadn't even realized in my spiral into this version of myself how much I had in common with Dad. And where I understood him better, I had promised myself I wouldn't become Dad. And if that's how people were seeing me... things had to change.

"No, she's..." I could hear Nate's mind starting to work, as he slowly started to put together what had actually happened. Reframing everything he had seen over the past few days. Realizing I wasn't a sixteen-year-old kid anymore, and he couldn't just tell me what to do and not expect me to push back.

"She's not fine, Nate," Toby quietly said, "and you going after her so hard when she's trying her best? It's not productive. She is so outside her comfort zone and the mirage of a life she built, she is throwing it out just to keep you safe. And that's why I'm not going to tell you where she is, because I do not trust you have her best interests at heart right now, when she's doing everything in her power to keep you from being murdered."

"You're right. He has not had my best interests at heart," I agreed as I opened the bedroom door, "but as much as I appreciate it, it's also counterproductive for Nate and the rest of the team to not know where I am. So, please tell me you didn't just leave Zain and Gray in that nasty rental car just to come fight with Toby."

"Wait... you've been here the whole time?" Nate asked, and I was impressed Toby hadn't given Nate any reason to think I might be here.

"I really needed to sleep, since you and Zain decided I didn't need to last night," I pointed out, "but that being said, Toby, I know this is your apartment, and I know it's a weird ask, but can I have a moment alone with my brother please?"

"Yeah, I have some work to catch up on," Toby noticed, before giving Nate another warning look, and going into what was probably a second bedroom.

"I heard Toby chew you out, and I'm not going to add on to it," I said, sitting on the couch, and motioning for him to sit next to me, "but I need to know you're not going to be a problem, or if I need to stick you in a safe house at the bottom of the ocean where nobody will be able to find you."

"According to Kitty, those don't exist," Nate said, though I could tell he was questioning how much truth his wife had told him.

"Honestly, I have no idea, it just seemed like the last place Nightshade would look," I said, crossing my legs in front of me. There was such a distance between us, and while he had been insufferable when we were younger, it had been loving. Now? It was *just* insufferable. I wasn't sure what to say to Nate. So much of what I believed to be true about my brother was a lie, which made it really hard to talk to him.

Maybe we were both seeing each other through new eyes.

"Nikki," he sighed, and I could see he was unsure about what he was saying. "What happened after I left? I thought they'd just put everything in a trust and let you decide when you were eighteen. Why do you keep saying you didn't have a choice?"

"Well, you were partially correct. Everything did go into a trust, and there wasn't a lot I could do until I was eighteen. But considering Dad wasn't officially head, and everyone just kind of covered for him, he still had a board seat and was still CEO, and we had to act like he was still in charge of those things," I explained. "But he had left instructions that his children could speak on his behalf in meetings. I think it was an 'in case he got injured' kind of thing, but it tended to create problems. There were a few times I had to lie and say I had to talk to you to make decisions, but the way Dad built the company, there were all sorts of things that couldn't be made without a Caldwell's input. So the day I turned eighteen? All hell broke loose. They finally had an adult Caldwell they could force to pick up the phone. They needed a new CEO, the charity had a major embezzlement ring running through it, and they tried to put off as many decisions as they could, waiting for me. If I had tried to walk away and wait for Zain, everything would have collapsed. And as much as I hate it, the company is important. We're leading in biomedical research and societal innovation, we even now have a few government contracts to help create better city infrastructure. The charity is helping so many underprivileged kids go to college. And as much as I hate Dad, I couldn't let all the good he had put into the world fall apart."

"I didn't realize the company does all that," Nate admitted. "I guess in all the preparation Sebastian did with me for the company, I never realized exactly the sort of things it was actually in charge of."

"To be fair, we also have a video game company and do a lot of movie producing just to make money, so things can stay affordable for the people who need them, much to the board's annoyance."

"Okay, I do remember multiple talks about diversifying your assets," Nate chuckled. "I just never realized you used the high-paying things to turn around and fund the things that would help people. Given our money, I thought the whole thing was about making money."

"There is a lot of capitalism in there, and everyone up top is paid entirely too much money," I relented, "but Dad's money, like the old mob money, it's not even used in the company anymore. It's fully self-sufficient, so the family fortune only goes up because of the investments Dad made for it. I haven't touched it."

"So, there had to be a Caldwell," Nate finally said after a few moments. "Dad was going to force one of us into it no matter what."

"And I just couldn't handle the guilt from letting it all crash," I sighed, wrapping my arms around myself. It was silent, the two of us staring at the floor.

"I had to make a hard break," Nate finally said. "It was the only way I could function because I was having daily severe panic attacks. Even before Dad left, it was to the point I couldn't function. Kitty was the one who insisted I leave, and why you all keep insisting I was micromanaging all of you. I was so busy just hoping that if you stayed on plan, nothing bad would happen, and then you'd all be safe."

"And you couldn't have figured out a way to set those boundaries without me thinking you were dead?" I asked, which I will admit was slightly hyperbolic, but I wasn't quite done making him feel bad for it.

"Nik, I know you won't believe me, but I thought you were fine," Nate admitted. "Thriving even. You were the one who stayed the public figure, who took over the business, who always knew how to have the perfect smile at the perfect time..."

"And who did I learn that from?" I asked him, and he grimaced.

"Dad. Right," Nate sighed. "Social media just makes it easy to forget how much of that we were taught."

"Nate, are you admitting to stalking all of those Nikki Caldwell stalker fan pages?" I asked, giving him a judgmental side eye.

"No, that would be Kitty, who will happily admit it," he countered. "She just showed me everything whether I wanted to or not. And I know I set some hard boundaries, and they probably were too hard. But I was twenty, and Kitty was pregnant, and I was scared and unprepared. Obviously, you were, too. But did you expect that I would have known what I was doing just because Dad had trained me for it?"

It was a hard question, because my gut said yes. But at the time, Nate was a year younger than I was now. And I have been thrown to the wolves. His being twenty wasn't quite the excuse he thought it was, but at the same time, I could see why he used it.

"Where did you leave Zain and Gray?" I asked, deciding it was better not to give him the answer he didn't want. I just didn't have it in me, not yet.

"Gray is currently introducing Zain to one of those weird hipster coffee bars," Nate answered. "It's across the street, and it was one that 3D prints your face on your coffee. They can come..."

"Sorry to interrupt," Toby said, opening his door with an urgency I hadn't expected from him. "Nikki, there was a break-in at your house. There are dead birds everywhere, there's blood on your walls, and your housekeeper is pretty shaken up. I'm not sure about property damage, but..."

"But he was there," I finished for him, taking a breath to recenter myself, "and he's decided I'm next."

Chapter Ten

T HERE WAS SOMETHING STRANGE about walking into my house knowing it would be trashed. But it was even stranger to walk into my house with three other people. It was without a doubt the most people who had been in my house at one time since I had bought it.

Most days, it was just me and my housekeeper, and we did our best not to bother each other. I just was glad she hadn't been here when Nightshade was—it probably had saved her life.

The shocking smell of iron and decay hit my senses as I took a step into the hallway. I flipped the lights on, and there were bird carcasses everywhere. More dead nightingales than I had thought were even in the city. Their glassy, dead eyes were open, staring at me from the floor. It reeked of murder, and I watched as the drone Gray made zipped over my shoulder.

"Yuck," I heard her say, looking over the dead birds. "Do we want to go in, or should we wait for the scanner?"

"Go in," I sighed, feeling the crunch of bird bones beneath my shoes. I winced at the way they broke under my feet. Each step, another crunch. The only relief I had was that he hadn't touched any of my art collection, which was the thing in the house I cared about the most.

"I didn't realize you were so into art," Nate said, following me in as I heard Gray walk in and immediately back out of the house. I couldn't blame her, I didn't want to deal with the smell either.

"Mom always said art was more important than money," I shrugged, getting through the main hallway, realizing the birds were making a path up the stairs. "And so I had always planned that once I could afford it myself, I was going to invest. This one was the first thing I bought with my own money that had nothing to do with Dad's," I said, lightly rubbing my thumb against the edge of the frame. In another life, I think I would have been an art history minor to go with the fashion degree I wanted to get.

I followed the birds past the shattered glass of windows and mirrors, which only added to the ominous cracking beneath my feet. The smell only got stronger, ending in my bedroom.

Birds of a feather don't fly together.

Since he didn't have my blood to create a canvas, Nightshade used birds as his paintbrush—the disposed carcasses in a pile under the words. The drone flew over my shoulder and started scanning everything around me. Clearly, his words were about us, how he expected to pick us off one by one. I wasn't sure if it was a clue or a warning, and with the smell of death permeating in the house, I didn't want to figure it out right here.

"He left the food in your fridge," Zain said as he walked in, carrying a few slices of cold pizza that should have been thrown out days ago.

"How can you eat looking at this?" I asked, both disgusted and impressed.

"Practice," he answered, and I suddenly had more questions I didn't want the answers to.

"Ew, ew, ew ,ew," I heard Gray mutter to herself as she climbed up the stairs to find us. "Um Nikki, I hate to disturb all this, but there's a body. Next room over."

I was terrified we were going to find Jacob in the next room, but as I ran in, it was Cece. My housekeeper, or former housekeeper, had her cleaning supplies around her and a phone in hand. Which just made the hand-shaped bruises around her neck so much more prominent. I had been hoping she hadn't been in the house when the call had come, but instead, she had been the one to make the call. And paid for it with her life, her blood used to write another sickening message on the wall.

I see you little birdies trying to mend the flock. Maybe you'll kill each other and do my job for me.

"How does he even know that?" I asked, not wanting to believe anyone was informing him. "That we don't get along. That we've been fighting. All we knew was he was stalking Brittney, and she didn't have that information. How long could he have been planning this?"

"If you have a security system, I could go through your system and make sure he didn't sneak in," Gray suggested. "But like...

preferably not in the middle of all the bird murder. If you don't mind."

"You know he probably deleted the videos," Zain deadpanned, his mouth full of questionable pizza, only for Gray to give him a look. "Hey, it's what I would have done!"

"It's still worth a try," I said, hoping there might be a way to get more clues. If he had been tracking us, there were so many other places he could have broken into: Gray's lab, Nate's school. He might even have an idea of where Jacob was, if he had been doing his research long enough.

"Any chance the videos were backed up on a secure server somewhere?" Gray asked, thinking out loud. And my stomach dropped, as I realized the answer was yes.

I hadn't been there in years, I was certain none of us had been. When I had left, I had closed down the house, and if anyone was there, it was our old housekeeper, Nancy.

"Sands Point," I sighed, and as if on cue, I heard Nate groan. "Everything's backed up there, uploaded in real time. If there's anything we can trust that wouldn't have been tampered with, it's there. Get any last scans you need. We'll leave once you're done."

Chapter Eleven

O N PAPER, SANDS POINT seemed like the place people would expect me to live. It was the suburb everyone had been inspired by—full of mob money, parties, and the romanticized version of the richest of the rich, not caring about the rest of the world. It was a fairy-tale beach on the coast of the Bay, and it wasn't uncommon for someone to spend thousands of dollars a day just because they could.

It was the world Dad had wanted us to live in, to use to our benefit. The richness of generational wealth was an excellent cover. These were the kinds of people who donated to charity just so they could go to a gala and show off their latest gowns. Or who wanted the world to know they were helping others, not because they wanted to, but because they wanted a philanthropic reputation. These were the exact people I had invited to my fashion show that seemed a lifetime ago, because I knew they wanted the prestige.

But seeing the gates to the house made me feel sick.

There was something truly awful about returning to the place that continually haunts your dreams. Where your life had completely fallen apart twice. And where it was threatening to do it a third time.

The mansion itself had been in the family for generations and was an architectural marvel. Family legend stated one of the architects had been a serial killer who had built a building people couldn't get out of, and as a result, there were tunnels, secret doors, and an entire basement that wasn't on the official blueprints of the house. It used to be a speakeasy, but growing up, it had been my father's secret base of operations.

I had called Nancy to let her know we were coming, but as I walked into the house, I was positive there was no way she could have gotten everything this put together in the forty-five minutes it took for us to get to the house from my place.

Or else Nancy had gotten supernaturally efficient at her job over the past five years.

"Nikki!" she exclaimed, running down the stairs, and engulfed me in a hug that caught me by surprise. When I was little, she had been my nanny—and a third parent to Nate, Zain, and me. "And Nate, and... Zain? Oh, that growth spurt finally hit, just like I told you!"

"Rude, right? He used to be shorter than me!" Gray piped in from the back, immediately going in for her hug after Nancy was done with my brothers.

"It's always nice to see you, Gray. I've told you to get out of that lab more often," Nancy said, booping Gray's nose. "It's so good to see you all here again. I wish it weren't under such sad circumstances. Brittney was entirely too young for this. When should we expect Jacob? It should be easy to get a flight from Acedonia Lake, so is he coming tonight?"

"I'm sorry, Acedonia Lake?" I asked, wondering how Nancy could have known that when an entire governmental organization couldn't figure it out.

"He moved there a year and a half ago. He always sent me a postcard any time he went somewhere new," she smiled. "Didn't you know that?"

"I haven't heard from Jacob in about... four and a half years?" I said, thinking out loud.

"Three for me," Gray admitted, with a much deeper sadness than I had expected.

"I hadn't talked to him since I left," Nate sheepishly admitted, and an anger flared in Nancy's eyes that made me take a step back from her.

"Nathan Caldwell, what do you mean you haven't talked to him since you left? You know that boy had abandonment issues, and he hung on to your every word." The majority of punishments we had as a child had come from Nancy, and so I recognized the tone well. I was just glad it was Nate and not me.

"I know, I just thought..." Nate attempted to explain, but he trailed off as he looked at me. I wasn't sure if he was thinking about earlier, or if he wanted me to rescue him.

"Nate's been learning his actions have consequences," I finished for him, "about five years too late."

"And it's Bartlett now," Nate admitted, with a wince.

"You grew up in this house. You can call yourself whatever you want, but you're still a Caldwell, it's in your blood." I could see Nate immediately think about countering how he was adopted, but he decided against it. If he picked a fight with Nancy, he was sure to lose. "Now, the living and dining rooms are ready, and food is arriving soon. Just looking at you all, I can tell you all need a good meal, so I ordered Thai. And none of your orders better have changed much in the past few years, because you're getting what you're getting. Nikki and Nate, both of your bedrooms are ready. Zain, yours should be done in the next fifteen minutes once I finish changing the sheets, and Gray, I can have your usual room ready within the hour. How long do you think you'll be staying?"

As much as I had dreaded coming back here because of the memories, seeing Nancy so excited made me wish I could tell her longer. Giving me a new layer of guilt, I wasn't sure what to do with.

"We don't know yet, Nance," Nate answered for me. "We need to look over some things in the Nest, try to track down Jacob, see if there's any information we can use in Sebastian's files." Nancy's face fell, and the guilt washed over me again. "But..." he continued, clearly feeling guilty, himself, "I promise I'll talk to Kitty about maybe having us and the boys come up and stay here for a vacation soon. Maybe this summer?"

"You and Kitty have kids?" Nancy happily squealed, looping her arm in Nate's as she pulled him into the kitchen and peppered him for more details. Oldest child help duty still was the top of Nancy's to-do list.

"Wow, the house hasn't changed at all. It's like walking into a time capsule," Gray muttered, turning around in a circle as if that would change how the room looked. Zain had completely disappeared, though I wasn't surprised. His social battery had to be hanging on by a thread, since he hadn't been alone from the moment I first found him. He had always been drawn to the secret passages in the house and had probably slipped into one the moment he realized nobody was watching him.

But Gray was right, it was a time capsule. Some flower arrangements were new, chairs were in different places, but the moment I stepped into the spot I had watched Dad walk out the door five years ago, my stomach turned over. It didn't matter that nothing had changed, because that meant this still was a house of nightmares.

I sprinted up the stairs, past the family pictures, the different vacations we all had, the normal memories that were meant to be a cover for everything in the basement. That I once thought were normal family things we did to bond.

But that was before Dad abandoned us.

And before Mom killed herself.

I didn't realize I could climb stairs any faster, but I had to get away from the time capsule of murdered dreams. My feet led me to my room, and I slammed the door, only to realize it was just as much of a time capsule as everything else.

The walls were a glittery purple, decorated with glow-in-the-dark stars that had been meticulously placed into constellations along the walls. Different awards from art shows were scattered wherever I thought was the place that showed them off best. I had loved this room when I was sixteen It was the first thing I had ever designed myself. But now, I could see my talents did not lie in interior design.

There was a safety in the cringe that brought me back to how things used to be. Especially after the state of my townhouse had left me so disoriented. Toby had promised the birds and Cece's body would be gone, and everything would be cleaned and sterilized by the next time I went there, but I honestly wasn't sure if I'd be able to step into my house ever again.

The doorbell rang, and I assumed it was the food delivery. And as much as I didn't want to hurt Nancy's feelings, I wasn't hungry. As safe as this house was, the combination of memories that kept popping up completely took away my appetite.

Because every memory was about Dad. And the way he was running from us, like we were something he could just escape. I realized Nate had done the same thing, not that I would tell him, because they both hadn't thought about how it would affect the people who had cared about them.

And the thought I had been trying to avoid slipped through: I had fallen into the exact same trap. But of the three of us, I was twenty-one, and it was still considered appropriate to be making these sorts of immature decisions. So while the realization of yet another family trait we had in common permeated through my mind, all it did was make me more upset.

I was mad. But even more annoying, I was mad that I missed him. That I had spent the past five years missing Dad, and he hadn't cared about me in the slightest. His lackluster apology as I caught him leaving didn't count for anything. But I still wanted to impress him, thinking that maybe if I did a good enough job balancing the things he left behind, he would come back and be proud. That if I had been more like Nate, he would have wanted to compliment me for it. I hated that I still wanted that validation from him when it was obvious he didn't want me.

Just like Mom didn't want me.

I didn't let myself think like that often—the little time I had spent in therapy, it was the one thing my therapist had tried her best to drill into me. But being in the house? Being in the place where she died? It just made me feel like she didn't love me enough to stay. She didn't want to see me grow up. I wasn't worth that.

She had been everything to me when I was little, but in her way, she chose to abandon us, too.

The ache of loneliness was compounded by the echoes of conversation coming from downstairs. I knew I could go down there and join them, but I didn't want to get off my bed. Instead, I opened my phone, scrolling through the texts from people who were concerned about what had happened at my house, and a few from Toby giving details on the investigation.

It felt wrong to be lonely in the midst of so many people. Especially when people started to reach out, and I chose not to respond. It was a loneliness of my own making, and I had almost decided to get up when I heard a creak, and a door I had forgotten existed opened.

Chapter Twelve

I T WASN'T AS STRANGE as it should have been to see Zain climb out of my closet. I had forgotten about the passage that connected our closets, but even as the memories flooded back, my brother finding a way to enter a room in the most dramatic fashion was entirely on brand. And with him came the telltale smells of the food I had convinced myself I wasn't hungry for.

And maybe my brain didn't want to be hungry, but my stomach growled in pleasure the moment the smell of Pad Thai hit me.

"Here," Zain said, handing me a bag with my order in it before he flopped into one of my old beanbag chairs—or really, if I was being honest, it was *his* beanbag chair. He had always been the one to use it, while I had preferred to sit on my bed. Though looking at him now was comical, considering he had been so insanely short the last time I saw him in it, the chair seemed to swallow him alive. And now, he was all legs and entirely too big for it.

"I didn't want to be down there either," Zain continued. "I missed Gray, but she doesn't know how to shut up."

I chuckled, opening the styrofoam container and digging my fork into it. We were silent, each of us picking at our food and trying to eat it. It wasn't exactly awkward, but it wasn't exactly calm either.

"Have all the ghosts come to say hello?" I finally asked, and Zain rolled his eyes.

"Yeah," he replied. "Betty's pissed we all left. Apparently, her favorite hobby was pretending she was our grandmother, and she couldn't do it with only Nancy here. But the rest of the ghosts didn't care. They just were glad they could be seen again."

One of the weirdest things that came from Zain coming to live with us was finding out the house was haunted, which shouldn't have surprised anyone. It was an old mob house, after all, and plenty of people died here. Murder victims, people who died of natural causes. Zain had told me there were about ten ghosts here, all tied to the house for who knew what reason. They didn't, and none of us had the skills to help them pass on.

Zain could only talk to them.

"You okay?" he asked again, after a long silence. "You've been pretty quiet since we got back."

"Not really," I answered with a sigh, picking up a piece of chicken "Who wants to come to the place where everyone you've ever loved abandoned you?" I hated to lump Zain into the category, as it was well established by now his leaving wasn't his fault. And to some degree, I had forgiven him... but *only* him.

"Yeah. I mean I know this place is full of ghosts, but memories haunting you are a completely different kind of thing," Zain nodded. I knew not to ask if my Mom was among the ghosts; I had asked so many times when we were growing up. She was never there, not even in spirit.

But I guess if she had the choice of staying and only talking to her husband's love child or passing on, the latter was the better option.

"Yeah. Honestly, sometimes it feels like, even though Mom's ghost isn't here, her emotions stayed and suffocated all of us," I sighed. "There's just something about this house that makes me feel lonelier than usual. Just being here unlocks all the melancholy she was hiding from us until she decided to leave."

Zain squirmed uncomfortably in his seat, and I couldn't tell if he was holding on to something, or if it was guilt from everything that happened.

"Your mom didn't commit suicide," Zain finally whispered. "I don't know everything that happened, the ghosts wouldn't tell me. They thought I was too young to handle it. But Katya didn't kill herself."

"Of course, she did," I scoffed, "I mean, Dad always said..."

"I think it's pretty well established that Dad's a liar," Zain said, rolling his eyes, "and he threw me under the bus in more ways than one. Like he never cheated on your mom."

I stared at my younger brother, who was clearly sitting on secrets of his own. Or ones Dad was forcing him to keep.

"His relationship with my mom was years before he even met yours," he explained, holding up his hand to keep me quiet. "He was right not to tell you how the Circle of Shadows worked, but with how intertwined he was with them, it was also a pretty stupid decision. Long story short: he was supposed to join the Circle and be my Mom's second in command. He said no. This was right around when he started as the Eagle and was determining which way he wanted to go. My mom, his girlfriend at the time, tried to convince him they were on the same page with trying to end corruption. But the murder cult part, well, it caught him by surprise. Anyway, I don't know how this next part happened, and I really don't want to know, but she ended up getting a ton of his sperm and figured the potential of having a kid raised in the cult would bring him back, and she could get her hooks in him again. Didn't work. She found out he got married and then had you and Nate, and then decided to play her next card: having twins. Zak was evil incarnate and Mom's favorite, so she tried to use him to set off Dad's whole 'everyone needs to be a good person and help humanity' complex. Didn't work. Then, when we were eight, she sent Zak on some complicated assassination mission he wasn't ready for, and he never came back. That's when she dropped me off here, because if she couldn't have him, then she was going to destroy his marriage. Which she hates to admit, also didn't work. Dad had told Katya about what my mom had done, had told her about our existence since Mom had tried to blackmail them with it. And yeah, we didn't get along the greatest, but we tried. And she was the closest thing I had to a mom, since she wasn't trying to kill me. She and Dad just came up with the cover story so the press had a reason that there was suddenly another kid. They just didn't want you or Nate to know and get mixed up in the Circle."

116

"Why didn't you tell me any of this sooner?" I asked, abandoning my food on the bed as I sat next to him on the floor, "Why didn't you think to mention it?"

"I was waiting for Dad to. He said he'd tell you and Nate when the time was right, and then Katya died, and... then he left."

The silence between us was deafening, heavy with the weight of the secrets of the house, the weight that whatever happened to my mother wasn't the reason we were told.

"Can I tell you a secret?" I asked, feeling like it was the best time. "I've always known that Nightshade would be back. When I read the aura of the person we thought it was, it was all wrong."

"You've mentioned that before, Nik," Zain pointed out, and I shook my head.

"That's not the secret," I sighed. "The secret is, I haven't used my powers properly since. I wasn't sure if I was trying to convince myself that I didn't see how wrong it was, like it would make it better. But any time I've read an aura, it's just to confirm what I already know. And even then, it's been rare. But... I think I'm scared that if I start again, the same thing will happen. Plus, it's a stupid power anyway."

"There's something about Dad's blood that just makes powers suck," Zain scoffed. "The only one of us who has a useful one is Nate, and that's because he's adopted... Wow, we really have issues. Why did we stop going to therapy again?"

"Because we started right before everything happened, and I don't think any of us kept going," I said with a dry laugh. The idea of going to therapy made me want to vomit, and the last thing

I needed was some Department Approved therapist listening to all my parent issues. I sat enjoying the silence until the echoes of frantic footsteps came down the halls.

"Nik, Mom was murdered," Nate said, bursting into my room, slamming the door against the wall.

"Um... yeah, Zain told me something..."

"Zain, what...?" Nate shook his head, clearly trying to get his thoughts to make sense again. "No, you don't understand. Mom was murdered by Nightshade."

Chapter Thirteen

W HILE THE HOUSE HAD created a host of unwelcome
feelings, coming into the Nest gave me an intense sense of
déjà vu. Probably from the adrenaline of running into this room,
just as we had done hundreds of times before, whenever there was
an emergency.

I ignored the training equipment and tried to keep my attention
to a minimum. Whatever evidence Nate found, the secret Zain
had shared with me kept echoing in my ears. And he had silently
followed me, even though Nate hadn't invited him, clearly ready
to find out the details the spirits of the house refused to tell him.

"Gray, what is he talking about?" I asked, trying to keep my
voice neutral to counteract the absolute panic that was Nate's.

"Apparently, Seb had two different files on Nightshade," she
said, pulling things up onto the wall of monitors so we could see
them. "There's the one we all had access to, and there's the one
he kept private. He created a timed lock on it that kept the file as a
ghost app on the computer, so we wouldn't be able to access it. He
had to put the password in once a year, and it wouldn't show up.

But considering he hasn't been here to do that, we've had access to the whole case file for years, and none of us even realized it."

A few more clicks, and the secretive folder was open, and the first thing I noticed was the pictures. Every single one was of my mother, in her favorite nightgown, hanging off the landing of the stairs that Nancy had run down to greet us from not even an hour ago.

We had been told she had hung herself, but looking at the pictures, it wasn't just that. She had put up a fight. She had wanted to stay living. The only thing that seemed to be missing was the notes on the walls, the bloody messages that indicated it was him. We scrolled more, until we found a note and immediately recognized the handwriting, despite it being much cleaner than the notes he left on the walls.

My dearest Katya,

I know you don't understand my decision, but my love, I've never understood yours. Why would you throw away everything we had together? Why would you leave in the middle of the night? Why would you ruin me? I knew you were a queen, I treated you like one, and you repaid me by disappearing.

But I learned from you, I was reborn because of you. While you thought you would never see me again, I watched. I waited. I knew.

Remember, as you watch from the hell you will burn in, everything that happens from this point on is your fault. I am now the poison that runs through your veins. You created me. You created this.

~Nightshade

I blinked as I read and reread the message, the language entirely too familiar to me. It was the same as the internet trolls, the self-identifying "nice guys." Mom had run away from this man, and he had been stalking her. But my stomach dropped as I glanced at Nate, and then looked back at the note.

Mom always acted like Nate's biological father didn't exist and that he was better off without him. There was a story there she refused to tell. It easily could have been a coincidence, but it didn't feel like one.

"Yeah, everyone's had the same thought You're not subtle at all, Nikki," Nate deadpanned, his eyes glued to the screen. "But there's no way to know if he was my sperm donor. This guy could have been someone she met at a bar or on a job. She didn't exactly run with the best crowds before Dad."

Nate had a point, and there was a good chance he was right. And I could understand why Nate needed to hold on to the thought that whoever Mom had slept with to bring him into the world had a regular, everyday life. But the more I thought about it, the less plausible that felt.

"Um... what thought?" Gray's voice split through the silence, looking between everyone. "I think I'm missing something."

"Nate was adopted by our Dad," I explained, and Gray's eyes widened to the point I was afraid her eyebrows would enter her hairline.

"Wait... you don't think..." she started mumbling, clearly finding this information a new puzzle for her to figure out.

"Absolutely not," Nate insisted, refusing to let her even finish the question. "There's no way." I let him have the final say. Of all the bombshells that had been dropped since we had come back, this one shattered his identity. If he wasn't ready for these questions, it was only fair to drop them.

"Nate," I quietly said, "you're allowed to have time to process. And you're right, just because Nightshade was one of Mom's exes doesn't mean he's your biodad. But you're allowed to process the rest of it too," I said, motioning at the screen. "You took Mom's death the hardest. You're allowed to sit with the fact that everything we knew about her death was a lie."

Nate's eyes went gold for a moment, and I wasn't sure what futures he looked into, but the moment his eyes went back to normal, he decided to ignore me. But it was pure Caldwell stubbornness. We all had it, including Gray and the twins. I was confident that one of the traits Dad looked for in recruitment was being stubborn to the point of ridiculousness. But with how much Nate ran from his emotions, I wasn't surprised for him to glance his few seconds into the future to figure out the way to avoid emotional conversations. It didn't mean I was going to always let him—this completely changed so much of our lives, and he had to process it, whether he wanted to or not.

Or if he wanted to pull a Dad, we would all wake up tomorrow to find he ran away from dealing with it.

And I also knew I needed to include myself in the needing to process things boat. Between what I had admitted to Zain and all this new information about my Mom, it just made everything in my life feel like a lie. They were lies that Dad was using to protect me, but in the end, they just made us more distant. And yet, at the same time, we finally got a piece of the puzzle that had always been missing: why Dad was willing to break his code. Why Nightshade was such a personal villain for him. Why Dad had become more and more paranoid, so stuck on vengeance that he seemed to lose sight of everything else. Why he had lost that giant part of himself after we all lost Mom.

"I can process it later. Right now we need to find this guy," Nate finally said through gritted teeth.

"No, right now we need to find Jacob," I countered. "I don't know how Nightshade's figured out the four of us are together, but it means he knows Jacob's the easy target."

There was no small part of me that wanted to lure Nightshade to us now, to try to bypass him on the hunt for Jacob that he could easily have a headstart on. But we weren't ready. We hadn't worked as a team in years, and there was so much new information that was already starting to cloud our vision.

"Gray, is it possible to open up Acedonia Lake's CCTV interface? Cross-check with security and traffic cameras with facial recognition to see if we can pinpoint where Jacob is?" If he was still even there, it was worth a shot to find him. "Then, see if we can find anything about him on the internet. Check police reports. Maybe we'll find some sort of pattern to see where he goes and how to find him."

"You do realize that was exactly what I did for Seb all the time, right?" Gray laughed. "I already have the algorithm written, so we can start running it tonight. Hopefully, get some results soon." She dramatically turned back to the computers, and it seemed like the world no longer existed to her. Her fingers flew across the keys, and I let her work. There was no stopping her when she started on a project.

"Alright, the rest of us need to train," I said, specifically looking at Nate, who I thought could use some getting out of the aggression that had been growing in his features. I blinked, and just to check, saw his aura was bright red. Anger and fury radiated off of him. I blinked again, figuring it was better not to mention it. "Zain, you're the professional. You have to run us through some things."

And the sick smile on Zain's face made it clear that I was going to hurt in the morning.

Chapter Fourteen

I HAD SLEPT IN, and I figured I had earned it. Between Zain putting us through the ringer, going through some of Dad's old holographic training modules, and rereading the Nightshade files over again to see if there was something we had missed, I was physically, mentally, and emotionally exhausted. I groaned as the soreness in every single one of my muscles reminded me that I wasn't as young as I used to be, even though I was still too young to be having thoughts like that. And I wondered how sixteen-year-old me had managed to do this on a daily basis. Probably the routine, and barring special occasions, Dad forced us to have a regular rotation of training, recon, and patrols each week so we wouldn't get burned out.

And we just crammed all three into a single night.

The more pessimistic side of my brain was screaming that it was ridiculous to have done this much work just so we could defeat one person. But even our plan on what we would do with Nightshade was still nonexistent. Part of me wondered if Dad was right and killing him—or at least trying to—had been the best course of action. I knew Zain would probably be on team "kill him," and Nate probably was too, based on how red his aura had been. Which just made me uncomfortable.

Nate had always been the one advocating for avoiding killing, no matter what. But the pain was too personal and too fresh—and I was starting to understand the conflict of interest guidelines the Department had put into place for these situations.

Gray, on the other hand, would be team "turn him in," but I wasn't exactly sure that was the right course of action either. He could escape, disappear again, and we would be going through this same exercise years in the future after another one of us had been hunted down and killed.

My phone started buzzing in my ear, and I realized I had put it under my pillow at some point. I answered it before I looked to see who was calling. I had been putting off both work and Toby all of last night, so the chances of it being one of them were high.

"Good morning," I grumbled into the phone, and I was relieved to hear Toby's laugh on the other end of the line.

"You know, I thought you were ignoring me when you didn't text me back yesterday, but it sounds like you had a long night."

"Zain gave us a training session," I explained. "Everything hurts."

"That would do it." I could feel him grimacing through the phone. "Brave of you to do that, but I don't envy you in the slightest. I'm pretty sure your brother would go harder than my Dad," he paused for a moment, and I could tell he was going from regular Toby into whatever his work persona was like "I was calling to check in on you after the break in yesterday, to see how you were doing." The sound I made at the question wasn't human; the mixture of a groan and a sigh was definitely enough to answer his question. "I'll take that as bad."

"More like, I have to ask you a question, and I need you to answer it before I give you more information," I said, realizing that someone had put a thermos of coffee on my nightstand while I was passed out. I wasn't sure if it was Nancy or Zain, but at this point, I didn't care. "Was my mother on your official list of Nightshade victims?"

"Of course not," Toby scoffed "Why would she...?" But he stopped, and I heard the clacking of computer keys before he answered, "No, she wasn't."

"That's what I thought," I said, taking a long drink of coffee, as a realization came to me. The reason as to why Dad would have kept Mom's true cause of death a secret, why he wouldn't even have told us. "We found a secret evidence file last night. My Mom was murdered by Nightshade. I think she was his first victim, and if not that, then one of the first."

"Holy..." Toby muttered under his breath. "That's breaking so many conflict of interest laws. Your dad never said anything."

"I think my Dad had her death ruled a suicide specifically so he could get assigned to the Nightshade case," I said. I had heard that sleep helped you figure things out, but everything was now falling into place. He had broken every rule, he had forced us into his vengeance mission, it had become an obsession. It was his way of getting revenge for Mom's death, and it had destroyed him. Dad was the very thing the Hero Code was supposed to keep from happening.

"Nickel, you know if that's true, which, knowing your Dad is very on brand for him, it also means you just reported a conflict of interest to this case." I could feel him treading lightly, especially since he had been there when everything had happened. He had experienced it with me, and the fact Toby could compartmentalize was impressive.

"You are also my handler," I pointed out, "which means it's up to you whether it's too much of one to let us continue."

"Right," he muttered, and I could feel his brain starting to think through the options. "Do you think you or any member of your team will have a problem with keeping to the Code in pursuit of Nightshade?" The question sounded so official, and I could tell he was reading from a script for whatever paperwork he would have to fill out. And I also knew my answer could get us pulled off the case.

"Yes. Nate," I answered, and it almost felt like a betrayal to my brother. "Zain and Gray didn't have the same attachment. And as for me, I honestly don't know. I'm still processing everything we've learned."

"You know, that's a fair answer, and more people should realize it is a valid one," Toby said, and it surprised me how reassuring it was. "Especially with this being a situation that kind of changes everything about your life." I could hear him typing again, and I wasn't exactly sure what he was looking up, or if there was something else he would have to report.

"Okay, we've got two options," Toby said. " The first is I can pull you off the case. And I know I was against you being on it in the first place, but with this information, I don't think that's our best option. Time is of the essence, and having to turn over all the evidence and start over could cost Jacob's life. And I don't want to risk it."

"Okay," I said, surprised at where the conversation was going. "What's option two, then?"

"Option two is that your handler can join you. Be present for all planning and recon aspects, and monitor all patrol and fights to make sure all parts of the Code are being followed," he explained. "It's a lot more oversight, and I have to stay with you, but it keeps the mission going, and with me there, it lets me stop things from going too far. Otherwise, I'm just observing."

Toby was absolutely right, it was the better option, and he was someone I actually trusted enough to have that responsibility with the rest of the team. Even though I wasn't sure any of them would be a fan of it.

"I'm not sure everyone else will..." I started before he interrupted.

"You're the official team lead on this, Nikki," Toby reminded me, and for the first time, I understood it had been me the whole time. Somewhere, I had assumed that with Nate being back in the fold, his seniority would cause the responsibility to transfer to him. But I had been the one putting everything together. I was the one regularly making reports. The one job Dad had insisted I could never do was the one I had stumbled into. "You are more than welcome to get input from your team, but this decision is your call."

"I think you should come," I said almost immediately. I knew in my gut it was the right thing to do, that Toby could see things I wouldn't. "Nate's going to hate it, but I think everyone else will understand once they get used to the idea."

"Cool, I'll be there in the next hour," Toby said, and I could hear him starting to pack.

"What, you're not going to teleport over here?" I asked. "I meant to ask when that new power developed, because you sure didn't do that when we were teenagers."

"It's not a power," Toby admitted. "For my birthday last year, my Dad gave me a Xatanian teleportation device. He's been pushing for me to come visit Xantania, so it had two charges: one to get there and one to get back."

"And you used it on me instead?" I asked, a little surprised—as complicated as things were between Toby and his father, he always talked about wanting to visit his father's planet and learn more about that part of his culture.

"It seemed more important," he admitted. "Nickel, I've known you since we were thirteen, and I've never heard you cry like that."

"And you've also been saying since you were thirteen how badly you wanted to follow your father to Xatania someday," I countered. "I'm not more important than that."

"Yes, you are," Toby said, and I could feel the blood rush to my cheeks. "You've always been more important to me, Nikki." I wasn't sure what to say, and my stomach seemed to have flipped at the idea. I was starting to second-guess agreeing to have Toby come on our mission, because it meant we were going to be together until it was over.

And whatever residual feelings I had, whatever he just meant by that, it would just get more awkward as we worked together.

"Well, you should pack then," I awkwardly said, eager to get off the phone call so I could recalibrate myself. "We'll see you soon."

I chugged the rest of my coffee as I tried to control the butterflies in my stomach so we could focus on finding Jacob. He was the priority, even if Nate would disagree. As Toby reminded me, I was in charge, and Nate could suck it. If he was going to refuse to process everything we had learned, then he was going to have Toby as a babysitter whether he wanted it or not. Whether Nate believed it or not, the idea of Jacob's death on his hands would be too much for him.

Once upon a time, the two of them had been like brothers. And I knew that deep down, Nate was going to need him. Maybe we all would.

Groaning, I forced myself to roll out of bed, figuring it was better to announce our new team member before he got here. I put on the slippers that were as ridiculous and fuzzy as they had been when I was a teenager and made my way down to the kitchen—cursing each and every stair I had to climb down along the way.

I was surprised to find I was the first one in the kitchen and to find Nancy making breakfast. I made my way toward the coffee pot and refilled the thermos, before going to the fridge to add the cream and milk that was sure to be there.

"I was hoping you all took your coffee the same way. I made a trip to the grocery store last night when you were all training," she smiled as she kept working on the giant pan of scrambled eggs she was working on. "I left some for each of you on your nightstands. Except Gray. I think she pulled an all-nighter in the Nest."

"You know, Nance, you don't have to take care of us anymore." I smiled at her, sipping my coffee as I curled into a ball on the chair, then immediately sat up straight because that hurt more than regular sitting.

Stupid Zain.

"Nikki, what else am I going to do?" Nancy asked with a seriousness I rarely heard from her. "I have been by myself for so long, and while I know none of you will tell me what's going on, I wasn't born yesterday. I can see how scared you are, so I know it's bad. And I promised your father that his children would be safe and taken care of, and even if he's not here, I intend on keeping it."

"I don't get how you could even want to keep a promise to him after he abandoned us," I mumbled, the words leaving my lips before I had a chance to filter them for Nancy's benefit. She sighed, looking down at the eggs, moving them around the pan so they wouldn't burn.

"Your father was a complicated man," she finally said, and I could tell she was choosing her words carefully, "and he loved and cared about all of you. But he sacrificed too much of himself in an

132

attempt to right the wrongs of generations. He took on too much, and it broke him. And on that last night, he did everything he told himself he would never do. Katya's death had already been so hard on him, and I think the only reason he kept trying to fight was for her."

I had no idea if Nancy knew what had happened to my mother, if she had known about the lie, but she didn't elaborate on it.

"She cared so much about the world. She spent so much money on the communities she came from and always wanted to uplift them. And I think it's what drew her to your father in the first place, their shared love of helping *everyone*, not just the people who could pay for it."

It made me wonder if Nightshade was someone who had come out of those neighborhoods. Maybe Mom had helped him out of some situation, and he had misinterpreted it. Like those guys who decided that women in customer service positions are flirting with them because they were simply being nice.

"I think," Nancy continued, taking out a large bowl and scooping the eggs into them, "losing the person who was his biggest support made your father feel like he was drowning. I never thought it was right that he had all of you going on patrols, but he insisted he couldn't do it alone. Your mother occasionally joined him on patrols, and she had always been there to give him advice and let him bounce ideas off of her. He hadn't worked alone in years, and I think he lost his moral compass along the way. And how could he teach you how far was too far, when he didn't even know for himself anymore?"

Nancy's compassionate take on Dad was different from anything I thought. I never thought of Dad feeling guilty. I had never seen that side of him. But out of all of us, Nancy knew Dad the best. She had been there from the start. But her version of the man came through obvious rose-colored glasses, and the truth of who Sebastian Caldwell was was probably more in the middle of our two varying opinions.

"He could have at least called. Or sent a birthday card," I muttered.

"I wish he would, too," she admitted. "I spent the entire first year waiting for a message from wherever he had settled. Waiting for him to remind all of you that he cared. And I am disappointed he never reopened those lines of communication and saved all of you from that."

I silently drank my coffee, not wanting to get into that landmine of an emotional discussion when I didn't have enough coffee for it.

"I am proud of you, though," Nancy said, setting a plate of bacon and eggs in front of me. "I know everyone always assumed it would be Nate who followed in your father's footsteps, but I always thought you would surprise everyone and show that you should take up his mantle. You always took after Seb the most."

"Please, we all know Nate's still mini-Dad, complete with running away from his problems and a one-track mind for revenge," I deadpanned, and Nancy gave me a look that made me immediately shove food in my mouth, just like it had when I was little.

"Nate may have been trained, but he's so much more like Katya, working well in supporting a team instead of running it. Once everyone is together, he is excellent at recognizing strengths and helping plan things out, but on his own? His anxiety causes him to second-guess everything, and he ends up in choice paralysis. You, on the other hand, know how to get people to work together, even if they don't want to. You're not here because you want to be, but because you need to be. And I've seen what you've done for the businesses. You have a lot of the same sense your father had."

I looked down at my plate, ready to take another bite to satisfy Nancy, only to realize half the meal was already gone. Apparently, I had been hungrier than I thought.

"I always saw the potential in you, and your father completely missed it, which was to his loss," she insisted, sitting down next to me and squeezing my hand. "But if he were watching you now, I think he would be incredibly proud."

I knew that Nancy was trying to be comforting, but a host of new feelings rose in me. I had always been in second place. Second born, second in dad's eyes, second in joining the team. I hadn't ever been seen, because nobody chose to see me. But Nancy did, and while the part of me that had always wanted Dad to see me seemed validated, the rest of me still felt the constant resentment.

"I guess we'll never know about that," I shrugged, shoving a whole piece of bacon in my mouth to keep from having to say anything else.

"Maybe we'll hear from him soon. Since Nightshade's back." I looked up at her, practically choking on my food. "Do not give me that look, Nicole Caldwell, I have ears," Nancy scolded me, "and none of you have been particularly quiet. It wouldn't surprise me if he was using all of you to lure out Sebastian and start the cycle all over again."

It was a good theory, one I was sure we all thought about a few times. But I felt like if those were truly Nightshade's motives, he would have been more obvious about it. That all of his messages would be taunting the Eagle instead of us. Yes, the villain was an enigma on purpose, and even Dad couldn't always put the messages he left behind together until the next murder had been committed.

"You know, Nancy, Dad didn't give you enough credit for your problem-solving abilities," Nate yawned as he walked into the kitchen.

"And I'm assuming you're still a walking garbage disposal, so I made you a double serving," she smiled at him, before shoving a plate into his hands. "But you're incorrect. Your father gave me much more credit than you knew, and I helped him plenty of times when he got stuck."

With Nate distracted, I blinked, allowing his aura to fill my vision. The red of his anger was more muted, so it thankfully wasn't as intense. But it was still the most prominent of his emotions. I blinked again, hoping he didn't notice I had been analyzing him.

"How are you doing?" I decided to ask, figuring it was a way to at least try to stop the awkwardness that had been growing between us.

"You already know," he shot back, "but I just want all of this to be over. It's bringing up a lot. And I'm getting a good reminder why this life isn't for me."

"And nobody actually wants a serial killer actively targeting them, either. I think we're all ready for that part to be over." I heard Nancy cough, but I was confident she was covering a laugh as Nate rolled his eyes.

"Sure, just generalize everything that's going on," he snapped, "We need to get this guy. I *need* to get him. It's the only way I'll feel like I've made it up to Mom for missing it the first time. I always had a feeling after she died Sebastian couldn't be trusted, and now I know why... Every single thing he told us was a lie."

"Nathan, your father was trying to protect you. You were fifteen, Nikki was eleven, and Zain was eight and still adjusting to being here. He was afraid Zain would run away, and that you and Nikki wouldn't feel safe in the house if you knew everything. And I agreed with him."

"Are you kidding me, Nancy?" Nate practically roared. "You didn't think we deserved to know our mother had been murdered?"

"Your father was going to go after Nightshade whether the Department gave him permission or not," Nancy shot back, with a bite I had never seen in her before. "I knew he'd find some loophole that would get him official permission. But if you had known she was murdered, you would have been thrown into your father's life before you were ready. I had hoped this would have discouraged you from following in his footsteps." This was a fight

I had not expected, and I took a long drink of my coffee and hoped everyone had forgotten I was in the room. "I never wanted this kind of life for you or your siblings, and I know that the three of you didn't get a choice. But you were so young, and if you had known... it would have consumed you. I know sometimes sidekicks are children, but even teenagers were too young for the horrors he put you through. And I was right, Nathan, because after twelve hours of the truth, you are ready to throw away all of your morals to get even."

"So, Sebastian's allowed to do that, but I'm not?" Nate asked, and I sank lower in my chair. I needed so much more coffee before I even entered this fight and let Nate know that this was the exact reason I had approved Toby coming on our mission."

"Nobody allowed your father to do anything—he just did it. And it destroyed him," Nancy said. "And I will not let it do the same thing to you. Not when you have a wife and children waiting for you at home. You need to remember who you are, and who your Mother and I raised you to be, because Nathan, you would not be able to live with yourself if you killed that man."

Clearly, Nate disagreed, taking his plate and immediately walking toward one of the secret passages that would get him to the Nest. I wish I knew what to say that would help, but nothing would change the fact that something so fundamental to all of us had been a lie. And nothing was going to bring Mom back from the dead. The anger Nate felt was burning in me, too—however, it felt different. I wanted to make sure Nightshade would never hurt anyone again. That nobody else would be one of his victims. I knew that Nancy was right—I couldn't let us kill him.

No matter how tempting it was.

None of us would be able to live with ourselves if our idea of vengeance involved murder. It would just start the cycle over, creating a new Nightshade through us.

"Why does Nate look like one of those old cartoons where they have angry smoke coming out of their ears?" Gray mumbled as she walked in, making a beeline for the food and coffee.

"He's still pissed about how much we didn't know about Nightshade," I answered, "and if you want to talk about it, I'm going to need more coffee first. I came down here hoping everyone was still asleep, and I've already talked to four more people than I was planning to this morning."

"Oh, is Zain awake, too?" Nancy asked, looking over the food to see if my brother had taken some and left without her realizing it.

"No, I was on the phone with Toby. He's on his way here," I said to Nancy. "He's our handler on the case."

"Great. No questions about Nightshade or Toby," Gray said, catching on fast. "Anyway, I left my algorithm running last night and woke up to a message from Kitty that she was offended I didn't want to collaborate with her, so she hacked the Nest and improved it, so we should have a decent idea of Jacob's whereabouts soon," Gray said before pausing for a moment. I could tell she had a question, one of the ones she had just promised not to ask—and I just refilled my thermos once again in preparation for the kind of day it would be. "Are you sure you have no idea where he might be?"

I could tell Gray was hurt by the fact that Jacob had dropped off the face of the Earth, but at the same time, almost all the information the two of us had was identical. Gray was the one who knew Jacob had started using again, and that Brittney had kicked him out for it. And it was strange that the twins were no longer a unit, because there was still a part of me that had a hard time remembering that "Brittney and Jacob" had shattered long before the murder.

"I just hope he's not dead," Gray sighed. "I tried reaching out a few times, but I never got a response." I nodded, but I wasn't surprised. Gray was the optimist and had been waiting for the day the team would get back together. And while Gray and Zain were instant best friends, Gray and Jacob had always been close—or at least *seemed* close. Maybe Gray had just decided she would also be besties with Jacob, and he never saw it that way.

"He's not," Zain said, coming in from the secret passage in the pantry and immediately shoving a piece of bacon in his mouth—not bothering to sit down and get a plate. "Computer found him. And there's good news and bad news."

"If the bad news is that he's using again, I already know that," I reminded him before Zain shook his head.

"He's homeless," Zain said, not bothering to swallow as he explained, "and jobless. So, no address or work we can track down."

"Okay, what kind of good news do you have?" I asked, hating that this was a needle in a haystack situation that would be so much harder than we had expected.

"He has a car," Zain said. "Cameras were able to get his license plate number, and Kitty is pretty sure she'll be able to track him through traffic cameras once we get into Acedonia Lake."

"See, we're going to find him," I smiled at Gray, though my enthusiasm felt entirely fake.

"Yeah, I hope so," Gray nodded, taking a long drink of coffee. "I just hope we're not too late."

Chapter Fifteen

"Nikki, why is Toby here trying to force me to take a mental health screening?" Nate demanded, barging into my room as I debated what to put in my bag to take to Acedonia Lake.

"Because conflict of interest guidelines state that in situations like the one we're in, heroes are allowed to stay on the case at the handler's discretion," I answered, "and considering you are being impossible, I made a call to have him be here. And he's worried about your ability to handle this, if he's starting a screening."

"I don't need a babysitter, Nik," Nate snapped, which was starting to prove my point.

"I don't think you're qualified to make that decision, Nate," I said, giving him an exasperated look, "and as the team leader, I get to decide what the team needs. And at the moment, what the team needs is someone with us who is not as emotionally tangled up in this situation." I shoved in a final pair of underwear into my backpack and walked out of my room, knowing my brother would follow.

"We don't need the Department knowing all of our business," Nate argued. "They already knew about..."

"I checked with Toby this morning. Dad reported Mom's death as a suicide to the Department," I interrupted, figuring the very predictable direction he was going in. "She was never listed as one of Nightshade's victims. And he purposefully did that so he wouldn't have this kind of oversight, and nobody would question his actions until it was too late. I am not going to repeat history."

"You don't know that, Nik," Nate argued, but I was already rolling my eyes at his one-track mind.

"You're right, I don't," I said as I walked into the front hall where Toby was waiting. He was in the form he typically was in, gangly and average height, with the glasses he didn't need sliding down his nose as he looked at some of the artwork that hadn't changed since the last time he was here, "and if you had wanted to make those kinds of calls Nate, you should have been in charge. But you don't want to be, so you get to deal with it."

"When did she get so bossy?" I heard Nate mutter under his breath, and I turned to see that Zain had appeared at some point when we were talking.

"Dude, she's not wrong," Zain scoffed. "If it was me, I would have kicked you off the squad last night. You're way too emotional, and I'm betting you're going to get one of us killed."

Nate's eyes bulged, and it was clear he had expected Zain to be on his side, especially since our younger brother had always been quick to jump to murder. But I was glad Zain saw the same things I did: Nate currently couldn't make any rational decision. All his hurt had bubbled up to the surface and made revenge seem like the sweetest solution.

"Okay, I think I'm ready," Gray said, somehow rolling three giant suitcases down the stairs. The luggage itself didn't surprise me—there were so many suitcases around the house, but it took a moment to realize that Gray was probably bringing all the gadgets she had made and had packed them in addition to whatever clothes she brought. "Oh, Toby, hi!" she smiled, before running over and pulling him into a friendly hug. "What are you doing here?"

"Nikki decided we needed a Department babysitter," Nate pouted.

"I'm not here to babysit you, I'm just here to observe and make sure you can handle the mission," Toby countered, with a stern look that made his eyes glow their natural gold for a second. "If you want to pretend I'm not here, feel free. If you want to bounce ideas off me, you can. Just think of me as here to support you in whatever ways I can."

"Cool, you can support me by growing yourself magic muscles and taking all of these to the car," Gray said, practically shoving all her luggage at Toby.

The ride to the airport our private plane was waiting at was short and tense, though Gray happily chattered about everything to fill the awkward silence. And thankfully, most people fell asleep once we were in the air.

"So, I did find these," Toby said, handing me some files as we listened to Gray snore from a few seats away. "They were filed incorrectly. There were some things Nightshade had done that weren't found out until after the warehouse..." I appreciated him trailing off and not finishing that thought, "so nobody put them in the investigation files."

"Thanks," I said, glancing over the files, figuring I would look at them more in-depth later. We would be in the air for another four and a half hours, so there wasn't much to do outside of napping or investigating.

"So... how are you doing?" he asked, and I shrugged.

"Depends. Are you asking as my friend or my handler?" I countered, not entirely sure which direction he was coming at this conversation from.

"Both?" Toby offered, though I could tell it wasn't exactly true—I just wasn't sure which one he was lying about.

"Better than last night," I answered, figuring it was better to be as truthful as possible after all of the drama that went down with Nate's refusal to cooperate. "We got a lot of information. Some things are making a lot more sense, but there are still a lot of questions," I explained, "but it also feels like we lost Mom all over again."

"Grief has a way of popping up like that," Toby agreed, taking the handler path of the conversation. Which was for the better, since my old feelings already were trying to peek out of the box in the back of my mind I had attempted to shove them in. "Especially in situations like this, where what you thought happened is completely different from the actual circumstance. I wish we had known, at the Department, even if it had been classified. I at least could have attempted to prepare you."

"You do not get to feel guilty for my father's terrible decisions," I assured him. "Yes, you could have prepared us. But there's also a chance this entire situation wouldn't have happened if Dad had followed proper protocol."

"That is an excellent point," Toby relented, smiling at me. "And it's too late to go back in time and fix it all anyway."

I nodded and let myself sit with the pain. And the truth and lies that caused it. But I found myself instinctively resting my head on Toby's shoulder, letting myself feel the safety that had always come with him. With the feelings I had been avoiding thinking about taking the wheel.

"I'm glad you're here," I whispered, those traitorous feelings fully controlling me. "I don't think I could have done any of this without you."

"Don't say that. I've barely done anything," Toby said, shaking his head, but not pushing me away. "You're the one doing all the hard work."

"And you're the only one who believed from the start I could do it," I said. "I know you well enough that if you thought I couldn't do it, you would have outright refused to let me take the case. Find some sort of rule that barred me from it. Especially with how long I've been out of everything."

"I knew this was important to you," he admitted, looking down at the ground, "and I thought working on it might give you some closure about how things went down with your Dad."

"Exactly my point," I said, forcing him to look me in the eye. "I've been looking out for everyone else, but you're the only one who's looked out for me. And it's been a long time since anyone has done that for me." I was still whispering, and I felt my stomach tie itself in knots. I couldn't remember the last time I had been this vulnerable, and that made me uncomfortable in more ways than one.

Especially since Toby seemed to be the only person who could bring these things out of me.

"That's what friends do, Nickel," Toby whispered back, but I wasn't quite sure he meant friends anymore. In the same way, I had ignored my feelings, it just felt like he was making an excuse. Especially with how close we were. I could feel his breath on my face, so close, so easily kissable.

The urge caught me by surprise again, but it was stronger. Our noses touched, and he was a breath away. Half a second away.

"Nikki, we can't," he whispered, his words right against my lips. And the rejection stung, even if he seemed to be convincing himself as much as he was trying to convince me.

"Right. Sorry." I said, immediately standing up and trying to find a new seat away from him to attempt to hide my embarrassment.

"Oh, I said that wrong," Toby exclaimed, loud enough I heard someone wake up but I wasn't sure who it was. "Nikki, it's not you. If I wasn't... If you weren't..." he was flustered, and I hated that it made him more adorable even while my cheeks were burning from the blushing, "Nikki, if we do this, I'll be taken off the case. Plus, you're grieving, and that's bringing a whole bunch of other emotions up. So, if we're going to try to do something again, I need you to be sure that I'm not a distraction or something to get your mind off of everything. And I don't think you can be sure right now, and I can't let myself hope and have you disappear again."

The embarrassment died down, because it was somewhat reassuring that this wasn't a rejection. Instead, it was Toby being right, even if he had wanted to kiss me. And he was right, because with how much I had going on, I couldn't make that decision. He deserved better than what I had done to him when we were sixteen, and even if I was positive at this second that I wouldn't do it again, even if I was working through my trauma. I just couldn't give him what he needed.

He needed to protect himself, too.

"No, you're right," I nodded, sitting down on the complete other side of the plane just to keep the temptation from bubbling up again, "I'm sorry."

"Nikki, you don't need to be sorry," Toby assured me. "I want to talk about it, but maybe after the mission? We'll just put a pin in it until then?"

I nodded again, picking up the folder I had dropped on the floor in my shuffle to get away from him. It was a fair boundary, an important one, and one I was glad he set so we could move forward for the sake of the mission.

Even if I still wished I had kissed him. Even if I was disappointed in myself that I was unable to give him the clarity he needed right now.

"So, I think now's a good time to read the files," I awkwardly said, flipping it open, hoping it would give me a few moments to compose myself. I went into the office of the plane, which was more of a mini-Nest Dad had installed to make sure he could work on a mission from anywhere. I had work to do, a file to read, and I needed to get Toby out of my mind.

No matter how badly I wanted to kiss him.

Chapter Sixteen

I F THERE WAS ONE thing I could always count on when
it came to any of Dad's stuff, it was that it would be
built for a workaholic. There were screens all over the office, a
holographic projector, and the most comfortable chairs on the
plane. I pulled up everything we had from the Nest computers,
the video we had of Jacob, and the file of evidence about Mom
I couldn't quite bring myself to look at again—but it was there
if I needed it.

I looked over what we already knew, just to see if looking at
it with new eyes would change anything. It didn't. But I now
had the context to look at everything in Toby's file and start
to analyze it.

The first thing in the file was a blurry picture of Brittney and her
"Twinge" hero profile that the Department had on her. Back then,
the twins had been such a unit they refused to get their official
pictures done separately. Twinge and Tribulation, the Pain Twins.
She could force people to feel endless amounts of pain, and Jacob
couldn't feel any. They had been the last recruited to the team,

and looking at the profile, it was hard not to have some of the old feelings of jealousy bubble up again.

Dad had tried so hard for Brittney and me to become friends—especially because, on paper, it made perfect sense. We had common interests, but our personalities just didn't mesh well. She was too perky and talked about nothing for hours, which grated on my nerves nonstop. And Dad had me train her, which, to everyone else, looked like he was finally giving me some responsibility. But it became clear it was less of an honor and more that he wanted to facilitate a friendship, because he still spent so much time training the twins by himself.

Jacob was more of a friend, though I doubted he would call it that. He took training to an entirely new level: oftentimes sparring with Nate and Zain for hours longer than necessary. It was the only healthy way he could get all the anger he was holding onto out, and the fact that he couldn't feel the hits only made him build an insane level of stamina. Sometimes Dad had to force him to stop due to him bleeding all over the floor, because even though Jacob didn't feel the injuries, it didn't mean they weren't there.

We knew they had a rough home life, though they refused to talk about it. And they didn't need to, because they had brought out a side of Dad we hadn't seen in years: the caring part of him that had gone dormant after Mom had died. It was hard to watch these strangers bring it out of him when his children couldn't. And when Dad finally seemed to start caring about us afterward, it was too little, too late. We had just started to trust him again when he disappeared.

But the reminder that I had been in charge of her training, even if it was a technicality, had brought a new wave of guilt for not keeping in touch with Brittney more. For not answering the phone when she called—even for not checking the voicemail sooner. I had to wonder if part of the reason I was blaming myself for her death was because Dad had trusted me with her training.

Her death meant my failure.

So many memories kept flooding back in, bringing me back to the warehouse, when something new from my memory cropped up.

Nightshade had all of us trapped. He told Dad to either kill him, or he would kill all of Dad's sidekicks. One-by-one. He taunted Dad, telling him he might be able to save one or two of us by sticking to his code, and had taunted me by saying it was obvious he would save Brittney. That she was his favorite.

But Nightshade knew our names. He knew who Dad's children were compared to the ones Dad had picked up off the streets.

And the exact thing he had taunted me with was something I was certain I had written in the diary I was keeping for my therapist at the time.

Dad had forced us to go after reading an article about the teenage mental health crisis. And it was someone who had Department access, since superheroes needed therapy, too, probably more than regular people. He had wanted to make sure it was someone who could have access to all parts of our lives. And I had left my diary with her during what had ended up being our last session.

She had resigned that Friday, and the last we heard, she had retired and moved across the country. It had seemed abrupt at the time, but once Nightshade blew up the warehouse and Dad disappeared, our therapist's disappearance was the last thing on our minds.

Toby had said some information he had was filed incorrectly, and I was shocked to see it was Dr. Persephone Graham, therapist to the heroes, staring back at me from a picture. If Nightshade had killed her, it meant he knew everything.

We now knew that he had held a grudge against Mom, and he decided the Eagle was his nemesis. Or maybe his partner. It was hard to tell at times what the villain thought their relationship was. But Dr. Graham fit his usual target: a successful woman in a field typically held by men.

It didn't matter why he targeted her; it just gave him access to a goldmine of information about us, especially with her having been killed two days before. And by the time Dr. Graham's body was discovered, our entire world was in disarray, and the Department had closed the case.

But I wondered if that grudge against Mom had been why he targeted her. If he saw us thriving and couldn't handle it. If Dr. Graham was just a stepping stone to his next targets: me and Nate. And if he had gotten all the information he needed to take down Dad completely by accident.

I needed someone who could confirm my thoughts, and even though he was still right there, I wasn't up for talking to Toby. Zain and Gray were still sleeping, and that meant there was one person I could talk to: Nate. And with his growing need for revenge, I wasn't sure if this would be pouring gasoline on an already out-of-control fire. I opened the door to the bedroom he had claimed the moment we stepped on the plane, balled up a blank piece of paper and threw it at him.

"What are you doing?" Nate groaned, his eyes not opening. So I threw another ball of paper at him, just to make sure he wouldn't fall back asleep.

"Do you remember Dr. Graham?" I asked, only for him to shake his head and attempt to roll over so he wasn't facing me.

"Yeah, Dad forced us to go to her. We didn't mesh well." Nate mumbled.

"She was murdered by Nightshade two days before we went to the warehouse," I said, and Nate immediately shot up out of whatever half-sleep he had been in.

"So, he had no idea Dad was the Eagle. He was after us," Nate said, thinking out loud. But his thoughts confirmed everything my gut was telling me. And I didn't like it.

"He had my diary, all her notes on us, and Dr. Graham was one of the few people who knew our secret identities," I pointed out. "What if we're looking at this all wrong? What if he's not after Dad at all, but we were always the targets? Nightshade just stumbled onto a way to kill us and hurt the Eagle at the same time."

"It's plausible," Nate sighed, realizing he wasn't going to go back to sleep as he came into the office. The video of Jacob was still playing on a loop, even though I had given up trying to find something new in it hours ago. I stared at the video, thinking about everything I had just learned about his last victim compared with our situation. I had so many unanswered questions and no way to find out the answers.

"You know, Dad always had that same look on his face," Nate said, and immediately my eyes shot to him in suspicion. I couldn't remember the last time my brother hadn't called our father by his first name. Like it was his way of punishing Dad for our mother's death. It came out now and again, but this felt intentional. Like he was trying the term on to see if it still fit. "I know you look just like Mom, but you have all the same mannerisms as him."

"Nancy said something similar at breakfast," I shrugged. "But you knew him better than I did, so I'll take your word on it."

"Listen, I know you're mad at him..." Nate started, but he didn't get to lecture me on Dad's choices when they mirrored his.

"I'm not just mad he left, you know," I snapped, but the words made me feel free. I realized it was the first time I had said them out loud, and once I started, I couldn't stop. "I'm mad he left me so much earlier than he did anyone else. You were always his second in command, so even when you were fighting, you were still close. Zain was younger and all murder-y, so he needed a lot of attention. And then Gray and the twins came, and he was focused on them, too. But never me. It was like you all were the apples of his eye, and I was forgotten and hoped for the day he would notice me."

"That's because you're just like him," Nate chuckled, ignoring the glare I shot at him. "He had a hard time connecting with you because you're exactly the same. You both strive to be better than who came before you, you both care too much and bury it under a mask of not caring at all. And you understood the duplicity that was needed to make the public adore you without knowing anything about you, and I still have no idea how to pull that off. I think Dad spent the least amount of time with you because he always assumed you were enough like him that you'd be okay."

"I have spent every single day since he left trying to prove I'm nothing like him," I sighed, "and now everyone keeps pointing out every single way I'm like him. And I hate it."

"And he spent the majority of his life and billions of dollars trying to prove he was nothing like *his* Dad," Nate pointed out, and I blinked for a moment. There were plenty of times I forgot I even had grandparents. I didn't know much about them past the fact that they were part of the now-defunct Di Vittorio mob. That mob was what had caused their death when Dad was a teenager, and instead of joining the Di Vittorio's, he took them down. The details of what my grandparents did were never clear, but with the money we had, it was very possible they were high in the organization.

"So, I'm the second coming of Dad. Great," I sarcastically deadpanned. "If that were the case, wouldn't he have tried to put me in charge instead of you? Since you were the one he wanted to be the leader?"

"Nikki," Nate said, looking at the looping video of Jacob again, "it doesn't matter. You put yourself in charge the moment it was necessary. Everyone on this plane would be dead if it wasn't for you. Just think about that." He yawned, clearly thinking about going back to his nap when the pilot announced we were about to land in Acedonia Lake.

"You owe me half an hour of sleep," he muttered as I sat down and put on a seatbelt. "I want that on the record."

Chapter Seventeen

D OING SURVEILLANCE IS ONE of the most boring parts of being a superhero. Sitting in the same place for hours, rushing to go to the bathroom, hoping you wouldn't miss the five seconds you had been waiting the entire time for. Everyone in movies always made it seem like it was fun, or over quickly. But it wasn't, it was just hours of not being allowed to do anything, hoping you eventually would find what you needed.

I was sitting on the glider Gray had made me, because after all the grumbling about the fact that I couldn't even drive a car, I finally relented to using it. It was easy to operate, but it was not comfortable to sit on.

It had been six hours of waiting, and I was cold, hungry, and cranky. And I wished I had brought something more to do than just designing things on my sketchpad. I had promised Gray a new suit, but had accidentally started designing new ones for the entire team after a few hours had passed. Dad's old supersuit designer had been old-school: complete with bright colors and easy-to-see motifs. But these suits I had imagined as sleeker, and easier to both hide and move in. If I had access to my 3D printers, I could easily create armor underneath like I had done countless times before.

While the armor was already designed and only needed to be fitted to everyone's measurements, the suits I designed had always been bright colors. Everyone had a brand. Most of them required them to be seen, and it was easier to do that if your costume had obvious colors and style.

It just also happened to be hard to sneak up on someone in a neon orange supersuit. That was just a fact of life.

If I were at my studio, I would have access to an entire floor of 3D printers and industry-level sewing machines, and could probably put the suits together relatively quickly. One suit per day would give us a week to get it done.

A project for later, as there was no way we would have time to get it done now. Not with Nightshade after us.

Sighing, I looked back over my sketches and hated how much I wished I could see them in action. I wanted to know if, after five years, people would still recognize us, or if they would see us as something new. If I could aim for a combination of that, it would probably be enough to get people talking. To let the world know we were back. But there wasn't a world we would all be back in after this. Zain probably would want to, Gray seemed like she wanted to, and I...was going to put a pin in that decision until after I was done with this case. But Nate wouldn't want to; he made that much clear, and I had no idea if Jacob would be willing to speak to us ever again.

I debated ripping up the sketches, as if it would be enough to get the designs out of my head and I could forget about the entire thing. But Gray's voice in my ear snapped me out of my thoughts, reminding me I was wearing an earpiece and was probably supposed to check in.

"Nikki, Jacob's car just pulled into a park near you," Gray's voice said. "I think he might be meeting a dealer. Someone is wearing a mask. Though it could be MysticKnight, we are in her jurisdiction. But it could also be... not good." I didn't need to hear more. Gray sent me the GPS ping, and I turned on the glider and started on my way.

And thankfully didn't fall off like I had the first five times I had tried it, getting onto the roof I had been perched on.

"How far out?" I asked, manipulating the glider in the general direction, and glad there was virtually no traffic at 2:48 in the morning. Even if I wasn't on the road, I didn't need an audience to witness me using this for the first time.

"Five minutes if you go fast, ten if you obey traffic rules—which technically you don't have to because you're not on the road and..." I cut off Gray's rambling, not wanting to let myself get distracted as I crouched on the glider so I could go faster. I did enjoy the flying aspect, even if I didn't want to admit it to Gray, and managed to get there in seven minutes.

I landed in the parking lot just in time to watch a man skipping away in a mask. It wasn't a hero. Instead, it looked more like one you would buy at a high-end costume store. Cuts with blood oozed out of the mask, and he stopped and saluted me from across the street. A truck passed as I debated running after him, and the man disappeared.

"Nightshade's here and just disappeared," I said into my comms, my blood running cold as I realized this was the first time I had been in his presence in years. He could kill me, but I think he wanted me to see he was here. To see whatever it was he had done.

To put me in an impossible situation: to try and save Jacob, or let the trail go cold.

I chose Jacob. I could hear chatter on the comms about whether or not they could see him on the camera, and if someone else was close enough to get to him. But I turned it off and ran through the parking lot, looking for the car I had only seen in videos.

It didn't take long to find it, as it was covered in Nightshade's trademark graffiti—though I was surprised to see it was paint and not blood. For once.

Tribulation now feels the pain. Do you?

"Jacob!" I yelled, sprinting faster as I read the message. I attempted to throw open the car door, which unfortunately was locked. I wasn't sure if he was alive or not; black spray paint had blacked out all the windows. I knew Gray was probably going to kill me, but I needed to get into the car, and the best way to do it was to get in.

I got on the glider, ran it full speed at the car window, and jumped off right before the glass shattered. A strange smoke came out of the car and immediately made me nauseous, and I didn't want to imagine what it was like for him.

But thankfully, Jacob was breathing. Just barely. His eyes were bloodshot, his skin was pale, and I could tell, despite his eyes being open, he wasn't conscious at all.

"Gray, call an ambulance, now!" I shouted, reaching my hand through the broken window and opening it. I dragged Jacob's body out and started coughing harder, the gas inside clearly a poison, combining with whatever it was he had just taken. I wasn't sure if the gas was making it worse or if they were fighting against each other, but I could tell Jacob didn't have long, and I didn't have enough first aid training to know where to start.

"Nickel," Toby's voice said in my ear, calming me down some, "I slipped a general antidote in your bag. See if it'll help with the poison, and it might slow the effects of whatever else is going on, too. I can't make promises, but it's better than nothing."

With some instructions, I at least didn't feel completely useless. I pulled out the needle and shoved it into Jacob's thigh, and within seconds, Jacob's breathing seemed more steady. Though if it was because of the clean air or the antidote, I had no idea.

"Jacob," I grumbled in his ear," you better live, because I will revive you if I have to. And if you think you can out-stubborn me and die anyway, you're wrong." It was a threat, but I could see the vaguest screw you on his lips, and I could at least tell the message was received. Whether or not he'd live to say it again was another thing entirely.

It was seconds later that the paramedics arrived, though it felt like hours. Even explaining the situation and what I knew didn't feel like enough as I rode with them to the hospital.

I had to hope we had done enough to save him. I had to hope we had gotten here in time. I had to believe we hadn't lost both Merrick twins for something I could have prevented years ago.

I had to believe we had gotten there in time.

Chapter Eighteen

"You can't all be in here!" I heard a nurse yell from the hallway, with Nate and Toby arguing with her so the rest of us wouldn't have to. Zain had turned himself into a pretzel so he could sit on the counter. Gray was in the chair closest to Jacob's bed, unable to say anything. And I sat in the chair by the window, looking out at the city, so I didn't have to look at him.

We had been told he might wake up soon, or he might not. There was a lot the doctors weren't sure of, and they needed him to wake up before they could run the tests they needed to on his brain.

"Ma'am," I heard Toby say, while I assumed he pulled out his badge, "we're on an investigation from the Department of Hero Affairs, and we are requesting you let us all stay here. However, I will take it up with the hospital president if necessary. Because you see that woman there?" I glanced at the door to see him looking at me, and I knew what card he was going to play. Even though it was risky to play it in addition to his Department card, with us all here. I just hoped the woman was too mad at our presence to put together the information she was getting.

"That's Nicole Caldwell," he continued, and the nurse peeked in as if she recognized me for the first time. "She's got enough money to buy this hospital, fire the entire board, and then fire you. The man in the hospital bed is a member of her family." I had to give it to Toby, that was a great way to bypass some of the suspicion he could have caused, "Do you really want to piss her off enough you'll never work again? Because she'll do it. I've seen it happen before."

The nurse glanced in, and I gave her my perfected ice queen glare, the one I had gotten plenty of practice in from board meetings and interviews I couldn't care less about. It was intimidating enough for the nurse, who immediately looked away.

"Fine," the woman grumbled, "but if he gets any worse, I'll kick her out first, followed by the rest of you."

"You know, Toby, I think I saw someone do that exact thing in a movie before," I scoffed at him, and Gray burst out laughing.

"What, I like movies!" He shrugged. "And Nate wasn't getting anywhere with her, and it seemed like something people would believe you would do. Even if it is ridiculous."

Nate had resumed pacing, and Toby was leaning by the wall next to me. I wouldn't say he was hovering, but it was still hard to look at him. I was still embarrassed by our almost-kiss, and I knew we would have to talk about it more. And I hoped nobody else was picking up on the awkwardness, even if it was a stupid bet to take.

I had been assured by doctors that I had kept him alive, and they had been able to neutralize the poison in his system. It was the Silence that was the problem. The drug was one I had heard plenty about over the years, especially from the Department. It was supposed to dull the powers we had, and as a result, became highly addictive to people who had undesirable powers.

I didn't know why Jacob would want to feel pain, but it would mean he wanted to suffer. Which made me worry about where he was mentally for him to have gotten to this point.

"Do you think if I throw cotton balls at his face, it'll be enough to annoy him into waking up?" Zain asked, throwing it at Jacob before any of us had a chance to answer. Though, of all the things that would annoy him, this seemed the most harmless, while also most likely. Just like if he were sleeping.

"Throw that at me one more time, and I'll shove it down your throat," an exhausted, low, gravelly voice said from the bed, and we all immediately turned to where Jacob was waking up. I could see Zain's pride that his idea worked, but as Jacob opened his eyes, he looked like he was trying to make us disappear.

"I don't know why you're here, but I don't want any part of it," Jacob grumbled, and I couldn't help but glance at Nate, considering said almost the same thing when we found him.

"Too bad, dude, you're already a part of it," Zain shrugged from the counter. "You were almost murdered, and the only reason you weren't was because Nikki showed up and saved your ass."

I could read the disbelief on Jacob's face like a book, and even though he was pale and weak, it was clear he was holding on to some extra anger at all of us.

"You should have just let me die. Everyone would have been better for it," he groaned, leaning back into his pillow. "It's not like any of you care about me anyway."

"Jacob..." Nate started, but Jacob's eyes flew open with a terrifying rage.

"Get. Out." Jacob snapped, venom dripping from his words. I understood it, considering it was the same anger I had felt plenty of times. The same thing that my Dad and Nate had done to him, I had done to Toby. The Caldwell cycle of abandonment was the cornerstone of our family, and we all were responsible and victims at the same time.

We all had to face the consequences.

"Hey, we just spent the last few days tracking you down so we could save your stupid butt, so the least you could do is hear us out," Gray quietly said, trying to smile at him. "Just give us ten minutes?"

"You're just here for your egos," Jacob huffed. "Britt couldn't even be bothered to show up. Did she try to talk you out of it? Say I was a lost cause? I can't imagine she's happy you're here." Toby sighed from the background, and it was the first time Jacob noticed him. The rest of us probably made some sort of sense, but Toby was the outlier—I was pretty sure the two of them hadn't ever talked before.

"Brittney passed away," he said, his words slow and measured in a way that was too rehearsed to be the first time he had given this type of news. "She was murdered on Monday."

"What do you mean murdered?" Jacob demanded, and an array of emotions played out on his face. Anger, hurt, fear, guilt. As if he had always expected that eventually his sister would be back and they would be reunited.

Maybe they would have, if Nightshade hadn't targeted her.

I tossed the case file at him, and he opened and immediately closed it as I mentally grimaced. I had left the picture of Brittney's crime scene at the top, so it was the first thing he would see. Probably not the best move, but I didn't have time to talk through it again. The file suddenly flew at the wall as he crashed his fist into the tray attached to his bed. The plastic splintered, cutting the edge of his hand, and it seemed like he hadn't noticed.

The Silence had worn off, and I wasn't sure if that was promising or not with Jacob in this state. Toby started picking up the papers that had scattered when the file hit the wall, and I couldn't blame Jacob. Not when it was his twin.

"He's after us," I explained, the news being better to come from me than Toby or Nate. "I can fill you in on the details later. But what you need to know right now is Nightshade survived, he's after us now, and he almost got you..." I looked down at my watch, surprised to see it was still the same day when it felt like days had passed since I had found him in the early hours of the morning, "this morning."

Jacob's face went blank, and I could tell he wasn't sure what I was talking about. And if I had to choose for him, I would have preferred he never remembered it. Knowing someone tried to kill you and remembering the attempt were two very different things, and if I could keep him from that fear, I would.

"Why didn't you go after him?" Jacob asked.

"Zain tried, but he disappeared," I answered. "We came here for you, and I wasn't about to let you die. You can fight us later on whether or not you want to be saved, but I think we're stronger together than apart."

Jacob scoffed, and I couldn't blame him. It had been five years, and any trust he had in my family was long gone. "Got the worst way of showing it," he mumbled, and I nodded in agreement.

"Yeah, we do," I agreed, "Nate can't handle being in charge, so he'll run the first chance he gets. Zain's over here being the one thing keeping a ton of murder cultists from murdering us in our sleep. Gray's been living in a dream world where none of our problems happened, and I haven't had any meaningful human interactions in five years. We're all a hot mess, we all have no idea what we're doing, and somehow, with it all stacked against us, we still found you in two days after the Department couldn't find you for six months."

"Nik, you didn't need to come for all of us that hard," Gray whimpered, and I couldn't handle everyone else's emotions anymore. Not when we were all holding it together by a thread.

"You're in charge now?" Jacob asked, looking between me and Nate.

"Yeah," I said, with Toby backing me up with a nod.

"She's registered as team lead with the Department as well," he continued, which made the closest I had seen Jacob smile.

"Good. You'll at least tell the truth," he grumbled, "but I'm not coming."

"Yeah, that's not a choice," Nate argued, and I immediately smacked his arm. I hadn't forced anyone to come, not even him—that honor went to his wife. And Nate didn't get to start changing things now.

"Don't listen to him, it is your choice," I said, figuring I could earn the few points I could by telling him to ignore my brother. "You can go to a Department safe house. Never see any of us again. But with everything we've learned, I think we're going to need to find my Dad, and if you skip out, you'll miss your chance to cuss him out for leaving." I knew playing into Jacob's anger issues could backfire. It wasn't my smartest idea, but we could get him more on our side later.

"I'm in," Jacob answered, biting the carrot I was dangling faster than I expected, "but only if I get to break Nate's nose too."

"Deal," I agreed, giving Nate a smirk as his jaw dropped. "I think out of everyone here, he deserves it the most."

"Nickel," Toby quietly warned, "I don't think this is the best way to build your team." I smiled sweetly and ignored him. Technically, it could count as training if Nate attempted to dodge out of the way. Which meant, technically, it still fell under the Hero's Code.

"She's not wrong," Zain scoffed. "Jacob would be doing us a favor if he did. Nate needs to be knocked down a few pegs."

And that was all Jacob Merrick needed to hear to become an enthusiastic member of the team.

Chapter Nineteen

C ONVINCING THE HOSPITAL TO release Jacob wasn't easy, and it took him signing himself out against doctor's orders to get him out of the building. I had assured the nurse, whom I was certain hated me, that I was taking him to some experimental treatment center in the Bay. A lie, though I wasn't against dragging him to one if he got worse.

I just was scared a hospital or rehab center would be an easy target for Nightshade, when we needed to keep moving.

I was certain Nightshade knew Jacob was alive; he had been baiting me and knew I had chosen to save him. And that was more information than I wanted the villain to have. It meant he knew we had fully reformed the team, and if he found us, he would make us all sitting ducks.

Nightshade's entire plan was what was puzzling to me. Part of me thought he wanted revenge on us for making our mother happy, and part of me wondered if he was trying to lure out the Eagle. Part of me wondered if he just thrived on the chaos from killing former sidekicks. Even Calder Bay felt too predictable, and

I didn't want to stay there. Same with Sand's Point, considering he had killed my mother there.

We needed to regroup, and we needed the Nest, which meant we only had one place we could go. And I hated that it was a risk we had to take.

Jacob was given one of the plane's bedrooms, and Gray was sleeping right outside of it. I was glad he was asleep, because I could tell he was starting the detox process. I had asked Toby to get us supplies to help him, but I feared we would have to get him medical attention.

And he would be targeted all over again.

It wasn't fair that I had to choose between his health and his safety—in fact, I would have preferred never to have made that kind of decision for him. But I wanted Jacob alive. It was the full reason that I had tried to find him in the first place—and unfortunately, it meant that we were in over our heads on how to help him recover from everything he had been through.

Toby was snoring on the couch across from me, Zain was nowhere to be found, and Nate had claimed the second bedroom. With everyone sleeping, I found myself wishing I could sleep on planes. The flight to Acedonia Lake had been easy to let myself get distracted with the file Toby had given me, but now that we were flying back, I was alone with my thoughts. I had already tried lying down, but all I could do was think. My mind was racing, trying to put together the pieces of the puzzle, and instead, only finding we had more missing pieces than I originally had thought.

It made me miss Dad. He couldn't sleep during flights either; it was one of the things we had in common. But not only that, it was one of the few things I could remember that were truly ours. Where we could talk, where I felt like he was actually listening to me. Any time we were on the ground, he was pulled between so many people, but in the air, he was mine.

It felt like it was a silly thing to miss, especially since I was never able to tell if he'd only been interested because I was the only one awake. But Nate's words were in the back of my mind: that the two of us were more alike than I gave us credit for.

I wasn't sure if I believed him, but as I looked at the country below, I willed myself to think like Dad. To try to look at the pieces of the puzzle differently. To step back from the individual pieces I was looking at and look at the entire situation as a whole.

Every single thing we were facing was the consequence of Dad's actions. Nightshade only got bold enough to go after us because of his rivalry with the Eagle. The Circle of Shadows had a personal vendetta against Dad for turning them down. Both situations were ones he kept close to the chest, and purposefully kept information from us—information he never would have written down for us to find. It meant we needed Dad. He could look over everything and tell us what we were missing.

I groaned, wishing again he had reached out to us. He let us know where he had gone. Nancy had been so sure he would have that it almost seemed like she thought it was out of character for him not to have given us something.

And then it dawned on me: he had.

I shot up off the couch and ran toward the office. Dad would have known his Nightshade file would fill in some of the blanks, but not all of them. Which meant there had to be more in there; there was a clue we had all missed at the shock of finding out about my mother's murder.

I opened up the files on the different screens that lined the wall. The pictures had been the only thing I had looked at before. But there were unofficial case files, journals, and spreadsheets he had buried. I started combing through everything, looking for a clue, when I suddenly had the feeling I was being watched. I glanced over my shoulder and found Jacob staring at me from the doorway.

"How are you feeling?" I asked him, offering him the chair next to me so he could see the screen.

"Like I was hit by the fucking comet," he grumbled, with a coldness that made me reluctant to ask more questions. There was a way Jacob always seemed to be carrying the weight of the world on his shoulders, and it only seemed to have intensified since the last time I had seen him.

"Yeah, you look like it," I finally decided to answer, but it was true. He looked terrible. He was covered in sweat and shivering, while dark bags under his eyes were so intense it looked like he hadn't slept in weeks. "Did anyone fill you in on Nightshade murdering my mom?"

"Gray," he nodded. "That's what you're looking at?"

"I feel like we're missing something," I admitted, "Some sort of clue that's going to help us. I just don't know what else he would have left in here for us to find."

"Yeah, Seb was always intentional," Jacob agreed, taking an uneasy breath as he blinked and tried to take in the information on the screens. "Why was he sending money to your mother after she died?"

"Wait, what?" I asked, pulling over the spreadsheet he had been looking at onto the main screen. And Jacob was right, every single month, he put away money he had labeled "For Katya," which made no sense. My eyebrows furrowed as I thought about what it could mean, before searching all of the information we had for my mother's name.

And I wasn't surprised at how many times her name was there.

There were thousands of financial transactions sent somewhere in Valterra, and I had no idea why Dad would be sending money there. We had been there on vacation a few times, with it being Mom's favorite place in the world. It wasn't exactly safe for us, though. It was a country with some of the strictest laws against powered people, and registered heroes here could easily be arrested if they used their powers on their soil.

But it wasn't just the money. So many of my father's journal entries were letters he wrote to her. Things he wished he could tell her, things about her he missed, promises that he would make sure her killer would never do to anyone else what he had done to her. It felt like I was intruding on their relationship with the way he bared his soul in some of the pages.

Everyone had always insisted my father loved my mother with the entirety of his heart. They made them sound like a fairy tale, and I think to some degree, I bought into it when I was little. But then Zain arrived, and it fractured my view of everything. But as I looked at the letters, it became clear I truly never understood how broken my mother's death had left him. How he struggled to live without her. What he had wanted most in the world was the opportunity to grow old with her, and it had been ripped away from him.

I scrolled through the journals, trying not to read too many of them, until I realized the date on the last one. The date everything went wrong. The date Dad had assumed he had killed Nightshade—and if there was anything about where he was going, it would be there.

Katya, my love, it's done. I'm done.

I thought it would feel like justice had finally been served. But when I saw the body, I felt empty. I didn't recognize myself. Instead, I saw a body, a gun, and years of broken promises. Promises I had made in your name, you would have hated.

I ruined the children. The ones you loved, the ones you would have taken in the moment you saw them. I told myself I did it for you, to help bring you justice. But I wasn't the father they needed. I turned them into warriors, and I can't fix it. I can't fix any of it. The longer with me, the worse it'll be. And I cannot do this to them anymore.

I failed you, my love.

I'll wait for you in our spot. I had it ready for you, even if you never got to see it. There, I will pay my penance, and one day, I hope to be worthy to see you again in the next life.

~Sebastian

"Jacob?" I asked as I finished looking at the letter, "Are there any property holdings or somewhere in Valterra that Dad was going to?"

"Why?" Jacob asked as he started playing around with the touch screens.

"I think I figured out where my Dad went," I said, as I started to look through some of my own files. "I think that's where he's hiding."

The two of us were silent as I started running another search, looking just for Valterra, while Jacob started looking at the more detailed documents. I was glad to have another set of eyes as we combed through the data.

"Did your Mom have a thing for Eagles?" Jacob asked. "Not like your Dad, like the actual bird."

"Not that I know of, why?" I asked, looking away from my screen to what he had found.

"There's just a lot of money that's gone toward this Eagle Sanctuary," he shrugged as he shook his head.

"That doesn't make sense, there aren't any Eagles in Valterra to begin with, and..." I paused as we both looked at each other. We had figured out there was one Eagle in Valterra, and as I pulled up the sanctuary on our satellite imagery, it showed not some animal reserve, but instead, the ruins of a castle and a hunting lodge that seemed put together enough that it was liveable.

"We found him," I whispered, looking at Jacob. "That has to be where he is."

"I don't have a passport," Jacob groaned, "and I doubt you can get him to come here."

"Passports sound like a Toby problem," I said, hoping this wouldn't be one favor too many. It was going to take some time, both getting the paperwork in order and figuring out a way to make sure we could operate safely in Valterra. The secret identity database was one that nobody but the Department had access to, but it didn't mean their government didn't have some way of knowing.

But that gave us time, and we had somewhere that was mostly safe to wait it out. Sands Point was looking better and better, and would give us all the time to rest. And gave Jacob a chance to start to recover.

I hoped we would bring Dad out of hiding, that it would immediately make it easier to lure out Nightshade with what he wanted most. And if we could pick Dad's mind about the Circle of Shadows, we could potentially find a way out of this situation without them trying to murder us all. We hadn't seen them since Annelton, but they were sure to catch up to us at some point. And we needed to come up with a plan of what to do when they finally did.

"You really think alien boy's going to pull a passport out of thin air?" Jacob asked. "He might work for the Department, but last I checked, he isn't magic."

"Fine, we'll go at it two ways," I thought out loud. "We can ask Zain to find someone who can get us a realistic fake passport that won't get you arrested. But we'll also work with Toby to see if we can get you a real one through proper channels in the meantime."

"Huh," Jacob said, looking at me with an expression I had never seen on his face before.

"What?" I asked, narrowing my eyes at him.

"Always thought you were more straight-laced than that," he shrugged, and I shrugged back. I probably would have been five years ago. But things changed, and things needed to get done. The least the Department could do in the long run was forgive me if I got Jacob a fake passport while we waited for a real one.

"I'm honestly not sure what I am anymore," I admitted. "Since this started, it seems to me like who I am and who I thought I was are two completely different people."

Jacob nodded in understanding but didn't elaborate. But there was a calm in the silence where I knew he did understand. I wanted to do the right thing, what Dad's mission had started as: to keep Nightshade from murdering anyone else. And even now, I was still on the fence as to if we actually needed to find Dad, or if we could find the answers here.

But all roads seemed to lead to Sebastian Caldwell's problems, to the messes we now had to clean up. And the least he could do was help.

"Doesn't really mean anything, but I think you're cooler now," Jacob said, groaning as he slowly stood up and started to walk back to the bedroom he had come out of. And while Jacob might have thought it didn't actually mean anything, it seemed, for the first time, that things made sense.

Or at least... almost did.

Chapter Twenty

"Jacob should have a passport in about three days," Zain told me as he walked into the Nest. I wasn't surprised he could find someone who could do forgeries that quickly. If anyone had the ability to press on criminal contacts at the drop of a hat, it was my baby brother. Toby wasn't the biggest fan of the decision, but there were already some hurdles with the Department bureaucracy that were making it hard for him to get through.

"Toby's hoping to get one soon, but it's looking like it's going to be two weeks," I sighed, looking at the satellite live stream on the computer. Gray had made sure we had a satellite camera constantly monitoring the location we found, just to make sure nobody left. Or that Nightshade didn't show up. Or that anyone else who could be a problem would show up.

But so far, it looked abandoned. And I was worried we were doing all of this work to get to Valterra, only to find Dad wasn't there when we showed up. True, we were rich enough and Dad had poured enough money into this where there could be an entire subterranean level nobody knew about, but at the same time, it just felt too predictable. Even for him. And I hated that I had to fly over the Celestia Ocean just to find out if I was wrong.

"How's he doing?" Zain asked, and I sighed. The last time I had checked on Jacob, I was worried he wouldn't make it through the day, let alone the trip.

"Bad," I answered, "He's fully in withdrawal, and apparently, Silence withdrawal makes all his nerves feel like they're on fire. So ironically, it's more pain than he would feel while he's high. Nancy's looking after him like a mother hen. I wish I could do more, but she's more qualified than any of us are in this situation."

"Yeah, years of patching us up will do that," Zain agreed.

"Speaking of Nancy," Nate growled as he stomped into the Nest, "either of you mind telling me how she got her hands on withdrawal drugs? For Silence, those are usually under lock and key because there's a shortage of them." The way Nate was talking, I wondered if he thought I was breaking all the laws I could think of, or if I had stolen the meds for Jacob, when everything we had done had been by the book. Mostly.

"My guess would be from Toby, but I didn't know she had those," I stated as I glared at him. "But why is it a bad thing he has them? You saw how he could barely walk when he got off the plane. And even if I had stolen them, which again, I didn't, I think Mom's spirit would have approved because that was the sort of thing she would have done before she met Dad."

"That was low," Nate snapped at me, "but Jacob should be in the hospital, not the house. Or rehab, since it didn't take the first time. But I guess nobody cares about doing what's right for Jacob right now—"

"Oh shut up," Zain hissed. "Don't act like you've got the moral high ground when you're on a one-man Nightshade murder spree."

"That's different," our older brother snapped.

"You're right," I agreed. "Yours is worse. I let Jacob decide for himself because he's an adult and has that right. You didn't want to be in charge, Nate, so you don't get to make these calls. You don't get to decide if us getting Jacob's life-saving medication is unethical, you don't get to decide to murder someone, and you especially don't get to act like we're criminals because we're doing things differently than what Dad would have done. Toby is monitoring us so we don't go outside the Code, and if he's fine with everything, then we're fine."

"Nightshade murdered our Mom, Nik," Nate pleaded. "Why are you so insistent on saving his life, when he ruined ours?"

"I'm not saving his life," I yelled, any control over my temper completely gone. "I'm trying to get justice, not revenge. Because that's all you want, Nate! Revenge. Like, how do you not even hear yourself right now? Murdering Nightshade is okay, but getting Jacob's life-saving medication is crossing the line? Make it make sense, Nate!"

"Right, I forgot, I'm just interrupting on the Nikki Caldwell show," Nate seethed, and it felt like I had been slapped in the face. "Everything has to be about you. What you want, what you think is best. You'll pretend it's about everyone else and letting them make their own choices, but it's obvious you think you're better than the rest of us and all our ideas are worth nothing."

"Oh really? What ideas do you have, Nate?" I argued, feeling any last control I had over my temper completely disintegrate. "Because all your ideas have been terrible. And if you don't believe me, let me list them: you wanted to kick Zain and me out of your house, drag your feet about coming, argue with everyone about everything like a toddler, and then jump straight to murder. Does that sound like a leader to you, Nate? Do you think any of us would even want to follow someone acting like you? I'm sure your sons would have better ideas, and they're four!"

"She's got a point," Zain muttered, loud enough for both of us to hear, but just quiet enough that he could act like he wasn't a part of this fight.

"Oh, shut up, Zain!" Nate snapped. "You've always just followed Nikki's lead!"

"Really? Because if that's the case, Nik would be a lot more murder-y than she is," Zain snapped back, mimicking Nate's tone. "But since you're so excited about murder, would you like for me to describe the people I've killed? The things my mother forced me to do? Would you like to know what it's like to watch the light go out of someone's eyes and know you were the one who caused it? You keep thinking of murder in the most generic terms, but I've done it, Nate. Over and over again. And if that's the path you want to go down, fine, I'll take you down it. Watch it destroy you. But I'm not following Nikki's lead, if anything, she's the one holding me back to try to keep me human."

There was a darkness to Zain we always knew was there, despite the fact Dad had always tried to shield us from it. He held it back, and in seeing it for the first time, I understood why. The way he talked, the fluidity of his movements as he became a weapon instead of a human, all of it was truly terrifying. For the first time, I saw the Prince of Shadows instead of just Zain. This was the first time he let us see the part of himself he worked so hard to rein in, and with how easily he slipped into it, I was glad Zain wanted me to hold him back. That he wanted to have a grasp on the humanity he could easily leave behind.

"That's enough!" I yelled, my voice echoing off the walls of the Nest. "Nate, you've made it clear you have no real ideas—you just don't like mine. Zain, I need you to take a walk because that was terrifying, and I'm glad we're working on reigning that in. And I would like to remind both of you that the only reason I'm in charge is because nobody else wanted to be in charge. So I will continue to make the tough calls, continue reporting to Toby, and Nate, I'm about five seconds from throwing you off this mission. Mom would be disappointed you can't accept a decent idea when it's looking you straight in the face just because you didn't come up with it!"

"Stop talking for Mom, not when you're betraying her like this," Nate growled. "But I can tell you what Dad would think, since you've thrown away his rule book. He'd tell you that you have no facts, that you're grasping at straws, and that all your plans are barely put together. He'd tell you that you're the reason we're all going to be killed."

"And he'd say you're too emotional and letting it cloud your judgement," I shot back. "He'd think we were on a time crunch, and if we didn't work together as a team, we'd be handing ourselves over to Nightshade one by one."

"I'm too emotional? Really? Says the little girl running back to Daddy the first chance you get?" Nate asked, and I let out a sigh. The fight suddenly made a lot more sense. Because it wasn't actually about Jacob. It was about finding Dad.

"You could have led with the fact you don't want to see him instead of making us suffer through that entire fight to get there, Nate," I said, after letting myself breathe and let go some of the anger. "I don't want to see him. But you just pointed out we don't have all the facts, and you're right. But unfortunately, he does. He's our best resource for information, and with what's going on, that makes him an asset we have to deal with."

"Oh, you children are so cute," a new, unfamiliar voice cut in, and the three of us turned to see the stranger. The woman had deep tan skin, thick black hair braided into a crown around her head, and the same glowing green eyes Zain had. "Naive, but cute."

"Mother," Zain said, quickly getting between us and the woman, his hand on a knife I hadn't realized he had on him. "What are you doing here?"

Chapter Twenty-One

"**I** SHOULD BE ASKING you the same question, child," Yasmine said, her eyes focused on her son. "I believe I told you to stay in Annelton, yes?"

"So I could wait for you to kill me? Or for you to be ready for me to kill you? Yeah, something like that," Zain countered, and I was impressed that he had the guts to sass the woman who was clearly here to kill us. If Yasmine Hadi was here, there was no other reason than that she decided she had to take care of this loose end herself.

"It was a lesson in patience you still refuse to learn," she countered, disappointment dripping off each of her words. "And a lesson in letting go of what holds you back. Which you failed." The insult didn't go unnoticed, but she flicked her eyes to me just to get the point across.

"Oh, so I'm the family disappointment again?" Zain asked with an eyeroll. "Great. Used to that. Now answer my question. What are you doing here?"

"I had to come witness your weakness for myself," she said, almost as if she were talking about the weather. "To not control my own Princeling, do you not see how that makes us look? Undermined. Insulted. How dare you refuse to show obedience where it is due?" The anger grew sharp, and I noticed her eyes seemed to be glowing brighter. "Your brother would never have insulted the Circle in this way."

"My brother has also been dead for over half my life, so playing the Zak card doesn't really work well anymore," Zain shrugged.

"Who's Zak?" I heard Nate ask me under his breath.

"Zain's twin brother," I answered. "Died on a mission when they were eight."

"Plus," Zain continued, blocking out Nate and my conversation, "since he was a homicidal psychopath, I'm pretty sure he would have killed you by now and have great-grandad possessing him."

"As he should have," Yasmine matter-of-factly stated, adding to the horror that was this conversation. "It's a shame you won't do what needs to be done. But also a relief I won't have you taking up the mantle, as you, Zain Hadi, are my greatest disappointment."

"So you've said, but I'm still here," Zain scoffed. "It's all words at this point, Mother. You're not going to kill me because you don't have another heir, and I doubt you're going to find anyone else worth reproducing with. You're, like, five hundred years old. Your eggs have to be so insanely shriveled by now."

"You will watch your words," Yasmine growled, and where I had thought the glowing of her eyes before had just been a trick of the light, it was clear now they were quite literally glowing. The whites of her eyes turned the same neon green as her irises, and I watched as her hair started to pulsate with the same green light. It was clear we needed to get out of here. Now.

"Make. Me." Zain smirked at her, flipping the knife as he challenged his mother.

"Unless you have a better idea," I muttered to Nate, unable to hide the sarcasm in my voice to let him know our fight wasn't over just because we were interrupted, "I think we need to get out of here."

Nate nodded in agreement as we started toward one of the passages that led to the top floor of the house.

"You truly think I would not find another as worthy as your father? A man who is too stupid to realize the power I offered him?" Yasmine asked. "You think I am not patient enough to wait another four hundred years for a mate who will give us the heir we deserve?"

"How old is she?" Nate muttered as we closed the door behind us and started running up the stairs.

"Entirely too old. No wonder Dad was terrified of her," I said, opening the door and climbing out of the fake painting we kept in the second-floor hallway. I bolted to the window to check if we were surrounded. I couldn't see anything outside, which didn't surprise me, but there were just enough signs to tell that Yasmine was not alone.

"We need to get out of here. Now," I said, before giving Nate a pointed look, "if that's alright with you."

"Really? Now? You're doing this now?" Nate deadpanned, clearly unamused.

"You've made it clear you hate my decision-making. It seems like a great trial by fire for you to be in charge if that's what you want so much," I snapped at him. "So, are you cool with leaving?"

"Hey, guys," Gray said, peeking out of the door, her curls falling out of the messy bun she had attempted to make on the top of her head. "Do you mind keeping this fight away from Jacob's room? He's trying to sleep." The more I looked at her, the more I realized Gray hadn't slept since we had gotten back. And while I had hoped Jacob would be in better shape, just a peek in the room showed he looked like he was at death's door.

"We need to go," Nate instructed, immediately going toward his room with no further explanation.

"Circle of Shadows is here, Zain's fighting Yasmine in the Nest, probably murder cultists somewhere. No idea where, so just be prepared for assassins," I grimaced. "Try to get what you can of yours and Jacob's. I'll see what I can get from Zain's room. Only take what we need. We needed to be out like ten minutes ago. Any chance Zain has those throwing stars you made, or do you have them?"

"I do... might be good to use them," Gray nodded, a new determination in her voice. "I'll grab what I can," she said, rushing across the hall into her room.

"Hey Nance," I said, peeking into the room, only to take in exactly how bad Jacob looked. He wasn't only deathly pale, he was completely covered in sweat and shaking so hard I was worried about having to move him. "Circle of Shadows infiltrated the house. We have to go."

"Of course, they have," Nancy grumbled under her breath, "I'll get Jacob outside. I've got a go bag in the hall closet. Can you grab it on the way out?" I nodded and ran into my room, trying to figure out what was necessary. I shoved the fabric Gray made and a few sets of clothes into my bag, as I tried to think if there was anything else I needed. I hadn't taken much when I left home the last time, but if the Circle was here, I realized the chances of us having a house to come back to were slim. So, I picked up every single picture I had of the family and Mom and shoved them into my bag, too.

"Nik, what are you doing?" Nate asked, clearly judging the fact that I had saved the pictures. I was sure he'd thank me for it later.

"Nothing," I said, running into Zain's room and grabbing a few of his clothes and shoving them in, too. Nancy and Gray were already helping Jacob down the stairs, and his footsteps were so wobbly I wasn't sure if they would make it, and we'd have a six-foot-seven giant tumble down the staircase. But I couldn't focus on worst-case scenarios, not when we needed to plan our best exit.

Or at least, I had attempted to when the wall that typically hid the staircase down to the Nest burst open.

The five of us were on the ground, covered in debris, as I noticed Zain had been thrown through the wall, and his mother had some sort of green weapon that matched her eyes.

"Can you do that?" I asked Zain, pointing at the weapon.

"Nope. Long story. I'll explain later," Zain answered, as he threw his knife at his mother. It should have hit her, but Yasmine flicked it away with her powers as if it were nothing. I gave a curt nod as I ran toward Nancy's room, determined to get her bag while everyone had a clear path to the front door.

There had to be cultists outside, but Dad's favorite car was, too. And if we could get to it, we'd be able to escape. Probably.

We affectionately called it The Tank growing up, because he had made it as weapon-proof as possible, and it had enough gadgets and trinkets that it put the stereotypical spy cars we saw in movies to shame. But the best part was it looked just like a minivan, which meant there was room for all of us.

"Do you think I don't know what you're doing, girl?" Yasmine asked as I ran back into the room. One of her green bolts barely missed me but startled me enough that I tripped into a vase. Another green bolt filled the room and narrowly missed the trio who were trying to make their way toward the door, leaving a huge gap in the wall where it used to be.

"I've been told you wanted the children of Sebastian Caldwell," I said, drawing her attention. It was a stupid decision, but I needed time for the others to get out.=. "Let them go, and you can have us."

"I have my plans for their deaths, as they are as much Sebastian's children as you are," Yasmine chuckled, her laugh sending a chill down my spine. "I saw how he treated them. How he ignored your pathetic pleas for attention. Did you think I wouldn't watch where my disappointment was raised?"

It was clear she was preying on my insecurities, that I had been desperate as a child. Anyone could have figured it out after a single day. But I didn't need to dwell on that; if anything, this mission was helping me move on.

"Well, I'm flattered you were watching me. It must have gotten pretty boring with how many hours I spent with my sketch book," I said, realizing I was close to the cabinet where Dad kept his emergency shock guns. Or at least where they used to be. There was a chance Nancy had moved them, or the batteries were dead, or something else had happened within the past five years.

"You overestimate your importance, little Caldwell, just like your father," Yasmine said as I inched backward, her gaze fixed so hard on me I knew I had to move as slowly as possible. Out of the corner of my eye, I saw Zain looking at me with confusion, and I hoped he would run out of the house and protect the others. "However, I will give you a lesson your father should have and will teach Zain what he should have learned years ago: never get attached."

I had made it to the cabinet, and as her hands became neon, I knew it was only a matter of seconds before one of those green bolts was flying right at me. I reached in, and luckily, the familiar grip fit perfectly into my hand. Where I had been slow moments before, I was now fast, and I fired it at her. I didn't aim, I didn't have time, but her shock that I fired at her was enough, the bolt she had been preparing flying wide.

I wasn't sure if it was a relief or not when I realized this wasn't a stun gun, but instead a rifle.

Yasmine was distracted enough that she didn't notice Zain sneak up behind her and hit her over the back of the head with a statue of some random person nobody knew who they were.

"Thank the comet for Dad's paranoia," Zain said, nodding at the gun. "Take that. We'll need it."

I picked up the bags and ran out the hole that used to be the door, only to witness an entirely different fight ahead of us.

I was relieved to find all of Yasmine's assassins had swords instead of superpowers. There was something easier about facing them. Yes, they could slice through me like butter, but they were easier to dodge than literal magic. Jacob was lying against the van, the trek there having spent all his energy. Gray and Nate were in a formation we had practiced plenty of times, but neither of them looked like they knew what they were doing.

And Nancy had an assault rifle, which was an image that felt so outside the realm of possibilities, I wondered for a moment if Yasmine's magic had somehow messed with my mind. But the number of dead humans around her made it clear, I was not imagining it.

"I don't think I ever told you kids about my time in the black ops," Nancy laughed, aiming her rifle and letting the bullets fly at more of the assassins. Brain matter splattered all over Gray and Nate, and Jacob threw up—though whether it was from the assassin's head exploding or the withdrawals, I couldn't tell.

"I thought we weren't supposed to kill people, Nancy!" Gray shouted, hyperventilating at the carnage all around her.

"Sweetheart, please just get in the car," she said, opening the van door like she was just a housekeeper again. "You have those rules, I don't. Nikki, do you mind driving?"

"Don't know how," I said, shaking my head as Zain dove into the driver's seat. Nancy slipped into the passenger seat and managed to attach her rifle to the window with an ease that showed she had done this before.

"Now, make sure you're all buckled up, it's going to be a crazy ride!" she instructed, with the exact same tone she used to give out her recipe for her favorite cookies after someone complimented her baking.

"Please tell me Jacob has a bucket," I heard Nate mutter as he climbed over the pile of puke and into the van.

"Driver picks the music!" Zain announced as he started blasting heavy metal out of the radio.

"Are you sure this is the time for that?" Gray asked, clearly hyperventilating.

"Honestly, this is pretty chill for my Mother," Zain answered as he heard the van door close and immediately floored the gas pedal. "When I was four, we used my favorite teddy bear to blow up a hotel and then immediately went out for ice cream to celebrate a job well done."

"We are going to need to talk about how casually you tell these kinds of stories," Nancy said, looking through the scope of the rifle as we swerved out of the driveway.

"Nancy, you just admitted you were black ops, and clearly killed people like five minutes ago. The fact that Zain did the same when he was raised by the Circle shouldn't be that shocking," Nate groaned. "Where are we even going?"

Nancy tutted at him and instructed Zain to go faster. I wasn't sure how fast the Tank could go, but it was clear we were going to be testing the limits.

"I need all of you to watch the windows, let me know if anyone's following us," Nancy instructed, "and if they are, Zain, I need you to get them in my line of sight."

"Hey, Nik!" Zain shouted with a smile. "This is just like Annelton!"

"No, Annelton had fewer superpowers, and we didn't have a Nancy!" I snapped back, which only made Zain laugh harder. It was clear his horrifying childhood was the one thing letting him find humor in this situation, I could barely wrap my head around anything that wasn't the constant repetition in my mind of the word "survive."

I had expected motorcycles, after Annelton, it seemed like they were what the Circle would use. However, it took about five seconds to find out this time, it was worse. Four SUVs and a helicopter found us quickly, and I groaned.

"Nancy, they're here. Four SUVs, and how do we take down a helicopter?" I asked, though I didn't recognize my own voice with the level of panic dripping through my words.

Gray opened up her laptop and started typing. I wasn't sure what she was doing—with Gray, it could be anything from trying to hack something to asking Cypher how to shoot a helicopter out of the sky.

"Nikki, just focus on the cars right now," Nancy instructed, and I was amazed at how calm she was, more like she was explaining how to make a bed with hospital corners. "We'll handle the big one when it's the only one to worry about."

"Nance, I've gotten into the traffic light system!" Gray announced. "If you tell me where we're going, I can make sure we have all green lights. Might be able to get a few to change so when they inevitably run the red, they'll get hit by someone." I paused for a moment and looked at Gray. That sort of thing shouldn't have been able to be done from a laptop. Gray looked up at me and read my confusion like a book. "Don't worry about it, it's my and Kitty's job. Also, Nate, she said you need to remember to take your anxiety meds later, and I agree. You've been a pain in the butt this whole time."

"Tell Kitty I owe her... something," I said as I took the stun gun and opened the window on the other side of the car. There wasn't a lot I could do with the gun, but it might at least make them wary and get them in Nancy's crosshairs. "Can anyone switch places with Zain? I feel like he's better with a gun."

"Are you trying to turn off my music?" Zain asked, as the rock music suddenly got louder as he cranked up the volume. "Because if you wanted to be in control of the radio, you should have gotten your driver's license." He stuck his tongue out at me, making sure I saw his reflection in the rearview mirror. He glanced at the cars chasing us, each of them swerving any time I tried to even start to aim.

"Aim for where the tires will be after the switch," Zain instructed. "There's a pattern, anticipate their next move, and you'll be able to get them."

Finally, some advice that was actually useful.

Patterns were easy to look for, something I should have realized on my own. While my near-death experiences for the week were quickly adding up, I felt how much of my training hadn't come back. There were plenty of things I needed to relearn, and I pitied whoever it was who would be teaching me.

Because I was back. There was going to be an after this mission. I felt alive for the first time in five years. I had tried to deny this part of myself, even as we started the mission. But it was different now. It fit better. I would continue, I would do the work, I would get my license renewed. I'd even make those redesigned suits.

Nate was right when he said I was like Dad, that I was built for the same kind of life he lived. I knew I was privileged enough where I could make a difference, both as Nikki Caldwell and as Nightingale. Everyone would have a choice to make later, whether or not this life was really for them, but as I looked down the scope of the gun, I felt the calmness that came with epiphany. And I watched for the pattern and shot.

Hitting the car right in the middle of an intersection.

Our pursuer flipped, and two others crashed into it. I hated how it caused a pile-up because, as Gray predicted, distracted drivers plowed right into them, making the scene worse than it had to be. But it was a barrier. It got us away from most of the cars. There was one left... and the helicopter.

"Zain, if we go right, we should be able to get to the city," I heard Nate suggest.

"Absolutely not, Zain, you're going to turn left in two turns," Nancy cut him off, and I realized she had been giving Zain directions the entire time. I had no idea where we were going, but as long as Zain did, I guessed we were fine. "The streets are horrible, traffic will be a mess, we'll turn ourselves into targets. I'm taking you to one of your father's safe houses."

The Department had plenty of safe houses, but if Dad had one, it wasn't on their radar. It didn't surprise me. With how paranoid he was, he probably kept it in case the Department turned on him. Or in case Nightshade came to the house again. After all, Sebastian Caldwell was a man with a panic room inside his panic room in his mid-city penthouse. A secret safe house? Completely on brand.

The car chasing us started speeding up, and the look on the driver's face was chilling. There was no emotion on the man's face, and I realized that was what Yasmine wanted for Zain. And it was probably why he chose now to goof off; it was his way of rebelling against his mother. And if that was the case, I was a little proud of him. Not that I'd admit it, now was not the time, and I wasn't going to encourage the behavior.

"Nikki, we're going to hit a tunnel soon, and if this plan is going to work, I need that car gone before we get there," Nancy said, and for the first time since everything started, I heard the slightest bit of stress in her voice.

I knew I should have aimed, but the muzzle of a gun pointed at me from the car, and I immediately pulled the trigger and let the bullets fly.

The car flipped. And burst into flames. I had no idea if any of the drivers had lived or died, but I understood why we couldn't check. Even if I still felt slightly guilty about it.

"Great job, sweetie," Nancy said as I rolled up the window. I couldn't imagine her plan involved me shooting at the helicopter.

"Um, Nancy," Gray said, looking back at a map on her computer screen, "I know you said we're going into a tunnel, but there are no tunnels in this area, but we *are* headed toward a cliff. Was that intentional?"

"Yes, I know where I directed Zain," Nancy claimed, "and sweetheart, I'm going to need you to drive full speed off that cliff, so floor it."

"*Yes!* I've always wanted to do this!" Zain yelled as the car took off.

"I'm sorry, we're going to WHAT?" Gray screamed, right as we hit a ramp that seemed invisible to the naked eye. For a moment, we flew through the air, right toward the face of an even larger cliff. I knew Nancy wouldn't have asked Zain to do this if she didn't think we would survive, but there was a moment I was sure this was it. We were going to die.

Only to, instead, go through a hologram of a cliff face and bounce onto a road that was built in the cliff. Everyone in the car let out a sigh of relief before it was interrupted by the deathly sound of metal crunching. Flames surrounded the car as I realized the helicopter had tried to follow us and crashed into the opening. Everything around us was on fire, and there seemed to be no way to put it out.

"Oh for goodness' sake," I heard Nancy mumble, just like she did when she left food in the oven for too long. She pressed a few buttons on the car's console. "Whatever you do, don't open the windows. I had to suck the oxygen out of the tunnel to take care of the fire, so it should die off soon. But the last thing I want is for anyone to suffocate.

Everyone nodded, not wanting to cross Nancy after she had just saved us. Everyone... but Jacob. He hadn't moved, he hadn't said anything the entire car ride, and he was slouched over in a way that looked like he was either asleep or worse.

"Hey, Jacob?" I said, nudging his shoulder to try and wake him up, "How are you doing?" No answer. I had a feeling he wouldn't, but it felt wrong for there to be no answer to the question. "Gray, is he still breathing?" I asked, putting my fingers to his neck to check for a pulse.

"Yeah, barely," Gray nodded, and I felt the faintest of heartbeats press against my fingers.

"Okay, still alive," I breathed. "When can we get him out of the car?"

"In a minute or two," Nancy said, giving me a reassuring smile. "Don't worry, we're all going to be fine."

Chapter Twenty-Two

W HEN I WAS A child, before I found out about the family business, I went through a phase where I was obsessed with spy movies. I loved the idea of having somewhere secret to go if there was trouble, and the idea of a safe house was one I had latched onto. I had made multiple blanket forts, each with designs to be a safe home away from home.

And looking around this one? Dad had never had that sort of thought. There were no decorations; in fact, it looked more like a warehouse with furniture than anywhere someone was supposed to live for any significant amount of time.

Jacob had been hooked up to an IV and was being monitored in one of the bedrooms under Nancy's ever-watchful eye. Gray was hunched over her computer, doing who knows what. Zain was who knows where. And I worked hard to actively ignore Nate.

Our fight had shaken me more than I wanted to admit, and I was trying to figure out if I had been the person Nate had been describing. I wasn't sure if I had been forcing my ideas on everyone or if Nate was jealous. Or if he was trying to derail the mission so he wouldn't have to see Dad. Nate had always been stubborn, but I couldn't tell where his head was at. And I was afraid that if I asked, it would only bring on another round of accusations.

So instead, I was working on the new suit designs in my sketchbook. If we were going to be stuck here for a few days, it gave me time to start working on them. Which made me relieved I had saved the fabric Gray had made.

I was using the corner of the paper to test color schemes, when I heard someone sit on the other side of the drab gray couch, picked out to match the walls. I glanced up and scoffed when I realized it was Nate, who, at least, had the decency to look guilty, though I felt petty enough that I was going to make him talk first, or he could just endure the silent treatment.

"What are you working on?" Nate asked, and I rolled my eyes. I did have an idea for a suit for him, but no details. I didn't want to put in the time and effort for him to disappear again.

"Nothing that would interest you," I answered, looking back down at my sketches. I wanted us to each have our own colors that fit within the scheme and was trying to figure out what would look best on Zain.

"So, it's for work...?" he asked, and I slammed my sketchbook shut so he couldn't get a good glimpse at it.

"What does it matter?" I asked. "If I tell you, then it's 'the Nikki show,' and if I don't, then I'm a terrible person who doesn't care about anyone. You keep putting me in no-win situations, Nate, and then get mad at me for it. So, if I choose, I'm going to be a terrible person. At least I know I'm good at that."

I hoped Nate was going to leave. I didn't want a heart-to-heart, and I didn't want to hear why everything I had done was wrong. Again. But instead, Nate shifted in his seat, looking like he was trying to find words. Which I assumed meant I wasn't getting an apology.

"You know, after Mom died, I never trusted Seb," Nate admitted, acting like this was new information despite the fact that it was common knowledge. "I always had a feeling he hadn't told us the whole truth, and I couldn't figure out why. And then finding out his story was a cover-up for her murder... I felt vindicated. There's a lot of emotions I didn't realize I was holding on to, and I never understood why, despite everything, he still trained me and emphasized my role was to make sure you and the others were safe. But it was always clear you and Zain were the priority—Dad was terrified of something happening to either of you." That admission caught me by surprise, and didn't quite feel real. Because I felt like if Dad had felt that way, he wouldn't have forced us into this life to begin with. "So, he wanted me to be the leader. To make sure my siblings never had to make the hard calls or run into dangerous situations. And now that we're back in? I've realized I failed at everything Dad wanted me to do. I just don't know what my place is in all of this."

The admission surprised me, and I wondered if that was the root of why he was acting this way. He was covering up an insecurity none of us would think he had. Growing up, I had always believed Nate was the most self-assured of us all, but after everything I learned, it was clear this was just a front. Just another thing he had learned from Dad.

"And now we're in the middle a Nightshade case, which shouldn't have even been possible," Nate continued, and as he looked at me, I realized this ramble was turning into his version of an apology, and I softened a little bit. "Everything I trained for and worked so hard to learn all seems to come to you naturally. And I'm starting to wonder if he realized you had a natural talent for all of this and was trying to keep you from the burden. So, I see you figuring out our next steps and finding everyone, and all I can feel is Seb's disappointment at how you're doing what was supposed to be my job. And now everything hinges on being able to find him, and all I can feel is the growing anxiety that he'll be disappointed that you're the one who stepped up. And it's stupid, because I shouldn't even care what he thinks. He lost that right five years ago."

"I get it," I said, the words leaving my mouth before I had a chance to think about them. "Almost everything I've done since he left was trying to prove I was nothing like him. Which backfired so spectacularly that I turned right into him. But all of us were hurt when he left, especially when all any of us wanted was to impress him. So, when he left, none of us had any idea what we were supposed to do next."

"Yeah," Nate agreed. "This whole time I've wished he were here to tell us what we should do and guide us toward the answer. Or even if he was here to bounce ideas off of, that's always what I felt like I was best at."

"You mean the thing I've been trying to do with you this whole time?" I asked, giving him a pointed look. "And I'm tired of being sassed, or insulted, or for you to accuse me of putting myself before everyone for attention. But I also understand that you need a job, so what do you want it to be, Nate? It's hard to give you one when everything falls into one of three categories: how you don't want to be here, how you don't want to be in charge, or how you don't want to be second in command to your little sister."

Nate's mouth opened like he was about to answer, and the cynical part of my mind wondered if it was the "little" part or the "sister" part that bothered him the most. I was used to the unfortunate combination of being the middle child and only girl—it was a recipe for ruining things when it came to reputations. I was used to it, and I hated that I was. And the longer Nate stayed silent, the more it stung. Our parents had raised us to be equals, so I never thought one of my brothers would sit in front of me and silently admit he thought I couldn't handle the responsibilities just because I was a girl.

"I see," I snapped, opening my sketchbook again, fully planning on ignoring anything that came out of his mouth. And checking with Toby about whether those underwater safe houses really didn't exist, or if there was one we could throw Nate into.

"It's not any of that," Nate groaned, though I didn't want to know how he would defend himself out of this situation. "It's not that you're my little sister. It's just hard watching someone thrive in the position you had been told you'd be perfect for your entire life. Watching you just shows me that every single second of the impostor syndrome I felt as a child was true. I'd feel the same if it were Jacob or Gray or Zain in your place. It has nothing to do with you, it's just that I'm struggling with the fact that it was supposed to be me."

"Well, if you want to have a pity party, feel free to have it somewhere else," I mumbled, focusing on my page instead of looking at him, "because the way I see it, you have three options. Stay and mope and keep doing exactly what you've been doing. Go home so you don't have me rubbing all of your inadequacies in your face every day. Or you can get over yourself and actually help. Your constant moping is dead weight right now, Nate. We've all been out of this for a while, which means we're all struggling. And we need to get as close to the top of our game as possible, or we're dead. Honestly, we're so in over our heads, we might still be dead. But nobody can cover for you because we can all barely cover for ourselves."

"And what about Jacob? You don't think he's dead weight?" Nate asked, looking at me with a serious look instead of the sad one he came to the couch with.

"Jacob's recovering," I countered, "and just because he's fighting a disease none of us can relate to doesn't mean we're going to cut him off again. Do you really think he would thrive at a hospital with a bunch of strangers? He barely trusts us right now, and if we did that, we'd lose any hope of being able to reach out to him again. And you, of all people, should know that, Nate! You were the closest to him."

"This just isn't what Dad..." Nate started.

"I. Don't. Care. What. Dad. Would. Have. Done," I stated, emphasizing each word in hopes Nate would finally understand what I had been saying the entire time. "We are following the Code. We are not breaking any laws. We are doing everything with extra supervision from the Department. Yes, that's different than what Dad would have done, but that doesn't mean it's wrong. We've had to make a lot of hard calls, and with Dad's glaring absence, I think it's obvious his way wasn't the best."

"Are you arguing the fake passport falls under the 'not breaking any laws' part?" Nate asked, and while he was technically right about that, leaving Jacob was the wrong thing to do. He hadn't even had time to process his twin sister's death yet, let alone detox from Silence. He needed a chance to get back on his feet, and for now, that meant he needed the reassurance we wouldn't abandon him this time.

"If Toby comes through, we won't even have to worry about it," I justified, "and of all the things I've done, I'm pretty sure this is the exact thing Dad would have done in this particular situation."

Nate didn't answer, and I knew it meant I had finally won the fight. I may not be like Dad, I may not do things the same way, but when it came to this particular decision? It's exactly what Dad would have done: find a way, make it work, do what was best for the person.

"Right, well, I should probably leave you alone. You are busy," Nate said, motioning at my sketchbook.

"Not yet. You forgot something," I said. "You gave, like, five long-winded Dad-speeches in a row, but somewhere in there you forgot the apology. Something like, 'I'm sorry, Nikki, I know I've been the worst brother in the world,' would work perfectly."

"I'm sorry I've been terrible," Nate nodded, and despite having to feed the words to him, I could tell he meant them. It was progress, even if it was small. "I promise, I'll try to work on it."

"Good," I said, giving him a smile. "Now, since you want a job, I have one for you. Go ask Nancy if there are any 3D printers around here. Like, the really good expensive ones, because I am pretty sure if I leave to use mine, she'll drag me back here by my hair."

"That I can do," Nate nodded. "What do you need them for, anyway?"

"A surprise," I smirked at him, "you'll find out when it's ready."

Chapter Twenty-Three

"**N**IKKI, HAVE YOU SLEPT at all?" I heard Toby ask. It took me a few moments to realize it wasn't a dream, and I turned in the chair I had dozed off in to look at him. Ten 3D printers were going. After I had convinced Nancy to go to my workshop with a moving van and grab all of my supplies, I had immediately started printing armor. There were multiple mannequins I had shaped to everyone's sizes slowly being mocked up. The inside layers of the uniforms were done, waiting for the armor to be attached, so I could create the top layers using Gray's new fabric.

In my mind, the way everything was laid out made perfect sense. However, I was confident that if anyone else looked at it, all they would see is a mess. I had heard it from plenty of assistants any time my studios and workshops were in the middle of a new design collection. Which, I guess, this fell under that description.

"Well, I was almost asleep until you asked me that," I grumbled as I looked over at him. I had no idea when he had gotten to the safe house, or who had told him where it was. But I also had no idea what time it even was. Glancing at the timers on the printers, my guess was around two in the morning.

"In a bed, Nickel?" Toby asked as he sat down in the chair next to mine. It felt dangerous, him being here. Everyone else was asleep, and every single time Toby and I had been alone in the past week, I'd almost kissed him, and he'd always rejected me. And with how tired I was, I felt like I was about to make a fool of myself again, and just cuddled into my chair and yawned, and made sure to look at his shirt sleeve instead of his face.

"I can sleep in a bed on the plane," I lied, knowing there was no chance I'd sleep on the trip. "I just got an idea for the suits, and I'm trying to finish printing the armor so I can try to finish them on the trip. Though, even though these are the ones I always use, I'm not sure any of them will be done in time."

"I've heard that about 3D printers. You go fast, they're more prone to mistakes. You go slow, they take forever," Toby nodded as he looked at some of the mannequins. "You know, I always wondered about your process and if it was as messy as I imagined."

"Oh, really?" I asked. "And how does it live up to your imagination?"

"It's so much worse," he teased as he stood up to examine them closer. "Is this one Gray's?" He used his powers to mimic the size of the mannequin, shrinking to about Gray's height. And I realized if I needed to test how any of them moved, I could ask Toby to shapeshift if someone was unavailable at the time.

"It is. I patented this armor design. It gives a good range of motion while protecting everything vital," I explained. "And most

214

importantly, every suit I make is really easy to go to the bathroom in."

"Didn't Gray end up with chronic bladder infections one summer?" Toby asked, and I nodded at the memory. It was one of the things the classic suit designers never thought of, and I hated how the one thing everyone would have to do in the suit was always the last thing people remembered when making them.

"So... are you planning on bringing back the wig?" he asked, shapeshifting back into the body shape he typically had, and my rebellious eyes took in his smile. And my stomach flipped all over again.

"Absolutely not," I laughed. "They're too hard to keep on in a fight, and helmets are better protection. I'm giving them to everyone."

I watched as Toby kept admiring my work. I wasn't sure if he could tell what I had planned, or if he was trying to guess what the end result would be.

"Why are you here, Toby?" I asked after a few more seconds of silence had passed.

"You mean, why am I at your safe house? Or why am I in your 3D printer room at 1:52 in the morning?" he asked.

"The second one," I shrugged. "I figured someone would tell you where we were once you realized the house was gone."

"I wanted to check on you," Toby said, and I noticed a twinge of blue fill his cheeks. "I realized yesterday was your first real rest day since all of this started, and nobody saw you all day. I got worried, and I was right to, because it's clear you have not been resting."

"I can rest when this is over," I said, turning my chair to look at Jacob's mannequin to avoid Toby's judgmental look.

"Or you can rest now," he countered. "Nickel, this sort of project doesn't even need you here right now. There are hours before they'll be done printing. I get you have inspiration, but what happens if you burn yourself out before you track down Nightshade?"

I knew he was right. Out of all of us, Toby was the one who had stayed in the superhero life, granted, in his way. He probably went to training on superhero burnout and how to effectively manage us. I knew he was just doing his job, and if I read too much into it, I'd make a fool of myself again.

"I know this is the part where I'm supposed to say you're right and go to bed," I admitted, "but I tried that. My brain just won't turn off. It starts spiraling, and then I start second-guessing everything. If I have some sort of project, it at least helps me keep those thoughts from taking over."

"You know, that's the reason I retired from being Meteorite," Toby admitted. "Those sorts of thoughts and second-guessing got to be too much, and I'm not good with my hands or artistic enough to make something special when my thoughts are too much. I just couldn't cope with it. With being a handler, there are flowcharts and protocols, I just watch and report on the people who make the decisions and give them support when necessary. It's still hard, but I know exactly what I am supposed to do. It makes it easier to process."

"How did your Dad take you retiring from being his sidekick?" I asked, it had been something I had wondered since I heard through the grapevine that Toby had joined the Department, but I felt too far away from him to ever ask.

"Terribly. It's part of the reason he went back to Xatanian," he sighed. "He yelled about how I had been raised to be a warrior. How our race thrives in battle, like he forgot my Mom had been a scientist. Honestly, I wonder how things would have been if she hadn't died giving birth to me, if she would have mellowed him out at all. He's tried to get me to come to Xatanian a few times, but it always feels like it's a trick to get forced into their military or some other training."

"Is that why you used that teleportation charm on me? So your Dad couldn't force you to go?" I asked, and he nodded.

"I did mean what I said, about the fact I had never heard you that upset, and I needed to get to you as soon as possible," he continued, "but being able to use it, knowing it would ruin my Dad's plan to make me some human-Xatanian hybrid super soldier... it was the icing on the cake."

"Yay, Dad issues," I groaned, which turned into a dry chuckle. "You know, I think I would have preferred your Dad's goodbye to mine's—straight up ghosting us."

"Yeah, plus I *expected* my Dad to leave," Toby agreed. "Like, he sucks, but at least I got some closure. You just got questions and abandonment. I at least know where my Dad and his disapproval are."

"Are you planning on coming with us to Valterra?" I asked, not sure if Toby felt like he needed to be there for this particular part of the mission. Plus, his job as a Department member would make it hard for him to be in the country.

"Do you want me to come?" Toby asked in return, even though I hated it when he answered a question with another question.

"Yes," I quietly said. "One of the things that's been keeping me up at night is the idea of having to face my father without you." The words left before I had a chance to filter them, to figure out the best way to say it without adding more into whatever had taken root between us all over again. It was clear Toby didn't know how to respond, and it was the self-fulfilling prophecy I had expected when I first heard him. I had made it awkward and pressed into something I shouldn't have. At least this time, I hadn't tried to kiss him before he rejected me.

Thankfully, one of the 3D printers beeped and let me know it was finished. All of the armor I was currently printing was for Jacob, and I bit my lip as I pulled up the next design I needed done and refilled the materials.

"Nickel," Toby finally said once I stepped away from the printer, "if you want me there, I'll be there." I wanted to believe him, but there was a strange pause after he finished speaking, like he cut himself off from saying something else.

"What's the 'but' you're not saying?" I asked, and I saw him grimace. "You're easy to read when you're like this."

"What do you want me to go as?" Toby asked, his words slow and unsure. "Your handler? Your friend? Or as... something else?"

The question caught me off guard, especially with how much we had been dancing around each other since the mission had started. And at least we could lay it out in the open when everyone else was asleep.

"I thought something else was off the table," I pointed out, folding my arms around my legs as I sat back down in my chair. "I heard you tell Nate you didn't think either of us was in a place for a 'something else.'" And you told me on the way to Acedonia Lake you didn't want to be a distraction. Which is fair, because you deserve more than that. So, what's changed, Toby?"

"Do you remember when we had our first kiss?" Toby asked, and the question caught me so off guard that I started to laugh at the memory.

"Of course. It's not every day you almost get your eye poked out by someone's glasses," I smiled, "but it's one of my favorite memories." I was blushing again, and I hated how everything felt hotter. Like my skin wanted my blush to cover my entire body and match my hair.

"First of all, if you had just tilted your head the right way, that wouldn't have happened," Toby teased, "but three days later, everything exploded. Literally. Figuratively. And I never heard from you again, Nikki. At first, I figured it was the situation, and you would reach out when you were ready because you lost everything. Except me. I felt so stupid to think that when it became obvious months later that you wouldn't. I was hurt, and I did everything in my power to get over you. And now you're back, and it's all back, but it feels so much more intense than before.

And I'm scared you're going to finish this mission, and I'll have to beg just to see you again. And I can't do that again, Nikki."

It wasn't fair what I had done to him. I knew that. Even back then, I had known it. And while I knew Toby would understand my reasoning, it didn't make it any less wrong.

"I'm sorry," I quietly said. "I wish I had handled it differently. I just... didn't know better. And by the time I figured it out, it felt like it was too late."

"You were sixteen I don't think you were supposed to know better," Toby assured me, scooting his chair closer to mine. "And looking back, it's easy to see that. It's just between your Dad and Nate..."

"My family has a well-earned reputation for being flight risks. I get it," I nodded. "And for locking up our emotions. And as horrible as this Nightshade situation is, there's been so much about it that's made me feel more like me," I continued, "and I realized I hurt myself more by blocking everything out. I was scared one day you would pick up and go to Xatanian and leave me, so I left first. And I'm sorry for everything. I just wish I could make it up to you."

"You can promise you'll talk to me," Toby started, "and that you won't shut me out again. And I promise I won't go to Xatanian without telling you. I think that makes us even."

"I don't know if that's true," I said, looking down at the floor, only to be surprised as Toby's hand cupped my chin and forced me to look back up at him.

"You don't get to decide for me," he quietly said, "but you never answered my question. Do you want me to come as your handler, your friend, or as something else?"

"Something else," I quietly admitted, and before I could comprehend what was happening, I felt Toby's lips on mine. In all the times we had almost kissed this past week, I hadn't realized I needed this like I needed air. His tongue touched mine gently before exploring more. I wanted to live in the moment forever. Even when I was younger, a part of me had known Toby was my other half, and with this kiss, I finally felt whole.

"Gross," a voice interrupted, and Toby and I pulled away to see Zain in the doorway, an open bag of shredded cheese in his hand as he poured a handful into his mouth.

"What are you doing?" I asked, blushing harder than I thought possible.

"Getting a snack," Zain shrugged, holding up the bag of cheese as if it answered all my questions. "But for someone who insisted she didn't want to kiss Toby again, you sure did seem to be enjoying it." I didn't respond past throwing a few fabric scraps in his direction, even though they weren't going to hit him.

"What are you doing in the doorway?" I reiterated. "I know you didn't get that cheese from there."

"I wanted to see if you were still awake," Zain shrugged. "Gray and Jacob have been talking all night, and every time I think I'm about to sleep, she starts laughing. And her laugh echoes through the entire safe house."

"You were lecturing me about how I needed to sleep, when almost everyone was awake?" I asked Toby, who responded with a meek shrug.

"You seemed like you needed it the most," he answered, and as if it were on cue, my body decided to betray me and gave out a large yawn, just to prove his point. "You're going to bed. The uniforms will still be there tomorrow."

"If you two are going to be all couple-y, I'm leaving before I barf," Zain said, shoving more cheese in his mouth as he walked back toward his bedroom.

"Thank you," I said, once I was sure Zain was gone and not going to offer more commentary on us, "for putting up with me. And all of this."

"I knew what I was getting into," Toby smiled, "and I know there's something here, Nickel. But we don't need to put a label on it or rush anything, especially when we have Nightshade to worry about. I just want us on the same page."

"I know," I smiled at him, glad there wasn't any pressure. That we had space to figure ourselves out, that we could work on things we didn't know how to when we were teenagers. I got on my tiptoes and gave him a quick kiss. "And before you say anything else, I'm going to try to sleep. But if I'm not out in an hour, I'm coming back to work on this."

"Deal," Toby agreed. "And Nickel... I probably should have started with this, but I'll have Jacob's passport tomorrow." I had a feeling that was Toby's original reason for coming to the safe house.

"Oh, so I can stay up all night to work on this, and then sleep on the plane?" I teased as Toby looked at me with a faux-annoyance.

"I will pick you up and put you in bed, Nicole Caldwell," he threatened, and I laughed.

"You will do no such thing," I insisted as I walked down the hallway toward my room. I was glad I brought my headphones, because Zain was right—Gray was incredibly loud. But as I closed my door, I felt like a weight had lifted off all of us. For the first time on this mission, things felt like they were finally coming together, and maybe having a second to breathe was going to give us what we needed for what would come next.

CHAPTER TWENTY-FOUR

"**I**'VE BEEN IN VALTERRA for two hours and I already hate it here," I grumbled as I closed the umbrella that had done absolutely nothing toward keeping me dry from the rain that had blown directly into my face.

We had flown into Wassecliff and immediately driven toward the ruins I had tracked down, stopping only to eat before what was either going to be a confrontation or disappointment. Everyone was on edge, and I was exhausted from not being able to sleep on the plane while everyone else had. I had spiraled with questions of how this could go. Would he be happy to see us? Or upset? Would he have kept up with how we were, or have pretended we didn't exist? I stared out of the window the entire car ride, but I barely took in the scenery we drove past. There were too many scenarios, all of them plausible. Each with a different version of Dad. The one from before Mom's death. The Eagle. The One Who Lived in the Shadows.

"We're here," I heard Nate say as he parked the car right in front of the ruined building. It looked exactly like I had expected from the satellite feed. Once, it had been a beautiful structure, but now? It was a crumbled mess that looked like it hadn't been touched in well over a century. "Are you sure this is the right place, Nik?"

"Not really," I said as I reluctantly got out of the car. Toby's hand found mine, and he squeezed it in reassurance. The idea had crossed my mind plenty of times that this entire trip would be for nothing, and as I looked around, I saw no signs of life. No humans, no animals. Everything was completely deserted. Gray started digging in her bag, probably for one of her scanners, while Jacob angrily kicked a rock at a sign, which caused it to fall from the post it had been hanging onto by a thread. Nate hadn't gotten out of the car, and I half expected him to drive away and leave us stranded.

"We've been expecting you," a new voice said from inside the ruins. A man who I could have sworn wasn't there a few seconds ago walked toward us. "For four years, actually. You're incredibly late."

"Who are you supposed to be?" Zain asked, one of his throwing stars in his hand, prepared to strike.

"And why were you expecting us?" Nate asked, deciding to get out of the car at the stranger's presence. I blinked, letting everyone's auras fill my sight. On our end, we were a fury of anger, anxiety, and resentment. But this mysterious man didn't have an aura. And that was concerning.

"You're not human," I said, blinking away my powers. "What are you?"

"My name is Baldwin. I'm Mr. Caldwell's personal android assistant," the man explained. "We have a lot to catch you up on, however, he doesn't have much time left. So I will ask that we hurry, as I am sure he would like to see you all. Where is the other girl?" the robot asked, scanning us.

"Dead," we all deadpanned, and if it could feel emotion, I was sure it would have been surprised. Or as surprised as its programming let it be. "And who are you?" he asked, looking at Toby.

"Tobias Asl'Hagt," Toby answered, and Baldwin's eyes seemed to be scanning a screen built into his eyes.

"Yes, you're on the list," Baldwin said, and I looked at Toby and shrugged. At least my Dad must have somewhat trusted him if Toby was allowed into his secret hiding place. "Please, follow me." The android went over to one of the trees that seemed to be growing into the building and opened a door that led down. My theory about the tunnels had been correct, and wherever Dad was hiding, it was underneath the ruins.

How it was built was a question for another time, because I had caught the one thing Baldwin had said that worried me. Dad didn't have a lot of time left, which meant he was dying. This didn't give me a lot of hope that things would get better from here.

The android led us through an underground corridor, which felt like it consisted of three basements, a very flooded tunnel I was sure was one storm away from a cave-in, and multiple turns. I wasn't sure how long we had been walking or if we were even going anywhere. The misdirection and length of the walk had Dad written all over it.

I blinked again and looked over everyone, trying to get a gauge on what everyone was feeling. Jacob and Nate seemed to be having a competition about who was angrier about the "Dad is dying" development, though Jacob's aura was more intense. Zain was upset, though you couldn't read it on his face. Gray's aura pulsed between excited and nervous, which felt on brand since she was the one who seemed to have forgiven Dad long ago. And Toby's aura was wary, an emotion I didn't see often, but it made me glad he was looking out for us. Especially since I was holding onto his hand like my life depended on it, certain that when we found Dad, I would immediately projectile vomit all over his feet.

"Remember to breathe, Nickel," Toby reminded me, placing a soft kiss on the top of my head. I tried to let out a long breath and release some of the tension I was holding, but it didn't do much good.

According to Toby's watch, we had been walking for about twenty minutes when we came into a sleek and modern living space. Unlike the safe room, this one had been designed for living, with the same decoration style as the Nest. The technology and future had a set place and purpose, and all of it seemed like it was rarely used.

"If you would please make yourself comfortable, I will let Mr. Caldwell know you've arrived," Baldwin said as he walked into a room off the main living area. Jacob immediately flopped onto one of the couches and groaned from exhaustion, clearly not having been up for the whole twenty-minute walk. I couldn't blame him. If I had known to expect that I would have worn different shoes.

But I smiled, because I knew Dad was going to hate seeing Jacob like that.

"Soooo..." Gray started as she sat down in a chair, only to squirm as she realized it had been built for aesthetic and not comfort. "How are we all doing?"

"Do you want me to tell you what everyone's auras say, or do you want us to lie to you?" I asked, though, if looks could kill, Gray would have been murdered at least three times.

"You know, it's on brand for Dad to be dying the moment we find him," Zain said, forgoing the furniture and sitting on the coffee table.

"Well... that's morbid," Toby said, his eyes wide at my brother.

"We were all thinking it," he defended. "What's the most dramatic thing Sebastian Caldwell could do after going missing for a half a decade? Die the moment we find him."

"Zain's... right," Nate slowly said through gritted teeth, almost as if it pained him to admit it. But with how many fights the two of them had over the past week alone, it probably did. "Think about it, now we have to act civil because he's dying. When he's the one who put us in the situation in the first place."

"You're planning on acting civil?" Jacob scoffed. "Dying or not, I'm telling him the fuck off. He's the reason my sister is dead."

The words seemed to suck the air out of the room, all of us wincing at the reminder of what brought us together in the first place. Jacob hadn't talked much about Brittney's death yet, and it was clear he was still processing it. Even if he had lived without her for over a year, her absence was eating him up inside.

"Well, I guess that answers my first question," a quiet, hoarse voice said from the doorway, and we all turned to see a sight I hadn't expected. It was one thing to hear a robot say my father was dying. For the past five years, he had been more concept than human. I remembered what he looked like from pictures and recordings, and his voice had haunted my dreams. His presence could scare any boardroom or bandit with just the smallest of movements.

The Sebastian Caldwell in front of me was none of that.

This one was entirely too thin. Gone was the strength and imposing stature of my memories, and instead it was replaced with sickly pale skin, a walker, and an oxygen tank. He sounded weak, looked like a strong breeze could knock him over, and I didn't recognize him. Not at first.

Once upon a time, this man had been the Eagle. Now, he was just a man.

"Oh, my god," I whispered under my breath as Toby pulled me in close, his arms giving comfort as a myriad of emotions flew through me. Regret. Betrayal. Guilt. Pain. Part of me wanted to hug the sick man in front of us, and the other wanted to yell at him.

"Well, don't all of you speak at once," the voice said out of the man who was supposed to be my father—the differences so intense it was taking my mind so long to merge the two together.

"Sebastian," Nate said coldly, trying to keep the professional tone that meant he was annoyed.

"Nathan," Dad nodded in return, punctuated by a deep cough as Baldwin seemed to appear out of nowhere to lead him to a chair. "It's nice to see you all."

"By the comet, cut the fake polite crap," Jacob growled at him.

"Then you get your shoes off my couch. I know you were taught better than that," the old man countered, and for the first time, I could see him. The wit, the conversation, the quick mind. Underneath all the sickness, he was there, and that seemed like permission enough for the anger that had been bubbling in me for years to come out.

"You also taught us never to disappear without a trace, but considering how terrible you were at following that one, I think we're all a little confused about which of your rules we're still supposed to be following." The words left my lips like poison, and clearly, Dad hadn't expected I would be the one to say them. The dark part of me was glad to see the hurt on his face, and yet the part of me that had spent most of my life trying to please him winced. It hadn't occurred to me that I had the power to wound him. He had spent so much less time with me, it had never seemed possible.

"I guess that was deserved," Dad finally said, taking a deep breath. "As is all of your anger. It's why I had hoped you would find me sooner, there would have been..."

"If you wanted to see us, you should have sent an invitation. You do realize that's what normal people do, right?" Nate asked, his hurt taking the wheel as well. "Because anyone else would have sent us an address, or a way to contact you, or some other sign you were alive."

"We've never been normal, Nathan." The words seemed to be the motto Dad had clung to, giving him the shield he had used to justify everything. But I knew Nate was about to completely blow through it.

"And whose fault is that, Sebastian?" It wasn't a question, but instead an accusation. The fire in Nate's eyes was one I had become intimately familiar with since we had found him. But I knew this anger probably went back further. Nate's disappointments, his distrust in Dad after Mom's death. There was so much he had held onto that it had become a part of him.

"Plus, you waited a year to give us a case file that barely gave us clues to this location? Mom kidnapped me the moment she realized you were gone," Zain scoffed. "We didn't even know you left anything until like... four days ago? Three days ago? What time zone are we in again?"

"Four days ago," Gray answered, doing the math in her head, "and honestly, none of us even realized those clues were there except for Nikki. And it still took her days to figure out they were there. You could have been a bit more obvious..." she said before trailing off, and I was surprised to see Gray criticizing Dad. That was something I hadn't expected.

"Your mother?" Dad asked, blinking as he realized what Zain was saying, then looked at us slowly as if for the first time. It was like he realized we weren't the teenagers we left behind, and where I had struggled to see the man, he was struggling to see us as anything other than children. "You didn't stay together?"

"No," Jacob scoffed. "Nate dipped like three days after you did."

"Nate, you were supposed to keep them together," Dad said, his voice rising to the almost authoritative levels of my memories. Almost. But it brought to light how much pressure he had put on Nate, and why my brother had collapsed under it.

"I was twenty!" Nate snapped. "And you wanted me to be the caregiver to my baby sister, your love child, Gray, who should have left for college already, a junkie, and a cosplayer who had no right being in the field. And have you even noticed which one of us isn't here, Sebastian? It's like you don't even care. Brittney died as a consequence of your actions."

"A junkie? Really?" Jacob asked, and I was sure if he was at full strength, he would have pinned Nate to the wall. "You're going to say that to my face and insult my sister in the same breath?"

"Maybe if you had stopped using long enough to talk to your sister, we would have been able to save her," Nate snapped.

"You don't get to talk to Jacob like that, Nate. None of us had even heard from you in five years," I warned. I had hoped Nate's attitude would have gotten under control after our talk, but it seemed like Dad was bringing out the worst in him. "So, don't act like you've been brother of the year when you left us, too."

"That. Is. Enough!" The bellow was followed by a coughing fit that almost made me feel bad for Dad. Though to his credit, it did get everyone to calm down. It was obvious he had figured out we all had issues with each other, and his presence was only making it worse. "All of you take a breath."

Everyone was quiet again, each of us looking at the floor like scolded children, except Gray, whose eyes were fixed on Baldwin. She clearly was trying to figure something out, and there was a good chance she had blocked out our entire situation.

"How did you make his skin look so realistic?" Gray asked, oblivious to the tension in the room. "If it wasn't for Nikki not being able to read an aura on him, I don't think any of us would have realized he was a robot."

"I prefer Android, but I can give you the blueprints later," Sebastian said. "He's been my companion since coming to Valterra. I figured it was safer for me if the only person who knew where I was had programming that wouldn't allow them to reveal my location."

"Wait..." Gray said, and it was clear she was putting something together we hadn't yet. "You knew, didn't you? You knew Nightshade wasn't dead. This whole time, if you were so secretive about your location, you had to have known he wasn't dead." I truly felt bad for Gray, seeing her have to knock Sebastian off the pedestal she put him on in real time. "By the comet, Sebastian! I have been trying to defend you to everyone. I'm pretty sure I'm the only person in this room who doesn't hate you, and you have made it really hard not to. How long have you known?" I blinked, and Gray's aura was the deep blue of sadness while Dad's radiated guilt. Even with his letter to Mom, I never thought he had actually known Nightshade was alive, and this added a new layer to his betrayal, and hurt rushed through me again.

"Gray's right," I said. "You did know."

"I had hoped that making him think he won would have caused him to back off. After Katya..." Dad started coughing again. "She turned to stealing to escape their relationship. To give Nate a life better than the one they would have had with him." Nate's face paled, which left all doubt we had about who his biological father was completely gone. "She kept it up to help those less fortunate than her. I figured it out as I wrote my last letter to her. I had hoped that if he thought he destroyed me, he would believe he won. That he would stop. I was wrong."

The coughing continued, and I noticed the drops of blood that sprayed into his hands that he subtly tried to wipe on his pants.

"Mr. Caldwell needs to rest," Baldwin said, refusing to let us say another word as he led Dad out of the room. It was silent, as nothing we had expected had happened once we saw him.

"That was uncalled for, Nate," Gray finally snapped, breaking the silence. "Reducing everyone down like that. You know better, especially after everything we've been through. I really thought you had more respect for everyone." I was pleasantly surprised it was Gray who said it, because Nate looked like he had been slapped across the face. All of my words had fallen on deaf ears, and if it had been Zain, the same thing would have happened. But Gray had always been the perky, optimistic, and levelheaded of all of us, and if she was calling someone out, it meant they had crossed so many lines they couldn't even notice how terrible their actions were.

"I agree," Toby said, though it was from a handler's perspective as he tried to balance his job with everything else going on. "I wasn't going to say anything, because I'm not entirely sure where my place is in this drama. But if that's how you've been acting this entire time, Nate, I shouldn't have listened to your wife's pleas to have you involved and stuck you in a safe house."

"I know," Nate groaned. "I just...hate this." He stormed off into the tunnels, and I was certain he would come back once he cooled down. And for everyone's sake, I hoped it would come with the apology we all needed.

"Well, that went exactly like I expected it would," Zain deadpanned from the table, before doing a backward somersault off of it. "Dad seemed incapable of thinking anything could possibly happen outside his plans."

"I mean, it's Seb, what do you expect?" Jacob asked. "Couldn't even look at me to tell me how disappointed he was. Got enough of those lectures as a kid."

The hindsight of remembering how Dad had treated us brought a new light on everything he had said. It was impossible not to feel like a disappointment after how he had looked at us, how he had talked to us, but at the same time, he hadn't treated us any differently than he used to. We had grown, changed, and he had stayed the same. It was the kind of distance that made me realize that even on the good days, he hadn't ever treated us that well.

Everything had always been Dad's plan. Our code names, our looks, and our becoming heroes in the first place. He had controlled every bit of it and still had managed to make us believe it had been our ideas in the first place.

"I have rooms prepared for each of you," Baldwin said as he walked back in the room. "Please follow me." He led us down a different hallway, each of us getting a room that seemed to reflect not who we were, but our codenames Dad had given us. By the time we made it down the hall, I was the last one there, and Baldwin froze.

"I'm sorry we don't have a room for you Tobsai'uwadshg'aoisdgha'sdglkha'oe Asl'Hagt," I almost choked at hearing Toby's full name, I wasn't sure I had ever heard anyone pronounce it before since it human vocal chords didn't allow us to speak the Xatanian language, "Do you mind sharing with Miss Caldwell?" Before either of us could answer, Baldwin walked away, and it was clear there would be no argument with the android.

"Was he close to pronouncing your name correctly?" I asked.

"No, we can add robots to the list of people who can't speak Xatanian," Toby chuckled, before freezing as he walked into the room, "Um, wow. This room is....something." And he was right. Everywhere there were nightingales. Pictures, posters, the color scheme, and more taxidermied birds than I cared to count. A wave of disgust rolled through me as I was brought back to the dead birds that had littered my townhouse. The entire room looked like a reflection of who Dad expected me to be, and I hated it.

"Yeah, it's... Wow," I finally managed to say, wondering if I was going to be able to move the birds, or if they were going to be watching us sleep.

"Are you okay?" Toby asked, closing the door behind us as he grabbed a few blankets and started to arrange himself on the chair in the corner.

"Yeah, I think so," I admitted, and I was surprised the words were right. "I hadn't expected Dad to be so sick, but everything else? It's like I'm not angry at him, I'm just disappointed."

Toby laughed, but as surprisingly calm as I was, I feared the worst wasn't over. That something Dad said or did would cause me to spiral, or would end up ruining the little progress the team had made with each other over the past few days. I wanted to believe things would be alright, but with Dad in the picture, that felt impossible.

"Honestly, I never realized things were so bad for you guys with him," Toby said. "I was jealous when we were kids, that you all not only had a team, but a mentor who played to your strengths. But there were a lot of expectations he put on you all that nobody should have had." I was glad Toby said something; it was validating to have someone on the outside notice.

But I was so tired, I didn't want to think anymore. The travel was catching up with me, because even though I had told everyone I had slept on the plane, I hadn't. And I was exhausted.

"Are you really going to stay on the chair all night?" I asked, sitting on the bed. "Or afternoon? Or whatever time it is?"

"I wasn't going to assume you wanted me on the bed with you," Toby admitted, as I patted the mattress next to me. "And sharing a bed comes with expectations that..."

"I know," I nodded, "but since we're still figuring out what we are, I don't think sex should even be on the table right now. Or honestly, preferably ever. The idea of it grosses me out and isn't something I want..." I trailed off, having never actually talked about it before.

"Really?" Toby asked, relief in his voice. "I've always been the same way. I just didn't know how to tell people."

"Let's just take it off the table," I smiled at him. "I don't need sex to know that I want this." I leaned over and kissed his cheek and rested my head on his shoulder. "As long as you hold me, that's all I need."

Chapter Twenty-Five

I T WAS ALREADY ROUGH waking up, so hot I felt like I was on fire. Apparently, Toby's body heat went up when he slept to unbearable amounts, and I was so drenched in sweat I felt like I had just jumped in a swimming pool. But it was even more unsettling as my eyes adjusted to the lights, and I was surrounded by birds, looking like they were straight out of a horror movie. All I could see were the reflections of their eyes, and I realized exactly how much taxidermy was in the room.

Either Dad had started doing it as a hobby or had started collecting it. And I didn't exactly care which reason it was, it was entirely too much. I wasn't sure what time it was. My phone had died, and I had forgotten to change the time on my watch, but I guessed it was the middle of the night.

I carefully untangled myself from Toby's too-hot arms, making sure I didn't wake him, and went to the living room. That room didn't have any decorations that would stare at me... unless Baldwin had a charging station in there. I tried not to shudder at the thought.

I had just started sketching when I heard footsteps, and I glanced up and saw a ghost. Or Dad. It was just so jarring to see him so sick. And it was hard to tell if he just couldn't sleep, or if he had coughed himself awake.

"You can sit if you want, it's your house," I said after a few moments of us staring at each other.

"I was waiting to see if you were going to start yelling again. I had a feeling you were holding back earlier," Dad said, settling onto the couch next to me. It was strange, being close to him and having a stranger stare back.

"I was. But you started ignoring me in favor of Nate, like usual, so I'm used to it," I said, the words coming out matter-of-factly, but they still stung him more than I had intended.

"Nicole, I—" he started before I shook my head.

"You don't need to explain yourself. You wanted Nate to be the next you, or you were trying to keep Zain from being a serial killer, or you were recruiting Gray or the twins. You were busy, I was the one who needed the least attention. So, that's just what I got," I had thought I would yell if I ever got to say my piece with Dad. I would get my revenge for him leaving for so long. But after leading the team, myself, I somewhat understood why he did it. I didn't agree with it, but I was letting it go. Not for him, but because it was exhausting to keep holding on to it.

And I had missed these quiet times where it was just Dad and me. And as this was clearly going to be the last time, I didn't want to ruin it.

"You were always the constant. I never thought you wanted any extra attention," Dad admitted, looking guilty. I couldn't remember a time when Dad ever had the decency to look guilty, and my eyebrows furrowed in confusion. Sebastian Caldwell wasn't one to have guilt or regret; he did what he thought was right, and that was that. Though I had read some of his journals, and seeing him now, maybe I was wrong. Maybe he just hid it where none of us could see.

"When it came to training, you're right, I was. But it never seemed to cross your mind that I needed my Dad," I pointed out. "We all did. Mom was murdered, you covered it up, and from that point on, all we ever did was train. We had to fight corruption, make sure people who hurt others were punished. None of us knew who we were outside of your little soldiers, not really. We were too young to have been thrown into your personal war, which we knew nothing about. And even if we had our licenses and passed the psych evals, we had no idea the fight we were even fighting."

"That's why I made sure you'd get the files on your mother," Dad sighed, and I could tell he was trying to figure out the right thing to say. Not to spin it in his favor, but to have the conversation. "I wanted you to know the truth. So you could see how eaten alive by revenge I had gotten. Losing your mother was the worst thing that ever happened to me, and for it to be him..." He paused and it was clear the two of them had talked about Nightshade—not as a villain, but as Mom's ex. It was a part of her past she hadn't wanted us to know, a secret Mom had kept out of love. A secret Dad had kept for her. "He stalked her for leaving an abusive relationship. He murdered her a decade after she left. It wasn't something I could forgive. Or forget. When I first met Katya, she was stealing not just so she and Nate could live, but in an attempt to help the other women who had just escaped similar situations. She wanted to make sure Nate would never have to know the monster Patrick was. I promised her I would protect her, and in the end, I couldn't."

"And in the process, you didn't give us a chance to find out how we would cope with the truth, or help us through understanding her loss. Or even be there for us, understanding what happened at the warehouse, because we didn't... Actually I need to have Toby awake for that conversation because there's something about paperwork that's five years overdue. But what happened?"

"Toby's your handler and your boyfriend? Is that allowed?" Dad asked, completely sidestepping my question.

"Yes, kind of, and no," I replied. "He was my handler first, which started when Brittney was killed. We're not exactly labeling things right now, but that started again a few days ago. And once this mission is over, he will no longer be my handler because we both know he won't be impartial. Now, back to my question, because I'm not going to let you avoid it." I could tell Dad was surprised and maybe impressed that I called out his avoidance, even though the only reason I knew to was because of the times I had done the same thing.

"I killed an innocent man," Dad finally stated, a faraway look in his eyes. "Nightshade, or Patrick McLaughlan, if you want to know his real name, got the best of me. It was bad enough that I had killed who I thought was him. But after I saw the body... it didn't take long to realize it wasn't him. He was too young, he didn't look like the few pictures your mother had shown me. And I realized I had been the weapon that created another of Nightshade's victims. It broke what little of me was left, and I thought you would be better off with Nate in charge."

"I can assure you that wasn't the case," I deadpanned, though I was sure that was obvious from everything Dad had already witnessed. "He and Kitty left within a few days. Got married, had twins. So, surprise, you're a grandfather. But I didn't even know all of that until this week because Nate cut all of us out of his life immediately, just like you did. He wasn't meant to lead the team, no matter how hard you pushed it on him. He's got crippling anxiety, he wasn't mentally equipped to deal with all of us, so he did what you did and ran. So, I was unprepared because you never taught me anything, and I had to take over the role you wanted for him. And I left the house the first moment I could, because staying alone with those memories wasn't something I could handle."

"But why didn't the rest of you stay together?" Dad asked. "I understand Nate left, and Yasmine took Zain. But the other four of you?"

"Gray left for school almost immediately, which was what she needed to do. I couldn't be mad at that. But the twins had abandonment issues and were so triggered by everyone leaving, they bounced, because why would they stay? So, everyone left me within a week of you."

"I see," Dad nodded, and I could see him finally getting a clear picture of the truth instead of whatever he had imagined happened after he left. "And what has Zain told you about Yasmine?"

"Everything," I admitted, "You could have told us that you never cheated on Mom. That she knew about Zain and Zak's existence the entire time. You kept so many secrets from us, and those secrets are all quite literally trying to kill us. Yasmine, Nightshade, everything leads back to you. It's the only reason we came to find you, because while we have safety in numbers at the moment, we have no idea what we're up against because you refused to tell us."

"I was trying to protect you..." Dad defended, but he trailed off with a dry chuckle. "But in hindsight, I can see you're right. You wouldn't be in this situation if I had told you everything."

"No, we wouldn't," I agreed. "And we wouldn't be in this situation if you had paid attention to us properly as kids. If you had seen that Nate wasn't a leader, if you had paid proper attention to me, if you had seen how many times you threw Zain under the bus with your secrets. If you had been our father instead of our commander."

"I didn't know how to do things without Katya," Dad admitted. "She brought out the best in all of us... and I was scared. For Nate, especially. I wanted him to be able to protect himself if Patrick ever came for him."

"It's hard to tell if Nightshade is after us, or if he's after you. I keep flipping back and forth as to which one it is," I sighed, "but he found our identities after killing our therapist. You wouldn't have known that; they found her body after you had already left. But if I had to guess, he wanted to take everything from you, because he saw you as taking everything from him. Like, do you think he even knows about Nate?"

"No," a voice said from behind us, and I saw a very tired and very wet Nate standing in the doorway. "Mom told me she had left before he found out she was pregnant. I doubt he put it together when he was obsessed with Dad stealing Mom away from him."

"Would you like to sit, Nathan? Or should I have Baldwin get you a towel?" Dad asked, and Nate shrugged.

"You two were having a moment, and I doubt my presence is welcome," he said.

"Nate, can you stop being an emo pain in the ass for five minutes?" I groaned. "You need this information too. You've been upset about all the secrets. Stop acting like you don't want them."

Nate looked at me with a mix of betrayal and shock before he sat down in a chair across from us.

"I know I owe you an apology, Nathan. Multiple apologies, it seems," Dad admitted, and Nate eyed him with suspicion. "I know I was hard on you, and my idea of you didn't align with who you are. I'm sorry I never truly saw you."

"Are we finally having family trauma time?" Zain's voice asked, before he jumped out of a vent and landed gracefully on the floor. "I've been waiting for this since we got here." He went and sat on the back of the couch, his feet resting on the cushions like they were a footrest. "Sorry, Nate, I know you're finally getting your well deserved apologies, but when's the last time we actually had just the four of us together?"

"And since when have you cared about the four of us being together?" I teased Zain, only for him to lovingly flip me off. I knew it was coming. It was nice to see this side of him. The side that showed his heart, the one his mother tried so hard to stamp out.

"I had always hoped I would get to see the three of you again. I had given up hope you'd ever come," Dad admitted, a sad smile on his face. The kind of smile you only saw on someone's face at the end of their life, with them looking back at everything they had done. None of us asked what he was sick with, and I doubted he would tell us. One last secret in his vault, one last thing he was trying to protect us from.

"I've always been proud of each of you," he continued, making sure to look at all three of us as he spoke. "I wasn't a good father. You don't need to tell me that—I already knew. I tried my best, but it wasn't enough. And I'm sure I could have tried harder. I kept too many secrets, and most of them I shouldn't have. But in all three of you, I see someone who is better than I ever would have been. And that's all I ever wanted, for you to have a better life. And for the three of you to always depend on each other."

"Yeah, about that each other part..." Zain started, before I gave him a look. "Okay, we've been better this week, but how do you know we're not going to fall apart again?"

"Have you met Nikki?" Nate asked, and for the first time since we found him, he gave me a genuine smile. "You really think she's going to do all that work finding us, and then let us get away with another five years of no contact?"

"Good point. She fought off the Circle to get me," Zain admitted, and Dad looked at me with a mixture of surprise and pride. As if he was finally seeing me through the lens he should have been looking through the entire time.

"So, you're in charge, Nicole?" Dad asked, and it was clear he was trying to figure out what the dynamics were now. Maybe he was trying to figure out how to help my team, because if one thing was clear, it wasn't his anymore. "What's your plan so far?"

"You don't get to keep any more secrets," I answered, looking Dad in the eyes and daring him to look away, "You need to tell us everything you know about the Circle and Nightshade. Anything you can think of that will help us fight them."

"Well, in that case, it's going to be a long night," Dad said, pressing a button on his watch that summoned Baldwin. "We're going to need coffee. A lot of it."

Chapter Twenty-Six

WAKING UP THE NEXT morning, or more likely the next afternoon, with how late I came back to bed, was a relief. I felt certain we had a decent game plan. Between the information Dad had given us the night before and the fact that we now had his expertise, I was certain that with a little bit of polishing, we would be able to pull this off. Toby had managed to get out of bed without waking me up, and I assumed he was finally getting the paperwork done he needed Dad to complete. His side of the bed was cold, and for the first time, I let myself lie in bed and relax.

But coffee was calling, and I wouldn't let it wait for long.

The moment I left my room, though, something immediately felt off. There wasn't any yelling, teasing, or arguing. There wasn't a lecture from Toby about the importance of paperwork or procedures, or Jacob finally getting his chance to tell Dad off. It was silent, and while I knew I had woken up at a weird time, silence wasn't something that was ever a good sign. I walked into the living room to find everyone sitting there. Everyone but Dad.

Something had happened.

"Miss Nicole," Baldwin said, and there was a sadness in the android's voice that felt out of place, "I am sorry to say Mr. Caldwell passed away early this morning in his sleep. He has left each of you a letter, and I am now required to give it to you."

It took me a second to understand exactly what Baldwin had said, and my stomach dropped. It had only been a few hours ago we got the answers we needed, and Dad seemed almost excited to get a chance to plan it out with us. He had seemed less like a ghost and more like the father I had barely remembered. The one we had before Mom had died. Finding Dad had been too good to be true, just like I should have expected.

I knew I should feel something, but an eerie numbness spread over my body. I had convinced myself for years that Dad had been dead; it had been how I had coped with his leaving. There was a fight in my thoughts: one that felt we should continue as usual, another believing I should have tried to find him instead of letting him disappear.

But it was too late to do anything. Too late to think about what I should have done.

I took the letter from Baldwin and shoved it in my pocket. I didn't have time for it now. I couldn't fall apart, not when we were in the middle of all of this. Not when I needed to be the support for everyone. I had to be the strong one because nobody else on this team would be.

"Okay, Dad gave me, Nate, and Zain some information last night, " I said, pushing back all my emotions with a deep breath, "and as morbid as it is, his death might be the way to catch Nightshade."

"Really, Nikki? Now? Dad just died," Nate snapped, surprising me with the amount of hurt in his voice. Of all the people here, I assumed Nate wouldn't have been this upset. "And you're just jumping back into the mission? You won't even take a second to process it?"

"If I take that second, Nate, I'm going to fall apart," I shot back, feeling the cracks in the hasty wall I had put up. "And if I fall apart right now, I'm pretty sure I won't be able to put myself back together." I took a breath and avoided everyone's eyes. "I know it sucks, and that what I'm doing isn't healthy, and I'm going to be making a therapist very rich unpacking all of this. But I want to save all of our lives, and at the moment, we have an opportunity to set the stage ourselves."

Toby got up out of his chair and wrapped his arms around my waist, his head resting against my shoulder. It was comforting, especially as I realized I was shaking from having no idea what was going on in my own mind. "Are you okay?" he whispered in my ear.

"No," I whispered back, and tears pricked behind my eyes. I knew I needed to mourn, and I would make sure I did later. I just wasn't sure if anyone else saw it that way.

"Honestly, Nikki's kind of right," Zain sighed. "Survive first, process later. Can't really do shit if we're all dead."

"At least you realized what you're doing is messed up, instead of Seb, who thought it was healthy," Jacob pointed out. "So, what'd you find out?"

"Nightshade needs to be our first priority, because he can't help himself and always makes things a spectacle," I said, pulling Toby's arms tighter around me,=. "The way he is with his costumes, theatrics, and his goal of always making the top story on the news. He would want to make sure if he won, Dad would be humiliated. So, what better way to lure him out into the open than Dad's funeral? His chance for a final showdown with Dad? Gone. But he can humiliate him by killing his children at his funeral. He won't be able to resist, which gives us an advantage because we know he's coming."

"Plus if he thinks we're grieving, he'll assume we're weak," Zain added, catching where my thought process was going. "So, he'll be shocked when we're prepared for him."

"And what about those of us who are actually grieving?" Gray demanded, and I realized she had tears falling down her cheeks. There was a quiver in her voice I hadn't ever heard. "I don't want to do that kind of fight at Seb's funeral. I don't think I can handle that. I know you all compartmentalize and turn off your emotions, but I don't think I can do that." She sniffled and wiped her eyes, and I was jealous. Jealous of how Gray had been close enough to Dad that she was devastated at his loss. Jealous of how Gray was going to miss him. And Nate agreed, which meant Dad's death was hitting him harder than anyone had expected.

"It's unorthodox, but if you need the closure, you could have a funeral right now," Toby suggested, kissing me on the head before he walked toward the middle of the room. "Each of you can say what you need to. We'll make sure he's laid to rest once we get back to the Bay by Katya, just like he would have wanted. Besides, does he have anyone else he would want at a funeral who isn't here in this room?"

"Mom," Nate quietly said, and he was right. The only person Dad would have wanted at his funeral more than any of us was Mom—and it was a comfort that they were finally at peace together.

"You know, Nate, funerals are for the living, not the dead," Toby quietly said, sitting in a chair, and forcing me into his lap. "You can start if you want."

"I guess..." Nate said, trailing off as he thought about what he wanted to say. "Obviously Dad and I had our differences. We didn't get along well, but despite all of that, I never had to question if he wanted me or not. Before he even met me, he knew Mom and I were a package deal. And he didn't just accept it, he embraced it. No matter what, no matter how many times we fought, I always knew he wanted to be my father. He was horrible at showing it, but I also never questioned it. So, that part of me is going to miss him. The part that knows he never stopped trying to be my father, that he chose it from the moment I met him. I'm always going to be thankful for that, and it's something I passed on to my own kids: making sure they know they're not only loved, but they're wanted."

Toby nodded at Nate's words, and I could tell there was relief in my older brother. He didn't exactly get the apology he wanted, but he could still see the good Dad did. Gray sniffled and wiped her eyes.

"Seb saved me," Gray quietly said, "I never mentioned how, because I didn't want you all to pity me. My home life was terrible. My mom had an endless cycle of boyfriends, and any time she was in a relationship, she'd pretend I didn't exist. And if the boyfriends found out about me... well, it was never pretty. I rarely went to school, and even when I did, I was so mentally checked out that my grades were nowhere near what anyone would expect now that you know me. I walked into the teen center the day I met Seb, knowing that if the Caldwell name was on the sign, there would be something I could steal so I could rent a hotel room for a few days to get away from my Mom's current horrible boyfriend. I hadn't ever stolen anything before, and instead of punishing me, he saw me. He taught me how to defend myself so I could actually sleep at night, he gave me a place to live that wasn't a chaotic mess, and put me in a school that recognized my potential. I know everyone thought I should have gone to college like two years before I did, but I needed to learn how to use my potential. And honestly, I don't think I'd be alive right now if it wasn't for Seb." The tears streamed down Gray's face, and while I knew that both Gray and the twins had a terrible home life, I didn't know how bad things were. I had thought she came from a mostly loving home that just didn't have the money to properly help her. "I don't think he even realized what he had taken me out of. And how much he changed my life. I know he messed up a lot, it's clear from the way the rest of you talk about him. But for me, Seb was the superhero, not the Eagle. I just wish he knew that."

"Yeah, Seb saved Britt and me from getting murdered by our stepdad," Jacob said. "The whole reason we met him was that the Eagle interrupted our Stepdad trying. I'd been stupid enough to bring a knife to what was a gunfight, and Seb made sure I never had to use it on the asshole. I was high as a kite, though I hallucinated the whole thing and tried to fight Seb. Lost. Obviously. He recommended we go to the teen center, got us help. Made sure we wouldn't have to deal with the asshole again, got me clean, got us somewhere normal. I was always pushing his buttons because it always felt too good to be true. That one day he'd bounce like our Dad did and leave us with nothing, and it fucking sucked that I was right. But he kept me and Britt alive, and I guess I have to thank him for that."

"I've killed a lot of people," Zain started, and the entire room winced at his words, "and yeah, I know you all hate hearing that, but it is what it is. Made my first kill at four, and by the time I was dropped on Dad's doorstep, I had already killed more people than I could count. I was more weapon than person and still managed to be a disappointment to my mother, who hated the fact I wasn't fully a weapon. Dad took me in anyway, forced me to get in touch with my humanity. He taught me how to care about people and respect life. I still struggle with it. Life's easier Mom's way—to turn off my emotions and become a murder machine. But Dad made sure I knew I could be more than that, and even though emotions are harder, it's important to still experience them. I'm soft now, at least by Circle standards, but if there wasn't Dad, I don't think I would have learned how to be human."

In listening to everyone talk about Dad, it was hard to figure out what I wanted to say, or if I even wanted to say anything. There was a theme in everyone's eulogies: how Dad had saved them from something. And then there was me: born into a happy family with a good childhood. By the time I needed saving, Dad was gone. I should have felt lucky I never needed it, but it was clear now that Dad always felt the need to save people. The ones he took in, my brothers, all of them needed him to save them. He had never seen me as a damsel in distress, so he never spent time with me. It was supposed to be a compliment, and maybe someone would take it that way.

But it was clear now that everyone else knew a side of Dad he had never shown me. The savior. And everyone's eyes were on me, expecting me to say something, like it would make me feel better. But I wasn't sure that was true. While they were mourning the relationships they had with my father, I was mourning the fact that we never actually had one to begin with.

"I think anyone who knew Dad had a complicated relationship with him," I finally said after the silence got too awkward to handle. "And growing up, my main goal in life was to impress him. Positive or negative feedback wasn't something he gave me, so I figured I was average at everything. And if I did better, worked hard, did everything perfectly, he might just tell me 'good job' once. We had our moments, ones that were ours, and those are moments I'll cherish. But I didn't need saving like the rest of you did, and so all those sides you all saw of him, I never did. Logically, I knew he cared about all of us; he cared about making the world a better place for everyone. But now I'm left wondering if I just wasn't broken enough for him. And now I'm scared that, now that I am broken, I'm destined to become just like him. That I'll lock away my emotions, push everyone away, and focus on the job. I've already gone down that path because it's what I learned from him. You all, to various degrees, learned how to be a good person because of Dad." My voice cracked, and the dam broke and for the second time in a week the sobs I had been holding in my entire life started to come out. "And now I just am left with the bad parts of him. And I'm disappointed in myself that I broke too late, and he wasn't there to fix me like he was all of you. Because I needed him, and he never came for me." Toby's arms wrapped around me again as I cried, unable to hide all of the brokenness inside of me, no matter how hard I tried. But with him, I was safe, and he gave me more comfort than anyone in my family had ever given.

"Let it all out, you're okay," I heard his voice whisper into my hair, "it's okay."

And, for the first time, I did.

Years of emotion bubbled to the surface. Hurt from the secrets and lies, how the moment he had finally started making things right, he had abandoned us. How I hated my father for leaving us, and how he had managed to do it again with his death, how I loved him and looked up to him at the same time.

259

"I'm sorry," I finally sniffled, wiping my eyes as my sobs turned into hiccups.

"Listen, Seb saved us, but he also fucked us all up," Jacob said, and I was glad for his harsh honesty. It was comforting, in a way only Jacob could be. "Well, except maybe Gray."

"And me. But only because I was already messed up when I got here," Zain added with a snort.

"You're already doing better than Dad, Nik," Nate said, and I could see how reluctant his admission was. It was written all over his face. "You can see where you're going, you can see how you're becoming Dad. And you've admitted you want to be different, to be better. You got us all back together, and that counts for something. None of us is going to let you go down that path."

"Until you all leave again," I whimpered as Toby's thumb stroked the side of my arm. He had told me he had no plans of leaving, but it wasn't until now that I truly felt it. "You all keep crediting me with getting us back together, but once the threat's gone, everyone's going to go their own separate ways again. And I'm going to be alone." I knew Toby wanted to counter, and I knew I would need to hear it again, but I appreciated that he was letting me feel what I needed to. It had been a long time.

And I hated that letting it all out did make me feel better. There was a giant weight lifted off my shoulders of admitting everything. That I was scared and lonely and didn't want things to go back to the way they were. I didn't think I could handle it.

"Like I'm going to willingly go back to my Mom after what we just pulled," Zain scoffed. "She'll just dump me back in Annelton, and I've had enough of cows to last a lifetime."

"And I should probably go to rehab or some shit like that," Jacob sighed. "I know the Bay's got a good one. And someone has to sort out Britt's apartment, so I'll be around for a while."

"Plus, I still live in the Bay," Gray chuckled. "I should be finishing my doctorate soon, you know, once I finally sit down and finish my dissertation. And from what I can tell, the Caldwell Foundation has a pretty sweet R&D department I would love to work for. You know, if the big boss lady on the board puts in a good word for me." She winked, and I knew he was well aware I would happily give her a job, even though I definitely did not feel like a "big boss lady" at the moment. I felt like nothing but numbness, pain, and exhaustion.

"I'm not making any promises until I talk to Kitty," Nate said, considering he was the only one of us who had a family and the kind of love that would be in major upheaval if he made any promises, "but I'm sure she would be fine with us coming up to visit more often." He paused for a moment, clearly trying to think of the correct words for what he wanted to say next. "But you're the glue that holds us together, Nik, and I think you got that from Dad, too."

I had never thought about it that way. I had been working hard to get everyone back together more than thinking about how to make them want to stay. But Nate was right—I understood everyone. Their strengths and weaknesses, their personalities. I could find the reasons we made sense to work together when others would struggle.

We were a family. A messed-up one, with more trauma than most people would ever have to deal with. We were going to fight. It was going to be messy. We needed each other, whether we wanted to or not. And I needed to relearn how to trust and let them all in.

"You're right," I nodded, taking a calming breath, though I knew I was about five seconds away from sobbing again. "But I think I need a couple of hours to myself so I can cry. Do what you need to say goodbye to Dad, and then we need to think of a plan. Work for everyone?"

I untangled myself from Toby's arms and sniffled as I went back to the room we shared, only to be greeted by the dozens of dead birds' eyes. It wasn't my best moment, but all of the birds were thrown into the hallway before I closed the door and let myself feel.

Toby had said funerals were for the living, but I never understood it until now. That even though I felt terrible, I felt lighter. There was something that had been lifted off, that being vulnerable let us come together. It was a reminder I had my family, that they were here, and I wasn't about to lose them again.

We were going to fight. Nightshade, the Circle, and anyone else who got in our way. They wouldn't stand a chance. That much, I finally started to believe.

Chapter Twenty-Seven

I F THERE IS ONE experience I could do without ever doing again, it would be traveling with a dead body. All of the paperwork, customs agents, making sure it was stored properly so we wouldn't open the luggage hold to the most disgusting sight ever, was more stress than I wanted to deal with.

And once the stress at the Valterrian airports and border was over, I still had work to do. While everyone was asleep, I started to think about the mission again. We needed to lure Nightshade somewhere we had control over while it still seemed like an appropriate place for a funeral. Funeral homes felt too impersonal, and none of us were particularly religious enough to feel like we needed it to be in one of the city's cathedrals.

I was almost desperate enough to look into the entirety of our property holdings, when I remembered the teen center had moved from its original location. Dad didn't get the chance to go to the other as much, and he was enough of an eccentric to the public where it would seem like it was his last wish to have his funeral in the building that started it all. And luckily, it was just being used as storage now, which gave us plenty to work with.

I had drafted a press release right before we left, and by the time we landed, Dad's death was everywhere. News stories, internet articles, a magazine cover, social media, and newspapers. It was impossible to miss that Sebastian Caldwell had disappeared to deal with his illness in private, and it was a battle he sadly lost.

I was glad my gamble that any news about my father after his disappearance would be big, because if I had been wrong, our plans would have been ruined.

By the time we got to the Bay, I decided we'd be safest at Dad's penthouse. I couldn't make myself go back to the emotionless safehouse, and every other potential place we could go was marred by more death than I wanted to be around. And it had a safe room. And a back-up safe room, just because Dad wanted a failsafe in case the first one didn't lock.

It was ridiculous, but I was glad for Dad's paranoia. It made coming home to the Bay slightly less stressful.

By the time we got to the penthouse, the Caldwell family was in full publicity mode. Paparazzi were waiting for us outside the penthouse, much to my annoyance, and managed to get shots of us all looking appropriately devastated. And the people my father had worked with were all calling to check in on us. Though by "us," it seemed just to be Nate.

"You know, it would be nice if the board actually called you instead of me. Since you're the one who works with them," Nate grumbled as he hung up the phone for what was probably the twentieth time since we had gotten home.

"Why would they do that?" I faux-innocently asked with an eyeroll. "You're the oldest, clearly that means you're the one holding us all together. I'm just a poor, sad little girl who must be sobbing uncontrollably into a pint of ice cream over the death of my father. Therefore, they have to talk to you instead of me." The sarcasm was dripping from my voice just like the fake ice cream that was melting in my analogy. "But I'm also terrible with the board, so I'm glad you have to deal with them instead of me. For once."

"Gross. Work," Zain deadpanned from behind us. "You know, I think that's what I liked the most about Dad. He got a job where he didn't have to show up every day, got to still fight people at night, and he could get away with ignoring people if he wanted to. Like, how do I get that job?"

Nate and I looked at Zain, trying to decide if he was serious or not. And it took him a second to realize exactly what it was he had asked, because Zain had known I would give him my seat on the board if he wanted it.

"No," he immediately started protesting, "I didn't mean I would take Dad's seat, also known as Nikki's seat. Absolutely not. Do not give them my name." And even though Zain was protesting, I saw Nate already texting someone. Between the two of us, I hoped we could wear Zain down. If the board thought dealing with me was rough, I would love to see what would happen with Zain in charge.

"You're lucky you don't have a phone, or else I'm pretty sure Nate would have told everyone you were the executor of Dad's will and to call you," I teased, before opening the bag of takeout we had picked up on the way to the penthouse.

"The day I do anything public-facing is the day Mother decides whatever building I'm working in needs to be blown up," Zain muttered. "Otherwise, I would gladly go nap through their stupid business shit."

"I will pay you ten dollars of Nikki's money to call it 'stupid business shit' to their faces," Jacob offered, entirely too excited by that idea. "I always hated those suits. They need to be knocked down a peg. Or five."

"Nate, just tell the board we're in mourning, and I'll be ready to come to work by the end of the week," I instructed, figuring some direction would help him out. And I added "talk to the board" to my mental to-do list of things I had to do once Nightshade was taken care of.

"I tried that already," Nate grumbled, right as his phone went off again, and he went into one of the bedrooms to take whatever this call was about.

"You know, I'm happy to help with the business stuff," Toby started, before I shook my head at him.

"No, you've got your job. You don't need to do mine," I insisted. "Plus, all they want me to do is sign my name on paperwork, and in true Caldwell fashion: Nightshade first, paperwork later. Just like Dad would have wanted." And with that in mind, I pulled up a hologram of the building onto the projection table.

"So, this is what we know the building looks like," I said, as I took away the walls so we could see the inside. "Back doors should be easy to bar shut, plus there are gates leading to the door. If we get some heavy-duty padlocks on those, it'll make it too hard for him to get in that way and will force him to go through the front. Takes away his element of surprise if he has to get through three locks and a locked door to get to us."

"We can expense the padlocks," Toby said, clearly trying to be helpful, despite the fact I don't think anyone on this team had ever expensed anything to the Department before. "Oh, wait. Stuff like that's not an issue for you all. Never mind."

"Anyway, we'll need to be prepared for him to be armed," I continued. "There's a high probability that there will be multiple guns shooting at us. I can't imagine he'll only come with one, but he won't have the upper hand like the last time we faced him in a warehouse. I think we flipped his exact trap on him." I smiled a little at that, feeling a bit like there was some justice in that. "He's going to want to be dramatic about it, so once he's inside, we need to make sure he doesn't leave."

"Are we sure he won't bribe any of the movers to lay a trap for us in our building?" Zain asked, his mouth so full of fried rice that it was nearly impossible to understand what he was saying. "It's what I would do."

"There's currently security guarding the building," I explained, before highlighting different parts of the building in red. "They run a full sweep every fifteen minutes. And we have security cameras with a twenty four-hour monitor. I made them check before we left that there weren't any blind spots from the cameras... However, Zain brings up a good point, and we need to be prepared for that possibility."

"Okay, that's a backup plan we're going to need," Gray nodded, writing something down on a notebook she had found, "but we still need to figure out plan A before we come up with plans B through Z. And even with all those backup plans, I'm still pretty sure we'll have something happen we never thought would."

"So, the goal is to get him in the open, disarm him, and take him into custody quickly and quietly," I said, demonstrating it on the hologram with the models of us I had placed on it. "It'll be five against one, with Toby hiding, which is not a fair fight for him. And honestly, I don't think it'll take that long because he's always worked alone."

"Seems easy enough," Nate said as he walked back into the room. "If we're coming at him from all sides, it shouldn't take long."

"Okay, that's the 'if things go right' plan," Zain said after a moment, "but it's too simple. Like, if getting Nightshade was this easy, don't you think Dad would have done it? He's smart enough to see right through this."

"And are we sure he's working alone?" Toby asked, his face furrowed as he looked at everything. "It's unlikely he would be able to vanish without a trace and then reappear without help. We know he's been able to get weapons, poisons, travel, and for that, he needs money. Who is funding him?"

"Yeah, Mom always talked about this guy like he refused to hold a job. There's no way he came from money," Nate agreed, with a wince. "So, where is the money coming from?"

"That's a great question," I sighed. "Especially since they've been letting him work alone. All footage we have of him since he reappeared has had him alone, which means that's our plan A."

"And plan B is Nightshade brought friends," Gray said, scribbling more thoughts into her notebook. "Don't like that at all."

"Great. So, do I get better armor when they're trying to shoot at me?" Jacob asked. "Since I won't feel it, I want that now before I'm bleeding out on the floor."

"We should have more than one person trying to draw fire. If we have two people being the distraction, it'll make it easier for everyone else to go for the target," Nate said, while we all looked at him. It was clear he forgot the first rule of suggesting the job nobody else would want to do meant you were volunteering yourself for it.

"Agreed. Thanks for volunteering," I said, adding Jacob and Nate to the hologram. "And we need Zain in the shadows. Guarding exists, making sure he doesn't find a way out we don't know about. Gray, I want you on the glider. I know you made it for me, but I think you'll be able to navigate it better in close quarters. Plus, having someone who is moving fast through the air is an asset, considering you also have drones to help you map out the place."

"Are you just saying because you think I can't fight?" Gray asked, looking slightly offended.

"Have you practiced fighting while at school?" I countered, and she immediately shook her head no, seeing my point.

"Okay, I think we've got a good start. We'll review and spar tomorrow," I sighed, yawning a little. "Plus, I have our suits to finish, so I will need some time to work on those tonight since I had Nancy bring over everything so I could finish them."

"On a scale of one to I need to start chugging cranberry juice now, how easily will I be able to pee in it?" Zain asked, and really, I couldn't blame him.

"When I first started designing suits, that's the first thing I fixed," I laughed. "So, super easy, won't be a problem." Everyone turned back to their food, and I felt like it was time for me to start working on the suits.

There was a deadline. They had to be done in four days. And looking at the helmets, I could see myself reflected back in the metallic coating.

The two sides of me were looking at each other. And as nervous as I was, I realized I was ready to finally let them both merge into me.

It was time for me to step back into my power. It was time to come back.

Chapter Twenty-Eight

I T WASN'T UNTIL I was getting dressed for Dad's funeral that I realized exactly how messed up this trap was. Everyone else's initial horror finally hit me, and using this kind of solemn event specifically to catch the man who had tried to kill us on multiple occasions was one of the most messed-up things I had ever suggested. Unfortunately, that was what made it all perfect.

Nobody actually wanted to interrupt a funeral, especially one they weren't invited to. And we had created a memorial for the general public to pay their respects outside the current teen center building, blocks away, and out of any potential danger.

As we walked in, there were a few paparazzi outside the building, but none seemed to be set up to stay there long. I guess they wanted a few shots of us going in, since the five of us together seemed like a novelty after they got the shots of us going into the penthouse after all these years.

I just hoped they were long gone by the time the trap was sprung.

Toby had taken the form of a balding minister about Dad's age, complete with wrinkles and a different eye color, and any time he spoke and his voice came out of the mouth of a completely different person, it always caught me by surprise.

But the moment we were safely inside the building, a wave of nerves between us all announced it was time. Zain started a perimeter sweep, Gray was pressing buttons on an arm piece she created for her suit to control her drones and the gilder, and Nate and Jacob started sparring to make sure they were warmed up.

Each of them wore their new suits, and it made the doubt creep in. They were muted colors of the ones they had before, each with a helmet that protected their heads instead of the masks we wore when we were younger. Sleek and metallic, we looked like the next generation of heroes. And it left me scared. I wondered if Jacob had recovered enough, if Toby should have followed his gut and stayed home. I worried Gray would freeze up after being safe in a lab for so long, or if I would have to explain to Kitty that something happened to Nate.

Everything we had planned suddenly felt like it was the worst idea we could possibly have, and I couldn't tell if it was first-mission jitters or if I had made a mistake.

"You know, you don't have to do this if you don't want to, Nikki," Toby quietly assured me, though his voice coming out of a sixty-something man was enough to snap me out of my thoughts. "It's not too late to call for help, and I'm sure that..."

"If you are even thinking about suggesting Miss Lumeriana, Dad will turn over in his yet-to-be-dug grave. The idea of her coming to his funeral is too much, even if it is fake," I said as I put my helmet on.

"I'm just worried..." he started, and I shook my head.

"We can do this," I said, turning on the display in the helmet. "We have to do this."

"Well, isn't this just a disgusting scene?" a new voice said from behind us, a voice we were too familiar with, but should never have come from the back of the building. "You know, security companies really will hire just about anyone these days. You might want to take a look at that."

We turned, and I saw the face of Nightshade for the first time. My mother's murderer. My father's downfall. No masks. No theatrics. He just looked normal. Clean-shaven, gray eyes, short salt-and-pepper hair. He didn't look like a killer, but as I analyzed his aura, he carried an anger with him that was so infused in his being that there was no doubt in my mind it was him.

"Oh, right. Boo," he sarcastically said, the gun none of us noticed going off. It's bullet hitting Toby. The only one here not wearing armor. The only one here who wasn't prepared for a fight. And to my absolute horror, Toby started changing shapes, colors, and convulsing on the flower faster than possible. It wasn't just that Nightshade was prepared, it was that he knew to target Toby specifically. Horror bubbled up in my throat, and I forced myself not to scream. Not to look at him, not to get distracted.

We could get him to the hospital later.

"Oh, right, I'm not supposed to know he could do that," Nightshade said, a demented smile filling his face. "I had thought you were smart enough to check for bugs, but you're so easy to spy on Nicole."

Zain had been right. I had been thinking too simply.

I had to snap out of my shock. I knew things were going to go wrong, we had to adjust. Now. But Zain should have warned us. This wasn't something he would have kept to himself. And Nightshade had never created a trap that could hold him. Which meant something was very, very wrong.

"Maybe," I said calmly, trying my best not to think of worst-case scenarios, as I noticed one of Gray's drones getting into position. "Or maybe this was just part of the plan." The drone tasered him, and the man fell to the ground. I put the handcuffs on him and a zip tie around his ankles for good measure. And he started laughing.

Green mist surrounded the man and flew into Toby's wounds. The same green that looked exactly like Yasmine Sadi's magic. Nightshade disappeared, and the clink of the handcuffs echoed through the room as he evaporated his way out of them.

He was magic now. We had guessed he had someone backing him, but it hadn't crossed anyone's minds that the two groups that were after us were working together.

"You see, Nicole," he said, teleporting to one of the balconies. "My friends give me money. They give me strength. And even though your father decided to die instead of being lured out, we'll still get our revenge. We're owed damages, and I don't care who has to pay for them."

"Shadow," I hissed through our comms, refusing to break eye contact with Nightshade. He was being dramatic, but if he was talking about Yasmine, then it meant we needed Zain. Immediately.

"It is cute the faith you put in my son," Yasmine's voice laughed as she appeared in front of me in a flash of green smoke, "but I think you forget, my son fights for us." I turned just in time to see a figure jump off the balcony and land next to Yasmine.

Zain. Helmet off. Eyes glowing green.

My stomach dropped with the shock of Zain's betrayal. It had to have been a plan that had gone through his mind. But it suddenly made things make so much more sense. How we had gotten out of Annelton so easily. How we all had been able to escape Sand's Point. Why didn't the Circle immediately track us down anytime we escaped their clutches?

Zain had been feeding them information the entire time. They didn't need a bug in our system, they had a face we all trusted. A mole we would never detect. A perfect double agent.

My brother. The Prince of Shadows.

Chapter Twenty-Nine

W E WERE CAUGHT IN a trap of our own making. Two Circle Assassins had knives to both Jacob's and Nate's throats. Gray was relatively safe, three stories in the air right next to the ceiling, though if everyone with the Circle could teleport, I wasn't sure it was safe for her to be up so high.

This situation was the exact reason why superhero licenses were required in the first place. It made sure we passed the tests and met the requirements to be in a fight. It was to keep people from dying, and I should have listened to Toby's gut.

We weren't ready. And I had led everyone to their deaths from the unholy alliance of Nightshade and the Circle. If we got out of this, I would be shocked if anyone listened to me ever again.

I froze, but everyone else made their move.

Nate and Jacob were able to get out of their holds as four additional assassins appeared out of nowhere. They had practiced for bullets, and a knife fight was different. But I had to trust their training, as both Yasmine and Zain lunged at me.

It had been years since Zain and I had a no-holds-barred sparring session; he had been holding back ever since I had found him. But now, I could see exactly how much he had perfected his fighting style. His mother let him do most of the work, watching with pride as her son attacked me. Which was fine, because I could barely keep up with one fighter. I would attempt a dodge, and like a snake, Zain had a counterattack ready. He knew my moves, he knew how I would fight, and I couldn't predict a thing he was going to do.

Out of the corner of my eye, I saw Gray's drones flying overhead. Most were attempting to provide cover for Toby's body, and I was grateful for Gray doing that. But she was after Nightshade, the only one of us in a position to even try. Electric bolts left the drones, and while none of them quite did what they were supposed to, they at least slowed him down.

Or at least it seemed that way until he disappeared in a puff of green smoke and reappeared on the glider with Gray. He ripped the control for the drones off her wrist and threw it on the floor, as it shattered into thousands of tiny pieces. And then to make things worse, he pushed Gray off the glider.

I pushed the panic button in my suit as I dodged another attack from Zain, sending an SOS out to anyone who was in the area. I prayed Miss Lumeriana wouldn't answer, I didn't want our defeat streamed on the internet for all to see. But we needed help, and we needed it fast.

I jumped over Yasmine, attempting to sweep my leg, and looked up long enough to see Gray hanging onto the third-floor guardrails. And as I dodged Zain's arm, I realized that the mother and son had a disadvantage: they hadn't teamed up with each other in years. They weren't working in tandem, their combinations were simplistic, and if you took away the magic, they were getting predictable.

And Zain was fighting in a way that didn't feel like him. He wasn't blinking, he wasn't smiling—typically in a fight, he would be smiling. He always enjoyed the violence. His eyes glowed slightly brighter right before he attacked, and as I collapsed to the floor, the thought hit me: Zain was being controlled.

Unfortunately, Jacob hit the floor, too, a giant bloody mess. He attempted to get up, only to get knocked unconscious. Nate was forced to fight six-to-one, and I did not like those odds for him.

"Zain, I know you're in there somewhere," I grumbled, as Yasmine dug her knee into my back. He didn't react to my words, I wasn't even sure if he heard them. A glance up, and I saw Gray had gotten herself onto the balcony there, and she was fighting Nightshade the best she could, having found a giant metal pole to defend herself with. Which was better than nothing.

"Zain," I said again, trying to get his attention, to break through the eerie blank look on his face. I twisted and managed to kick Yasmine off of me and stood back up, barely dodging a punch from my younger brother. "You are strong enough to snap out of this."

"Oh, Nicole, it does not work like that," Yasmine laughed, all but confirming Zain was being controlled. I backed up, only to hit the wall. I hadn't realized how close we were, and she had me cornered. These would be my final moments. My situational awareness had failed me. Jacob was down and maybe dead, Toby was still seizing, and I watched Nate get punched so hard I was sure it broke his jaw. "I always could take my son's mind. I was a gracious mother, I let him keep it. But he has been too disobedient, and it is your fault. What you taught him is too much to erase. And for that, Nicole Caldwell, you must die. And I will enjoy watching my son be the one to do it."

There was a terrible irony; this was my fate, because I was sure that if Zain ever regained control of his mind, the guilt would eat him alive. It would break him into the person his mother wanted him to be, so she could mold him into who she had always wanted. She'd take away every good thing about him.

She would make him a monster. Just. Like. Her.

"My darling boy, take care of it," Yasmine instructed, a sick smile on my face as she handed Zain a knife.

"Yes, mother," Zain's voice was robotic, but he caught my eye for the first time and gave me the slightest wink. And like a flash, instead of slitting my throat like his mother had wanted, he stabbed her in the stomach. Then again, through the throat. Then again, through the heart just for good measure. She fell off of me and onto the floor, green smoke pouring out of her wounds, her eyes, her mouth.

All into Zain.

The sounds of otherworldly chanting filled the room, and all the fighting stopped. The assassins bowed to Zain, as Jacob and Nate picked themselves off the floor in confusion. Yasmine had said Zain wasn't strong enough to do what needed to be done, and it had been implied she meant killing her. But there was a transfer of power happening, something that needed her death to be released. And all of it aged her so rapidly and distastefully, she looked like what I expected a mummy would beneath the wrappings.

"I taught you well," she rasped, looking up at Zain with a sense of pride.

"You taught me nothing," Zain sneered back. "Dad did. Nikki did. And if you think I'm going to let your precious Circle last another generation, I hope you enjoy watching me dismantle all your hard work from Hell." Panic filled Yasmine's face as the light faded from her eyes. Her last thoughts were defeat, and I felt it fitting.

"Zain, what did you do?" I whispered, but he didn't answer, instead, he now had control of the green smoke, and it erupted out of the assassins and Nightshade and into him.

"Okay, I'm in charge now," he yelled at our enemies, ignoring my question. "So, first order of business stop fighting my brother and my friends and get the fuck out of here." The order came with an authority I didn't expect from him. It was too mature for an eighteen-year-old. But the assassins immediately nodded and left, Zain's word now being law. No questions, no thoughts, only obedience. It was terrifying to see the brainwashing at work, and I hoped Zain was up for the task of deprogramming them.

"That's it?" Nightshade asked, looking down at us with a chaotic laugh as he punched Gray in the nose and knocked her to the floor. "You kill your mother and think I have to listen to you?"

"You're a member of the Circle of Shadows, are you not?" Zain asked, using his new magic to fly up to where Nightshade was laughing, hovering in front of the balcony. "You made a blood oath to serve the Center. The Center has been replaced, the blood oath remains." His voice started changing, turning into something deeper, ancient, and terrifying. "I feel that oath running through your veins, I feel your betrayal, your lack of belief. So, I will remind you of the consequences of breaking your oath."

I watched, horrified, as Nightshade's life force seemed to be pulled out of him. He started aging as rapidly as Yasmine had, his wrinkles deepening, his eyes sinking in. But it was clear Zain had no control over what was happening; whoever belonged to this voice, that was the one who was speaking now. And while there had been the argument the entire time about whether or not it was better if Nightshade was dead, I knew Zain was against it. Deep down, this wasn't who Zain wanted to be.

"Zain!" I shouted, just enough to get his attention. "This isn't you. You agreed we weren't killing him. That's not justice, it's revenge. You. Need. To. Stop."

A conflict played out on Zain's face, an internal struggle in his mind. Zain screamed, attempting to regain control, and dropped to the floor. Nightshade groaned, decades older than he had been less than a minute before.

"What did you do?" I asked, running to him and pulling him into a hug. While Gray might have struggled against the magically-infused Nightshade, I had no doubts she could handle the now ninety-year-old man who looked like he broke a hip.

"We didn't have a chance," he quietly said, tears streaming down his face as his voice was muffled from him pressing his face into my uniform. "We couldn't beat them, and they knew it. But my mother spread out her magic to thin, and she didn't have the control over me she thought she did. I had to pretend to be under her control, it was the only way to save everyone. I had to... take over." He barely breathed the last words, and I knew he was right. I wondered what the cost of his decision would be. It was already clear, after that display, that the more he used these powers, the more it would take away the humanity he had worked so hard to hold on to. That eventually he would turn into what Yasmine was by the end: a shell for whatever was now residing inside him.

"Thank you," I whispered, stroking his hair. I had never seen Zain so terrified, and he was shaking uncontrollably. I was worried, and I didn't even know what had happened. And now wasn't the time to get those answers.

Gray was sitting next to a now-restrained Nightshade as Nate helped Jacob up. But the sound of a groan in the corner made my stomach drop. Toby was still alive, and the magical seizing had stopped. He was hanging on by a thread. I kissed my brother's forehead and went over to Toby, taking his hand. His skin had settled to its natural aqua, but his skin was cold to the touch—the equivalent of a fever for Xatanians.

"Toby, you need to stay with me," I whispered, squeezing him.

"Nickel?" he asked, attempting to look at me but his eyes refused to focus.

"Yeah, it's me. You're not allowed to die, okay?" Toby attempted to nod, but his eyes closed, and his hand went limp in mine. And it was at that moment, our backup arrived.

And of course, it was Jeannie Michaels in her stupid Miss Lumeriana cheerleading outfit she insisted was a supersuit.

"Oh, my gods, chat, look!" she squealed into the camera that was hovering behind her, broadcasting the streaming chat to her. Thankfully, we were all masked, since Zain had seemingly disappeared. "You've seen it here first, the Eagle's little birds are back in action!"

She was lucky she was filming, because otherwise, we were all going to kill her. But the announcement was made, the truth was out there, and I truly hoped she hadn't announced our location to her millions of followers because otherwise our secret identities would be gone in an instant.

"But since you have everything under control, thanks for the exclusive!" she said, blowing us a kiss before flicking her blonde hair behind her. "Toodles!" she said with a little finger wave before flying off.

And I was so glad to hear the sound of the ambulance, I didn't have time to think about how much I hated the word "toodles."

Chapter Thirty

T HERE WERE BRUISES IN places that weren't supposed to be bruises. I had a set of bruised ribs that made it hard to breathe. And eventually, I would get them checked out.

But I had been in the same outfit for twenty-four hours, waiting for Toby to wake up. His Dad was off-planet, as I had expected, and he didn't have any family. I had to stay. I refused to let him wake up alone. He had known the risks, he had been terrified of them, and had tried to do his best anyway.

Thankfully, this hospital had an Xatanian doctor on staff and was contracted with the Department, so there were no questions about what had happened. I was curled in a ball next to his bed, wondering if he was going to blame me. He should.

He almost died because of me. It even felt wrong to fall asleep, even though I needed it. Toby would have done the same thing for me if I was the one in that bed, and I wasn't going to leave him. Not this time.

Though I was positive that if he ever woke up, he would lecture me about my stupidity and dump me.

He was a handler. He had no right to be in an active scene like this. He saw his office and the work he did for the Department as heroic. And it was. Because who cares for the heroes who don't care for themselves? Toby.

My Toby.

I had just found him again, and I couldn't bear the idea of losing him now. Not when he had been the only constant in my life since I was twelve. Not when he always saw the best in me, even when I couldn't see it in myself. Not when I had finally made my way back to him.

According to the doctor, he should have woken up hours ago, and while the steady beating of his hearts said he was alive, there was no change to anything else. It was hard not to wonder if, at this point, alive for him meant he would never wake up. Nobody knew what the magic had done to him, and the other tests they needed to do had to wait until he was awake.

But even if he didn't wake up, I was going to be here.

Because I loved him.

I had denied it for so long, but I had fallen in love with him as a teenager, before I even knew what love was. I didn't understand what I had been feeling back then. I had pushed him away because I didn't want to damage the most important person in my life. I had fallen for every snippet of information I had heard about him over the years. I had fallen for him when he held me when I cried, and let me know I was allowed to feel.

Every single time I had seen him throughout my life, I had fallen in love with him all over again; I just didn't know it.

But now I did. I knew that love meant I wouldn't ever leave him again. That I would believe in him. That I would support his decision, even if they were bad ideas. He had always done that for me, and maybe it was because he loved me, too.

A terrible decision if it was true, because I had done nothing but hurt him. And yet, I hoped he would come back to me, anyway. It just felt like it was too much for me to ask this time when I had landed him here.

I should have just held on when I had the chance.

I instinctively curled myself more into a ball and wished there was some magic I could do to wake him up. I had checked on Jacob and Gray, though they had both been released from the hospital. I had Kitty giving me updates about Nate, though I hadn't been able to give her the lack of updates on Toby. Zain had gone radio silent, and I wasn't sure if it was because of what had happened or if he was just being his normal self.

"Hey, Nickel," a weak voice whispered, snapping me out of my thoughts as my eyes shot up to look into Toby's golden ones.

"You're awake!" I breathed, as relieved tears fell from my eyes. "The doctors thought you would have woken up hours ago."

"I think I did?" he said with a wince that I think was supposed to be a smile. "I remembered you holding my hand, and then I fell back asleep. I'm kind of sad you're not still doing it."

"Sorry, I've been spiraling," I admitted, lacing our fingers together. "It turns out you don't react well to magic-infused bullets." I wasn't sure if I should have said it, if I should admit how close to death he was after he had only just woken up. I knew I shouldn't stress him out anymore. "How are you feeling?"

"Numb. Tired. Like I could nap for a thousand years," Toby slowly said after thinking a moment. "But I think once the drugs wear off, I'll feel like I got hit by a truck. What happened?"

"I'm glad you don't remember. It was a mess," I admitted. "Short version: Nightshade joined the Circle of Shadows and spent the past five years training under them. He shot you. Zain's mom showed up, attempted to mind control him, we all got our butts handed to us, and then Zain killed his mom."

"Please tell me you're joking. That is the last thing he should have done," Toby attempted to shoot up in bed, only to groan in pain and lie back down. It was clear he knew something more about what this meant, something Zain hadn't told me. And that whatever it was had been on the Department's radar and files on Zain without us knowing.

"He did it to save us," I quietly said. "If he hadn't, all of us would have died."

"Well, I'm glad he did something, since impressing you went off the table immediately," he groaned, adjusting himself on his pillows.

"Toby, you did not need to do this to impress me." I smiled at him. "And I'm sorry I forced you into it. Because you don't need to be a superhero to impress me. You have your quiet bravery, and your love of paperwork, and you always know what to say to make my days better. That's all I need, considering I think I've got the stupidly rushing into things we're not ready for covered for both of us."

"I just... I was scared if I didn't you would..." he quietly said, letting go of my hand and brushing his against my face, like he was scared my being there was a dream. "With all of this bringing you back, I thought..."

"Stop talking," I interrupted. "I know I pushed you away, and I was a ghost. I think you were the only reliable thing in my life, and that's why I was scared you would leave. So... I left first. And I've regretted it for so long." I wasn't sure if it was too much for Toby's drug-hazed brain, but I hoped he would remember it.

"So, it was easier to hurt me so I would leave than to trust that I wouldn't," Toby thought out loud. "Once I'm out of here, I'm going to give you therapist suggestions for all of your abandonment issues, because the first thing I learned as a handler is former sidekicks all need therapy. We're a really messed-up bunch."

"Yeah, we are," I agreed. Back when this all started, I would have refused to admit that. But if there was anything I had learned through the whole thing, it was that I wasn't going to shut down again. Even if the world decided to take everything from me again. "Just promise you won't go into the field again, even if I stupidly suggest it. You mean too much to me to lose you like this."

"I promise I won't," he said, stroking my cheek one last time, "as long as you promise not to stand me up for the dinner you've owed me for five years."

I laughed, not even thinking that was anywhere comparable to what I had just asked him. But in his mind, I knew they were equal, and that was another thing I knew I loved about him.

"Hey Nickel?" Toby said as he yawned and started to drift off again. "Thanks for staying. You know, when it counted."

He immediately fell back asleep, and I left a kiss on his cold, blue hand. I hadn't thought about the fact that Toby understood. His father was off-planet to the point I wasn't even sure he could be contacted. That maybe our fathers' leaving was just another thing we had in common.

I understood him, and he understood me. Together, we'd make it work. And with that, I finally allowed myself to follow him into a dreamless sleep.

Chapter Thirty-One

T HE NEXT FEW DAYS that passed were a blur. I had to constantly check up on the team and deal with Kitty's anger that she had to hear about Nate's broken jaw from Jacob and not me or her husband. Gray got a call from the school that she needed to come and finish her dissertation or leave the program and immediately started writing. And even though things were calmer, there weren't enough hours in the day to do what needed to be done.

Mostly because Zain was still missing. A day or two made sense for him, but a week? It was worrisome.

I had no idea where in the Bay he would go to hide, or if he was even still in the city. I had the distinct feeling Zain didn't want to be found, and a familiar fear crept in that I would never see my brother again. That he had abandoned us, after he had saved us.

After he had promised he wouldn't leave.

Zain had promised he would tell me about his mother's magic, and from what Toby had said, it was clear that killing Yasmine had been a sacrifice bigger than any of us knew. Zain had been scared, and if he was scared, it meant the rest of us should be terrified.

I had temporarily moved into the penthouse after Gray had found and destroyed the rest of the bugs and done a full reset of our system to make sure the Circle was fully out of our electronics. And I had taken to sleeping in the panic room, just for a little extra security.

And because it had the best bed out of all of them here.

I had locked myself in and started through the list of homeless shelters to see if any of them had any leads on Zain when I felt a tap on my shoulder. In the locked penthouse panic room. Where I was supposed to be alone.

I screamed and threw my phone, and Zain successfully dodged it.

"Where have you been?" I demanded, pulling him into a tight hug. His eyes seemed to permanently have the green unnatural glow now, almost like a cat's.

"Fighting my inner demon," Zain deadpanned, and even though he was attempting to play it off as a joke, it gave the impression he meant it literally instead of figuratively. "Don't worry, I won. For now."

"What do you mean by 'you won?" I asked, forcing him to sit next to me on the bed, terrified he would disappear again. "What exactly is happening, Zain? You promised me answers about your mother's magic before everything went wrong, and now I think we need them. The Department's already threatened to put you on every watch list known to man, and I've done everything in my power to get them to wait."

"Okay, I'll start from the beginning," Zain sighed, clearly choosing his words carefully. "The best way to explain it is I am possessed by a ghost. A genocidal ghost of the founder of the Circle who attempted to rule the world from the shadows, almost succeeded, but made sure nobody actually knew who he was, so he could continue being under the radar. He made some sort of immortality pact that ensured his soul would live on when his body died. So his son, my grandpa, ended up killing him, and then it passed down to him. Mom killed her Dad, I killed her, the ghost keeps passing on. With it comes all of these extra abilities. Summoning weapons, teleportation, mind control, and flight. Honestly, I think there are others I haven't even figured out yet. But with it comes the whole thousand-year cult thing, which is why the Circle is so hard to fight. Most people in it are born into it. They've been trained and indoctrinated over generations. And now that I'm in charge, ghost grandpa thinks we're ready to step into the light and rule the world. I'd rather not."

I blinked a few times as I processed everything Zain told me. I was sure the Department knew all of this, and it made them right to be concerned. Even if the brother sitting in front of me was acting like he always had, this wasn't something he could just pretend didn't exist.

"What happens if you lose control? Like what happened with Nightshade?" I asked, and even Zain couldn't hide the echo of fear that passed over his face.

"If I don't use the magic, I don't grant him any power that he can then take over," Zain explained, though I wondered if he was trying to convince himself that instead of me. "Plus, like I said. I won. We've agreed. For now."

"What kind of agreement could you possibly come up with? Especially with a, and remember these are your words, genocidal ghost?"

"Nik, I just... I don't know," Zain whispered, and for once he sounded like he was the lost teenager he always had been., "I didn't have a choice... and I made it to keep you all safe. And I'm going to keep you all safe."

"I'm sorry my decisions led to a sacrifice you shouldn't have had to make," I quietly said, and Zain nodded, flopping dramatically back on the bed. It was obvious the conversation was over, that he didn't have the answers to the questions we needed. I knew he was going to need to tell me the details of the agreement someday, but right now? Zain's lips were sealed.

"How's everyone else?" he asked after a few minutes of silence.

"Toby's still in the hospital recovering from surgery, but he's through the worst of it. Doctors are expecting a full recovery," I said, and I smiled as he relaxed. "Kitty's decided Jacob's moving in with her and Nate, so she's been doting over him. Nate's jaw is wired shut because he broke it, so Kitty's also kind of pissed about that, so I'd recommend not talking to her about it. She's still terrifying when she's mad."

"Wow, we really fucked this one up, didn't we?" Zain asked, "Like, Dad had us convinced we weren't in over our heads."

"Yeah, but he wasn't here," I pointed out. "I was the one who made the terrible call. So, honestly, I think it's time we focus on us and what we want and what's best for us instead of trying to live up to a dead man's expectations."

"Aww, my big sister's all grown up," Zain teased as he gave me an impish smile. "So, what's best for you? You back in? Or was the disaster your big sign that this was your last mission?"

"I don't know," I answered, lying down on the bed next to him. I knew I needed to make the decision soon, but I had to think about it. Nate said I had thrived as our leader, but the weight of leading everyone into a disaster was hard to hold. It would happen again, and it would still be on me. I had to decide if I could carry it.

Toby also said it was like I was back, and I felt more like myself than I had in years. Even though I loved the design work of my job and everything I had built for myself, the loneliness of it all had been mentally crippling.

I loved being the Nightingale. She was everything I had wanted to be when I was growing up. But there were pros and cons to coming back, and there was a steel someone needed if they were going to fully embrace this kind of life. I hadn't realized it, even back when I was a sidekick. There was a chance I would only lead people into disaster. I would watch the people I care about get hurt over and over again.

But I could also make a change. I could help people, just like Mom had wanted. I could uplift the people who couldn't defend themselves. I could continue breaking the cycle of corruption that went hand-in-hand with the Caldwell name. Dad had tried, and he lost his humanity in a cycle of vengeance. But there was a line between vengeance and justice, and I realized I hadn't ever been taught what that line was.

"What about you?" I asked, only to hear Zain snort in reply.

"Do you think they're going to let the Center of the Circle of Shadows keep his hero license?" Zain asked. "I don't think there's enough strings in the world Toby could pull to make that happen. But if I had a choice, I'd stay in. A last fuck you to my mom. Probably not the best reason, but I could start doing actual good in the world."

"You know, they might," I pointed out. There were reformed villains and various other people who had managed to get their licenses. I knew the process was different, but I wasn't convinced Zain would immediately be shut out. "You can try."

"Sounds hard," he said, before his lips curled into a smirk. "But I'll try if you do." It was a dare, plain and simple. I knew him well enough that Zain would leave a giant life decision to a dare.

Dad had always said there were pros to making split-second decisions: that you would go with what feels right to your gut instead of overthinking. And that advice... it felt right.

"Deal," I nodded, feeling more confident than I expected to. "I'm in if you are."

Chapter Thirty-Two

Acknowledgements

I TRULY CANNOT BELIEVE this book is out in the world. The character of Nikki came to me in high school, and while her story is completely different, I'm thrilled other people finally have a chance to know her. So, thank you, High School Ash—this book never would have happened without you and your spiral notebooks having lunch by yourself everyday trying to figure out how to write a novel.

The first people I want to thank is the amazing Finch Benson squad. Fionn, you believed in this story when I had been told over and over there was no audience and wouldn't sell—and for that I will be forever thankful. Chase, your cover designs are beautiful and I am so in awe of your talent. Elle, your kindness and big heart do not go unnoticed, and I am thankful to have you as a role model each and every day. August and Asher, thank you for the edits and your endless efforts to making everyone's stories as strong as they can be. Carly and Alex, the two of you are the best hype squad anyone could hope for. And to the Finches new to the Nest, we are stronger with you here and I cannot wait to see what you all can do.

A giant thank you to Cam and Jess who read the book and promised me it didn't suck. Your reactions and excitement were enough to kill any anxiety I had over this book.

To Lorne Balfe—I know the chances of you ever reading this book are slim, but thank you for writing the *Dungeons & Dragons: Honour Among Thieves* score, as it was the music I wrote this book to. I truly do not think I could have finished this book without this album, and now whenever I hear the music I am more likely to visualize my own plot points over the movie.

And to anyone who picked up this book, thank you for reading it. It means more to me that you'd choose my book than you probably understand.